Full Figured 3:

Carl Weber Presents

Full Figured 3:

Carl Weber Presents

Brenda Hampton and Nikki-Michelle

www.urbanbooks.net

Urban Books, LLC
78 East Industry Court
Deer Park, NY 11729

ISBN 13: 978-1-60162-372-0
ISBN 10: 1-60162-372-0

First Mass Market Printing January 2013
First Trade Paperback Printing September 2011
Printed in the United States of America

10 9 8 7 6 5 4 3 2 1

Distributed by Kensington Publishing Corp.
Submit Wholesale Orders to:
Kensington Publishing Corp.
C/O Penguin Group (USA) Inc.
Attention: Order Processing
405 Murray Hill Parkway
East Rutherford, NJ 07073-2316
Phone: 1-800-526-0275
Fax: 1-800-227-9604

Who Ya Wit 2

By

Brenda Hampton

Chapter 1

The verdict wasn't in yet about Roc being the man I needed him to be. At the age of forty-two I had allowed very little room for error in my relationships, and the drama Roc had previously brought my way, he could do no more. Somehow or someway he managed to get out of the ten-year bid he was sentenced to at Bonne Terre Correctional Facility, only completing a year and a half. He mentioned that his lawyer had gotten the sentence reduced, but there had to be more to it. Either way, I was very glad about that, and the thought of him being able to be a father to our daughter, Chassidy, truly pleased my heart.

It was only two days ago that Roc stepped into my kitchen, claiming to be a free man and asking if I was still down with him. I really didn't know what to say, but I remember my mouth hanging wide open.

"I'm not sure who I'm down with right now, Roc. There is a lot at stake and I just don't know if I can trust you again. I know that your son's mother, Vanessa, is still in the picture, and what about your conniving uncle, Ronnie? I don't know if I can deal with some of the mess I put up with before, and I'm sure you understand my concerns."

"I do, but let's face it . . . you've never trusted me. Vanessa won't be no problem for us and neither will Ronnie."

I could have laughed at his response, only because he knew that was a lie. "It would be so wrong of me to go there with you, so I won't. Just . . . just give me a hug, and the only thing I will say right now is that it's good seeing you."

"Same here, especially since you only came to visit me once. You were wrong for that, as well as for not bringing my daughter, either. But you're right . . . our issues need to be put off for another day and time. I'm here, so come give me the hug I've been waitin' for."

I moved closer to Roc, and as soon as his arms eased around my waist, the feelings for him that I was unable to release came back to life. I wasn't sure if this connection I had with him would be everlasting, or if it was just me wanting to make this thing work because of our child. That answer would come soon, but there was no doubt whatsoever that I was happy to see him.

It was scorching hot outside that day, but Roc spent much of his time trying to get to know Chassidy. He played with her in her swimming pool, chased her around the spacious backyard, watched TV with her in her *The Princess and the Frog*—decorated bedroom, and even cut the grass for me. It was good seeing the two of them together, and for her first time seeing him, she took to him very well. Later that day, we left my home in St. Louis, and followed my son, Latrel, back to college at Mizzou. After staying with him for a couple of hours, Roc, Chassidy, and I returned home. Chassidy was exhausted, so I laid her down for a nap, and then went into the kitchen where Roc was sitting shirtless at the glass-topped kitchen table, sipping from a Coke can and eating some barbecue-flavored potato chips. The calories would do him no harm, and the muscular frame that he had before did not compare to the one he now had. His biceps looked bigger, his chest was carved to perfection, more tattoos covered his arms, and the daily iron pumping had definitely paid off. He was dark as midnight, still very sexy, and clean-cut as ever! I couldn't ignore the fact that seeing him always made my panties moist and my palms sweat. Aside from the way he made my insides tingle, there was so much that I needed to say. I didn't quite know how to say it, but it was now or never.

With Roc being in prison, certain things came to my mind about what kind of person he now was. Was he still the young man who lived in the fast lane, selling drugs and having sex with many different women? Was he still willing to do whatever his Uncle Ronnie wanted him to do, and was Roc willing to do jail time for Ronnie again? Was movin' and shakin' still his occupation, and what could he offer me? Basically, had he matured at all, and, at twenty-seven years old, did being in prison redeem him? I sat across the table from him, eager to continue our conversation from earlier.

"So, in other words, you're telling me that you're a changed man. I don't have to worry about Vanessa ringing my phone or confronting me, as she did before. I don't have to concern myself with Ronnie calling me out of my name or putting a gun up to my head, right? And what about you? Can you promise me that you are done with shaking and moving? If not, Roc, I want no part of this."

Roc squinted, staring deeply into my eyes. "You don't have to worry about nothin'. All of that shit is in the past, ma. I'm done with all of that mess, jus' . . . just give me a chance to show you what's up. I promise you won't regret it. I've had time to reflect on some things, and my goal is to live a better life. I tried my way before, so let's roll with your way."

I wasn't sure if Roc could handle doing things my way. My way consisted of him getting a job, helping me take care of our daughter, leaving the drug game behind him, making sure there was no drama from his son's mother, and distancing himself from the people around him who helped bring him down, particularly Ronnie: the uncle who Roc had looked up to as a father figure. The one who supposedly made a way for Roc and had gotten him in to the drug game. He was the one who Roc had taken the fall for and wound up going to prison for. I hated Ronnie with a passion, and I could never see him being an inspiration to Roc, or Roc distancing himself from an uncle he loved more than life itself.

That night, all I allowed Roc to do was hold me in his arms, while questioning his early release and his future plans. He insisted that with lots of money and a damn good lawyer, anything was possible. As for his future, he wasn't sure. Lord knows I wanted to have sex with him, but I wasn't sure about us yet. My life had changed in so many different ways since he'd been gone, and honestly, I hadn't forgiven him yet for choosing to take the fall for Ronnie, instead of being there for his child. I was in a different place in my life and I couldn't afford any setbacks.

My career with the STL Community College was going strong, I had pulled myself out of debt, and my children were happy. Latrel was now a junior and I was as proud of him as any mother could be. He drove home almost every other weekend just to be with me and spend time with his sister. He also spent some days with my ex-husband, Reggie, who had divorced me because he'd fallen out of love. That's what he'd said years ago, but he was now regretting his decision. We rarely spoke to each other these days because he remained upset with me about Chassidy. In no way did I care about how he felt about me, and his only worries should have applied to his messed-up life.

According to Latrel, Reggie was in the midst of tying up his second divorce, which was more costly than the one he had with me. I only asked for what was due to me, but his new wife, she wanted it all! The house, cars, part ownership of his real estate business, and $10,000 a month in spousal support. I couldn't believe all that she was asking for, and, to my recollection, Reggie didn't have that much money to dish out. I truly wished him the best with his situation, but that's what he got for marrying a woman he had only known for one year.

That situation, in itself, made me wise up even more. I didn't want anyone to take what little I had, and I wasn't trying to share much, either. My house was for me and my children. My car was for me only to drive. I was perfectly fine with the way things were going, but I couldn't help but sit at my desk at work, thinking about how Roc would impact my life going forward. I had briefly spoken to him yesterday, but he seemed busy, trying to move his things from the penthouse he once had to a condo he was now living in on the south side of St. Louis.

I wiggled my fingers on the side of my face, eyeballing the phone on my desk and contemplating calling him. Why? Because he said he was busy, and since he hadn't called me back, maybe that meant he was *still* busy. I wanted to allow him all the time he needed to get settled, so I quickly dropped my thoughts about calling him and got back to work.

Working for the vice president of Student Activities was challenging. My boss, Mr. Anderson, was a serious black man who kept me on my feet. He was in his mid-fifties, and had a wife and three kids, but made little time for them. Normally, he worked six days a week, hoping that I would do the same. From the beginning, I made it clear that I could only work Monday through

Friday, never on the weekends. My family was too important to me and they definitely came first. Mr. Anderson understood that, and that encouraged me to give him my all. We got along very well and it turned out that losing my previous job was the best thing that had ever happened to me. My salary increased by $15,000, it helped with my bills, and I was in no way upset about that.

As my mind was consumed with calling Roc, the ringing phone interrupted my thoughts.

"Mr. Anderson's office. How may I help you?"

"Desa Rae, this is Sherri. Is my dad around?"

Mr. Anderson would never tell his kids when he was going out of town. And it wasn't my place to tell them, either. "No, he isn't, Sherri. He's out of the office today, but you may want to try his cell phone."

"Okay, thanks. I'll do that, but, in the meantime, how's Latrel doing?"

"He's fine. I had hoped the two of you would go out on another date, but he told me how busy the both of you are."

"Unfortunately, but I had every intention of calling him soon. You know I'm in med school and I never have time to do much of anything."

"Oh, I understand, sweetie, and you definitely don't have to explain anything to me. I'm sure

Latrel understands too. Call him when you can. He did mention you the other day and I'm sure he would be happy to hear from you."

"I sure will. Let me call my dad now, and be sure to tell Latrel I'll call him soon."

I told Sherri that I would, but shame on me for lying. Latrel hadn't mentioned her at all, and he actually told me that the two of them didn't click. Personally, I thought Sherri was perfect for Latrel. She was smart, funny, cute, and had goals that made her family proud. The fact that she was a virgin made me appreciate her more, and she reminded me a lot of myself. I made a mental note to call Latrel to see if he would be willing to take her out again. I knew it was none of my business, but I would forever and always be looking out for who or what was in my son's best interest.

Mr. Anderson was out for the entire week. I was pretty much caught up on all of my work, but just to keep busy, I started merging a letter that wasn't supposed to go out to the students until next week. Next to me was a pretty red basket, filled with chocolate chip cookies. I had already eaten three of them, and I couldn't believe how much my appetite had increased since Roc had been home. I'd probably picked up five pounds in two days, and couldn't stop snacking.

It was probably my nerves, and even though I hated to go there, I wondered if he was still okay with the *weight* thing. He did compliment me on how beautiful I was, but it was hard to hide the ten pounds I had packed on over the last few months. Since Latrel had been coming home a lot, I was cooking and eating more. Chassidy loved pizza, and it had become one of my favorites, too. Surely, it was hard to get those pounds off, and the once/twice-a-week workout that I was doing appeared to be a waste of time. My hips were more curvaceous and my thighs had gotten thicker. I guess the weight was going to the right places, and, for that, I really couldn't complain.

Double checking, I pulled a compact mirror from my purse, gazing at my reflection. Yeah, I still had it going on, and even the chocolate on my teeth from those cookies wasn't enough to make me think otherwise. I licked the chocolate, then pressed my lips together to spread my gloss that was barely there. I teased my feathery, long hair and batted my lashes at the prettiest woman I knew—me. I smiled and placed the compact back into my purse. Ready to finish up my letters, I scooted the black leather chair up to my cherry oak square desk that was neat and spacious. I barely had to leave my desk for anything, as the four-in-one HP printer, fax, copier, and scanner was right beside me. Stack trays for my letters were to my right, and pictures of my children were to my left. My drawers included everything that an administrative assistant would need to do her job, including the chocolate Hershey Kisses that I had stashed away for my cravings. I shook my head, knowing that I needed to stop.

Instead of resuming with my chocolates and the letter, I reached for the phone to call Roc. *What the hell?* I thought. If he was too busy to talk, then he would say so. The phone rang twice before he answered.

"Say, baby," he immediately said. "I'ma hit you up in about ten minutes. I'm in the middle of doin' somethin'."

Well, crack my face, why don't you? "Uh, okay. I'm at work, so call me here."

"Will do."

He hung up, leaving me to wonder what was up. Seemed like that spark he once had for me wasn't there anymore. I knew that the time we spent away from each other would make us feel differently, but was he still excited about me? I hoped that my small transformation from a size fourteen/sixteen to sixteen-plus wasn't a factor, but with men you just never know. Just in case, I grabbed my basket of cookies, aiming it toward the trashcan to throw the cookies away. When the aroma of sweet and thick chocolate chunks hit me, I quickly changed my mind, putting the basket back on my desk. I put one of the cookies in my mouth, closed my eyes, and let it melt. No need letting the cookies my best friend, Monica, had made go to waste that.

"Mmmmm," I said, indulging myself. "If you don't like it, Mr. Roc, too darn bad."

Less than five minutes later, the phone rang again. By looking at the caller ID, I knew it was Roc.

"Desa Rae Jenkins," I said, wiping my mouth with a napkin.

"Dez, it's Roc. I was just callin' you back. What's up?"

"I didn't want anything. Just checking to see if you got settled into your new place. Did you?"

"Just about. I still have a few things to do, but for the most part I'd better get used to makin' my condo feel like home. It's a li'l cramped for my taste, but a nigga gotta do what he must do to stay out of jail."

"I'd say so, and changing course, as well as leaving the drug game behind, will be very beneficial. You think?"

Roc was silent and all I heard was a deep sigh on the other end.

"Roc, are you there?"

"Yeah, I'm here. But, before we get off on the wrong foot, let me say somethin' to you, all right? I know I've made some mistakes, but there are no guarantees that more mistakes won't happen. All you need to know is that I'm goin' to do my best to stay on the right track, but even my best may not be good enough for you. If we hook up again, and I truly hope we do, please don't nag me about my decisions in life. They are mine to make and mine only. If you can't handle that, then don't waste your time."

Oh, no, he didn't just try to tell me off, did he? I knew he was busy trying to get everything in order, and I figured his situation could have been frustrating. In knowing so, I remained calm. "I just want the best for you, that's all. If my comment offended you, I apologize."

"Yes, some of your comments, with an s, offend me. Especially when I wanted to taste your pussy the other night, and all you wanted to do was tell me what you expected me to do. That shit is a turnoff, ma, and I'm not down with nobody tryin' to give me orders. I've been takin' orders for the last year and a half. Had enough of that shit and it's timeout."

Okay, I messed up so I had to lighten the situation. "Forgive me, as it's the motherly thing in me that always kicks in. So . . . does this mean I'm in trouble? I hope so."

Roc laughed out loud, and it put a smile on my face as I visualized his deep dimples and Lance Gross attributes.

"Big, eleven and a half . . . maybe twelve inches of trouble."

"Wow, I'm impressed. Didn't know a penis could grow that fast, but I'm willing to take whatever you got. When can I get it is the question?"

"It's all yours and all you have to do is say the word. My place or yours? Today or tomorrow? Morning or night? A bed, table, shower, or the floor?"

"I'll let you decide. Just let me know, so I can make some arrangements with our beautiful daughter."

"Yeah, you may have to do that because I don't want her around to witness all the hollerin' and screamin' I may cause you. Come to my place tonight and I will make sure all of the floors are clean."

"Can't wait," I said with excitement, picking up a pen. "Address, please."

Roc gave me his address and directions to his place near Tower Grove Park. Afterward, I called Monica to see if she would watch Chassidy for me and she told me to bring her over for the weekend. I thanked her and told her I would drop off Chassidy around 6:00 P.M. I couldn't wait to see Roc, and, unfortunately for me, yes, I was in trouble. The only person I'd had sex with was a man from work I'd met named Greg. We went out a few times, but I wasn't feeling him at all. He was boring to be with and I had to pretend as if I were enjoying our dates. I thought that having sex with him would help to break the ice, but that did nothing but turn me off more. He was the same age as me, very nice, but not for me. He continued to pursue me for a while, and just recently backed off. Thank God. I guess Roc had spoiled me. I knew it would be difficult to find a man who was capable of making my body do what he did, and, for the record, it was time for me to have some fun that seemed long overdue.

A few hours later, I was at home standing in front of my bed and observing the three outfits I had laid out. One was a red stretch dress with a V-dip in the front. It came with a black belt that tightened around the waist, and I had the perfect black heels to match. The other outfits were a one-piece, strapless white jumper, and jeans with a burnt orange button-down shirt from Ashley Stewart. I must have stared at the

outfits for an hour, debating which one would fit
me best. While in thought, I snapped my fingers
and hurried into my walk-in closet. I scanned my
clothes, then came across the flowered sundress
I wore the first time Roc and I had sex. He loved
my dress, so he said, but more than anything he
appreciated the easy access. I slid the dress over
my body and stepped into my yellow flip-flops
that matched. *Now, why didn't I think of this
before?* I thought, and hurried to grab my purse
and keys so I could go.

On the drive to Roc's place, I couldn't stop
thinking about what the night had in store for
us. I hoped like hell that I was still capable of
pleasing him. I mean, with Greg, my sexual per-
formance was just okay. In no way did being with
him encourage me to give it my all. Roc always
got the best sex out of me, and right about now, I
needed something good in return. I couldn't wait
to see him, so I put my foot on the accelerator
and sped up.

By the time I reached Roc's place, it was about
8:15 P.M. I told him I'd be there around eight, but
the battle with my clothes delayed me. I wanted
to check on Chassidy again, so I dialed out on my
cell phone to call Monica.

"She's perfectly fine," Monica said. "And if all
you're going to do is call here the entire weekend

to check on her, then I'm going to stop answering my phone."

I smiled, as my best friend knew how protective I was of my children. "What is she doing? Did I forget to put her *Princess and the Frog* pillow in her bag?"

"No. She's cuddled up next to me, resting peacefully with her pillow beside her. We were watching *Up* and those beautiful little eyes were fading by the minute. Tomorrow we're going to go check on my parents and I'm taking her to Incredible Pizza with my two nieces. They're spending the night, too, and the girls will have lots of fun. Trust me."

"I do trust you and you already know that. You know how I am about my babies."

"Yes, I do, and I'm the same way. Have fun with Roc this weekend, and don't worry about Chassidy. I hope everything goes well, even though I'm not sure yet about his return."

"I'm not sure, either, but I'm here. And the way my hormones are raging, there will be no turning back."

We laughed and Monica knew exactly where I was coming from. "What did you wind up putting on?" she asked.

I looked down at my sundress with blooming flowers, fearing to tell her. "A simple sundress."

"A sundress? Which one?"

"The yellow one with the white flowers and thin straps."

"Ugh, the one that looks like a balloon? You couldn't find anything else to put on? Girl, that dress is for cleaning up around the house. I can't believe that was the only—"

"Good-bye, Monica. I'll call to check on you and Chassidy tomorrow."

Monica was still talking and laughing about my dress. I hung up on her, but I was sure she would understand. Feeling a bit nervous, I looked at the address I wrote on the paper, comparing it to what looked to be a newly built two-family flat: one upstairs, the other down. The landscaping was beautiful and the huge picture windows on the front gave the property a luxurious look. I slowly walked to the door, already biting my nails. I couldn't understand why I was so uncomfortable with this, especially since I had gotten to know Roc so well. I took several deep breaths before ringing the doorbell. Almost immediately, I could hear Roc's hard footsteps coming down the stairs.

"Who out there ringin' my bell?" he playfully asked.

"Desa Rae."

"Who?"

"You heard me, Roc. Stop playing."

"You're late."

"And?"

"And if it were me, you would be all in my shit. So I'm gettin' in yours."

"Well, that's why I'm here. I was hoping that you would get into . . . well, something."

He opened the door with a heart-melting grin on his face. He wore a pair of dark denim jeans that hung very low, showing his light blue boxers and rock-hard abs. His eyes scanned my dress and his grin got even wider. So did the door. "Damn, baby, you . . . you out here lookin' like a dyme piece. Please come in."

I stepped inside, blushing. "I thought you would like my dress, and I have no complaints either."

Roc shut the door, and then turned to face me. His eyes dropped to my lips, and even though we had kissed the other day, this time was starting to feel different. I was feeling a bit more at ease, and when his hands went underneath my dress to touch my bare ass, I felt relieved. He backed away from our intense kiss.

"Did I tell you how much I love this dress? Seein' you in it always makes my dick ready to aim and shoot."

I rested my arms on his shoulders, already feeling his hardness. "I think you appreciate what's underneath my dress more, but that's just my opinion, of course."

He winked and continued to feel my ass. "Both. And to be honest, I appreciate all of it. Every single inch of it."

I could in no way argue with that, and his tongue went in for the kill again. My hands roamed his rock-hard body and I could feel my temperature rising. As we were both indulging ourselves, Roc eased back on the steps, pulling me on top as he leaned back. I could feel cool air on my butt, as every bit of it was now exposed.

I paused from the intense kiss, looking eye to eye with Roc. "Aren't you going to show me around first? We could talk about how your day went or how mine went before we start screwing each other's brains out, right?"

"As hard as my dick is right now, we gon' have to save the chit-chat for later. And trust me when I say you will get the tour you've been waitin' for in just a few minutes."

Roc attempted to raise my dress over my head, but I backed up. I stood, looking at him leaned back on the stairs, resting on his elbows.

"Can we at least get up the stairs? I need way more room than this and it's not like I weigh a buck-zero-five."

"You were the one who always told me to be creative, and work with what space I have. You do remember tellin' me that, don't you?"

I couldn't deny my own words, but the stairs were not my cup of tea. I started up the stairs, ignoring Roc as I passed by him. When I reached the top, he stood closely behind me. I could see into the small living room that was to my right, and the bedroom that was down the hallway to my left. Roc wasted no time removing his jeans and tossing them down the stairs. He pulled the top of my sundress apart, ripping it straight down the middle. Wondering if I cared? Hell no, I didn't. My thick breasts were now exposed and so was my shaved pussy. Roc peeled the sundress away from my body, tossing it down the stairs as well. In no way could I make it to the living room or his bedroom, so I lay back on what I assumed to be a very clean, carpeted floor. Within seconds, Roc rested his body between my trembling legs, allowing me to feel a big piece of hard meat that I couldn't wait to enter me. He started in on my wobbly breasts, squeezing them in his hands and sucking them at the same time. I was on fire, and all I could do was rub my hands all over his sexy dark body that had me hooked! I could already feel my juices boiling over, and when Roc slipped his finger inside of me, I gasped out loud. He made many rotations, causing my groans to increase. I couldn't take the foreplay much longer and was in a rush to receive the satisfaction I had waited on for almost two years. I reached down, touching his monstrous dick that made my mouth water.

"Baby, pleeease put on your condom. Hurry, okay?" I begged.

Roc removed his fingers from inside of me, bringing along a small flood of my juices. He sucked his wet fingers and kneeled between my legs. Putting me into position, he placed my legs around his back. He lightly rubbed his hardness against my slit, causing my eyelids to flutter. As he toyed with my insides and circled his head around my clit, I felt so weak for him.

"Do I have to use a condom?" he asked. "I really don't want to and I'm dyin' to feel the real deal."

The foreplay he delivered was feeling so good to me, and stopping the action would have been a crime. I guess I was about to commit one, because there was no way in hell he was entering me again without a condom. Him being incarcerated put a bit of fear in me and having sex with numerous women in the past concerned me too. I reached down, moving his hardness away from me.

"Please. Let's do this the right way. I know you understand my concerns."

He shrugged. "I don't, but when we're finished, I'm sure you'll tell me."

I kept quiet, as I in no way wanted to ruin the moment. Roc stood up, making his way down the long hallway and into his bedroom. I sat up on my elbows, observing him open his drawer and break open a condom package. I was in awe looking at his side profile, and the sight of his bulging muscles made me hungry. I got off the floor and made my way to his bedroom. He had barely put the condom on before I moved him back to the bed and kneeled on the floor in front of him. I held his hardness in my hands, preparing myself to please him in every way possible.

"Nice room," I said, not paying much attention to the room, but more so to my grip on his stick.

"I knew you would like it," he replied, looking at his goods with a wicked grin.

I covered his package with my mouth, making sure it hit the back of my deep throat. Due to his size, that wasn't an easy task. Roc dropped back on the bed, allowing me to have my way with him. Almost immediately, I brought him to an eruption.

"Dezzzz," he whined. "Daaaaamn, baby, you're guuuud at that shit."

I gave him minimal time to regroup, expecting him to return the favor. I eased my way onto the bed, straddling my thighs across his face. My pussy lowered to his thick lips and he already knew what to do with it. As his tongue dipped into my overly heated tunnel, all I could shout was, "Welcome home, baby, I'm so glad you're home!"

Thing was, would I feel the same way tomorrow?

Chapter 2

I slowly opened my eyes, slightly remembering parts of a dream I'd had about my mother. All I remembered was her sitting at a table, telling me to be very careful about my choices. She was holding Chassidy in her arms, and, for some reason, Reggie was standing beside her, laughing. It was a very weird dream and I was so glad to come out of it. I yawned and sat up to observe my surroundings. I was still at Roc's place, but he was nowhere in sight. His room was lit up by a picture window that had no curtains at all, letting the bright rays from the sun come in. In front of me was a flat-screen television, sitting on an entertainment center. A microfiber wavy black chaise was next to the queen-sized bed I was in, and a dresser with a mirror was to the left of the bed. A ceiling fan in the shape of a palm tree hung from above, and the beige-colored walls looked freshly painted. The whole room was quite simple, and, to be honest, it was nothing like his penthouse.

Feeling a bit woozy, I pulled the soft blue sheets
away from my body and sat up on the edge of
the bed. Yes, Roc had sexed me all night and my
coochie was real tender. More than anything, I
needed a shower. I also needed to find something
to put on, since my pretty flowered dress was now
history. There were two doors in Roc's bedroom,
also the exit door. I didn't know what was behind
the other two doors, but when I opened one, I saw
a very long closet lined with clothes. Shoes, main-
ly tennis shoes, were everywhere and so were
plenty of boxes. I could tell Roc still had some
unpacking to do. I reached for the first thing I
saw, and that was a long purple and yellow Lakers
T-shirt. After I put it on, I opened the other door.
That one led to a bathroom. Inside was a stand-
up shower, double sinks, and a toilet. Toothpaste,
cologne, and soap were on the sink, and I only
saw two towels. I looked at myself in the long mirror, teasing my wild hair. I didn't have a brush to
straighten it, but my fingers were doing the job.
Once my hair was in place, I splashed cold water
on my face, patting it dry with my hands. I wanted
to brush my teeth, but my toothbrush was in my
purse. I couldn't remember where I had left that,
and I assumed it was somewhere near the stairs.

I left the bathroom and started down the hallway to find Roc. Almost immediately, I could hear voices. The floor squeaked a little, but I halted my steps just to listen in on the conversation.

"I'm tellin' you, them fools had me fucked up," Roc said. "I was one nigga they didn't want to pull them gates open for, and I wanted to spit on that white son of a bitch who opened it. But all I did was smile at his ass and salute! Adios, muthafucka, I'm out!"

I heard hand slapping, then another voice chimed in. "That's how you gotta do 'em. And the fact that you never showed fear, nor did yo' ass get in any trouble, it fucked them up. I told you Watts was gon' make a way out of no way, but I had to pay that fat sucker a bundle of dough. It was worth it though, baby boy, and you know I will always have yo' back."

Hand slapping sounded off again, and, unfortunately for me, I knew that voice all too well. It was Ronnie. Why Roc would want us underneath the same roof, I don't know, but I continued to listen, hearing another voice.

"I do think it's a good idea for you to lay low for a while. Ronnie, me, and BJ got this and you know we gon' hold it down for you."

"Just like you held down Vanessa while I was away, right? Sippi, you know I'm still bitter about that shit, but it takes a ho to show her true colors when a nigga locked up."

"I hit that bitch twice and if you got a beef about it, take it up with her. She the one who came at me. I'm not gon' turn down no available pussy. Besides, you told me she was just your baby's mama, nothin' more, nothin' less. Correct?"

I inched forward, waiting to hear Roc's response.

"She ain't shit to me no more, but a long time ago I would have given her ass the shirt off my back. She couldn't get a damn gummy bear from me now."

I heard laughter and that's when I decided to make my presence known before I got busted for creeping. I also wanted to make Ronnie aware that I feared him in no way, and since Roc had no intention of keeping him away from me, why not show my face? I took a deep breath, but just as I made my way to the living room, the floor loudly squeaked. Everyone turned, looking in my direction. Seeing Ronnie made my flesh crawl, and the other young man who Roc referred to as Sippi, oh my God! I wanted to run! If Vanessa had slept with him, she was out of her mind! He was tall, muscular, and had long dreads and a rugged goatee. His hazel eyes were frightening and damn near matched his gold grille. I didn't mean to stare, but I sure wouldn't want to see him in a dark alley.

Roc stood up, tugging at his cargo shorts to pull them up. "Say, baby," he said, sucking on a toothpick. "You already know Ronnie, but this is my boy, Mississippi. Sippi, this is Dez. Chassidy's mama."

Normally, I would have extended my hand, but . . . okay, what the hell? I reached out my hand and Sippi barely touched it. He threw his head back. "Sup. Glad to meet you."

Ronnie hadn't said a word and I ignored him, turning my attention to Roc.

"Honey, I was looking for some towels so I could take a shower."

"Damn, ma, you wasn't gon' wait for me?"

"No. Besides, you're busy."

Ronnie stood up, face twisted and cutting his eyes. He reached in his pocket, pulling out a wad of money that was too thick for his ashy hands to hold. Diamond rings were on each finger and a platinum and gold watch glistened on his wrist. He cut the wad in half, dropping money on the table. "My move," he said, looking at Roc. "You already know what I told you and I won't say it again. The next move is yours."

Dressed in an all-linen, cream-colored suit and diamonds in both ears, Ronnie proceeded toward me. He put his hands back into his pockets, jiggling his keys.

"Desa Rae, risk-takin' Jenkins. I see you back in business, but I wonder for how long. This time, I suggest that you don't overstay your welcome." He winked, looking very identical to Roc. "As that would please me more than you know."

Ronnie going to hell would have pleased me, and it was obvious that he still had a beef with me for taking up too much of Roc's time. Particularly keeping him away from the drug game. Before I could say anything, Roc intervened. I was sure he remembered what happened the last time the three of us were together, and I knew he was in no mood to see another gun upside my head. Trying not to go there again, I kept quiet, giving Roc an opportunity to address his out-of-control uncle.

"Man, lighten up and chill," Roc said, moving next to Ronnie. He kept staring at me, and I stared back. Roc swayed his hand in front of Ronnie's eyes, and he smacked Roc's hand.

"Don't put your gotdamn hands near my face, nigga! I don't give a fuck who you are. You out of line."

I was surprised, as Roc in no way backed down. Now his face was twisted up and his forehead showed thick wrinkles. "Muthafucka, yo' ass the one out of line. If I didn't touch you, nigga, don't touch me. Show a man some respect in front of his woman and don't be treatin' me like no punk."

Sippi got between Roc and Ronnie, but from the way he was gazing at Roc, I could tell he had Ronnie's back. Lord knows I didn't want to get into the middle of this, but I had to put forth some effort to calm the situation.

"Look, Ronnie, I apologize if my presence makes you uneasy. I will do my best to stay out of your way and I don't want you and Roc arguing—"

"Shut the fuck up talkin' to me, bitch," he spat, keeping his eyes on Roc. "I see you done got some extra balls in prison, but you'd betta cut them suckers off and get back to just havin' two. Watch yo' tone with me, youngblood, and the next time you slip up at the mouth, I will bust you in it."

Roc tapped his lip with his finger. "Are you threatenin' me? Right here, old school, go ahead and put it right there."

I witnessed the mean mug on Ronnie's face and saw his fist tighten. My stomach dropped when he slammed his fist into Roc's mouth, staggering him backward. In no way did he fall, but as he quickly charged forward, Mississippi stopped Roc dead in his tracks. He placed his gun on Roc's heaving chest.

"Don't touch him, Roc!" Sippi yelled. "Back the fuck up!"

There was no way for me to just stand there, and when my eyes shifted over to the phone, Sippi turned the gun toward me. All I could think was, *Not again.*

"If you move, you die."

"Y'all muthafuckas trippin'," Roc said, wiping a dab of blood on his lip with his hand. He seemed calm as ever, but I wasn't. My stomach was rumbling and my hands had a slight tremble. All kinds of things were roaming in my head and all I could think of was my dream. Why did I continue to inject myself into this mess? I didn't know.

"Put that shit down," Ronnie said, giving Sippi an order. "You need not act unless I ask you to. As long as that fool got my blood running through his veins, don't you ever pull a gun on him! You got that shit?"

Sippi nodded and had already lowered his gun. Ronnie turned to Roc again, poking at his chest. "You and me gon' holla later. We don't do this, Roc, 'cause you ain't bigger than me yet. A wise man can go a long way in this world, and he also knows to never put pussy before partna. I hope you understand what I'm sayin', and don't you ever bite the hand that feeds you and feeds you well."

Roc cocked his neck from side to side, saying not a word. Ronnie and his goon headed down the stairs and I was relieved when I heard the door shut. Roc stormed by me, making his way down the hallway and into his bedroom. When I got to his room, he was laid back on the bed, looking up at the ceiling with his arm across his forehead. I figured it was time for me to go.

"I'll be out of your way in a minute. I had a nice time last night, but I'm discouraged by what just happened. You know how much Ronnie despises me, so why didn't you just wake me up and ask me to leave?"

"Good-bye, Dez. I'm not up for a bunch of your irritatin'-ass questions."

Roc was as stubborn as stubborn could get, but so was I. I was also a person who had to have answers when I wanted them. I walked over to the bed and lay sideways next to him. To put him at ease, I dabbed the blood on his lips with a Kleenex, then pecked his lips and put his arms around my neck.

"Listen, can we please not get off on the wrong foot? You just made that suggestion yesterday and I don't want my feelings for Ronnie to get in the way of what I feel for you. I hope you don't either, and for the sake of our child, let's do our best to get along. It would really mean a lot to me, Roc, and I promise that I will not pressure you about our relationship, or about what you decide to do with your life. I just want to be happy and have fun. I can't think of a better person I would enjoy myself with more than you."

Roc turned his head, then used his finger to touch the side of my face. "You're right. I'm sorry that happened in front of you, but shit like that happens all the time. We'll be drinkin', smoking herbs, and laughin' about that shit tomorrow, so no big deal. I apologize for how Ronnie is, and I really need to make sure the two of y'all keep your distance."

"Please," I laughed. "And how can you laugh, drink, and smoke blunts with someone who treats—"

Roc placed his finger on my lips. "Let it go, Dez. Puttin' my hands on Ronnie would be like fightin' with my own father. He's dead and you know Ronnie's been like a replacement. So sometimes I gotta chalk that shit up and take it. You would never understand and I'm not goin' to waste my time explainin' it to you. Now, if you're leavin', good-bye. If you prefer to stay, I have some other suggestions."

I smiled, wondering what his *other* suggestions were. "You're right. I don't understand, but tell me about your other suggestions. I have some idea, but I just want to be sure."

Roc rolled on top of me, playfully kissing down my neck. "I have to straighten out my closets, get my kitchen in order, bring my dinin' room table up from the basement, and unload a few more boxes. Will you help me?"

"Hmmm, don't know yet. I thought you may have something in this for me."

Roc stopped kissing my neck and pecked my cheek. "I always got somethin' for you. Once we get finished with the house chores, I intend to tackle some of your sweet pussy all night long and into the next morning."

"Wow. Are you sure about that? If my memory serves me correctly, you were the one who threw in the towel last night because you were tired."

"No, I wasn't tired. I was just givin' you a break. You were startin' to lose your voice, and I assumed you got tired of screamin' my name."

"That's because your dick is sooo good and I love hearing myself say your name."

Roc blushed. "I like hearin' you say it too. Hearin' you say 'Ohhh, Roc, baby' is like music to my ears. Let's go ahead and handle our business with the unpackin' first, then I'll let you turn on your music. I'll turn on mine too, and the way your snatch talks to me, my music may get a bit louder than yours."

"Tuh, it always does. You just don't know how loud 'Daaaamn, Dez, baby, keep fuckin' me like this' is. Your words are way louder than I could ever get."

Roc chuckled. "I don't be sayin' no dumb shit like that. And if I do, that's because I be under the influence."

"Under the influence of what?"

"A sexy-ass, lovin' woman who I couldn't stop thinkin' about while I was in prison. We gon' do this shit, ma, and before all is said and done, I'm goin' to make you my wifey. For better or worse, no doubt."

"And I'm going to enjoy watching you try."

We kissed, and before I made another move, I got up to take a shower. Roc left me at peace and I stood in the shower thinking just how much of myself I was willing to give. In no way did I know, or even want to predict my future with Roc, but being with him again felt special—with the exception of my setback with Ronnie.

***

For the next several hours, I helped Roc get his place in order. Like I'd said before, it in no way compared to his penthouse, but his new place was nice. It was shaped like an L, with the living room, dining room, and kitchen being on one side, and his bedroom on the other. He had two bathrooms and a basement that had to be shared with the other tenant. Not much furniture adorned the space, and Roc said that was because he wanted to keep it simple. He wasn't sure how long he was going to live there, but it was imperative that he removed himself from his previous location.

Around 4:00 P.M., I took a break to eat some barbecue from Red's that Roc had gone to get us on West Florissant Avenue, and to call Monica. She didn't answer, so I left a message on voice mail, telling her to call me soon. I wasn't sure if she was trying to avoid me, but I was a little worried since I hadn't heard from her all day. Roc was still going from room to room, making sure everything was to his liking. He had no organization skills at all, and since he kept stopping to answer his phone calls by hitting the Bluetooth on his ear, I gave up. The loud hip hop music was working me, too, and I could feel a headache coming on. I plopped down on his bed, and turned on the TV to watch the news. I could hear Roc talking to someone on the phone, cursing and laughing some more. I closed my eyes, trying to soothe my headache, but that's when he came into the room.

"Uh, what are you doin'? I thought you were supposed to be helpin' me."

I yawned. "I was, but I got a headache, plus I'm tired. You've been slacking anyway, and you have talked on that phone more than you've done anything else around here."

"Nigga, let me get at you later," he said, then hit the button on his Bluetooth. "I ain't talked to some of my boys in a while, so they were just callin' to see what was up. Sippi out runnin' his mouth about me and Ronnie, too, so everybody just wanted to make sure everything straight."

"Is it?"

"Yeah, I already talked to that fool. We good."

I had no comment, but I did ask Roc to turn down the music. He did as I asked, then sat on the bed next to me.

"Say. If you don't mind, I want to take Chassidy and Li'l Roc to a picnic with me. They need to get to know each other and I hope you don't have a problem with that."

The thought of Chassidy being anywhere near Roc's crew in no way sat right with me. I didn't know how to say it without offending him, but Chassidy wasn't going anywhere with him, without me. "I don't mind Chassidy getting to know her brother or relatives, but where is this picnic supposed to be? Am I invited?"

"It's next weekend at Fairground Park. He havin' a barbecue bash and I want to bring my kids to show them off. I don't care if you come or not, but you don't really click with my peeps. You know how we get down, and I don't need you there watchin' my back and rollin' those pretty eyes."

"Yes, I witnessed today how you get down, and unfortunately, Roc, I don't want Chassidy exposed to that kind of foolishness. Have all the fun you want, please, but I'm not comfortable with her being surrounded by a bunch of people getting high, drinking, pulling guns on each other . . . You know what I mean. I would love for us to have a picnic, and the kids can join us. How about that?"

Roc got off the bed, seeming a bit irritated. "Chassidy is my daughter too, Dez, and whether you like it or not, she will get to know her peeps. All of them ain't ghettofied Negros and plenty of them are down-to-earth, normal people. I have a serious problem with people who look down on others, so correct yourself on that, all right?

I'ma do this picnic thing with you, but there will come a time when you gon' have to ease up on our daughter."

I was already getting to a point when I knew it made sense for me not to comment. This was one of them, but Roc was so wrong about me easing up on Chassidy. No way, no how would I subject her to anything like what happened today. Roc would have to come to grips with it, and this was the one thing I wasn't willing to budge on.

After I took two aspirin, I lay back on the plush pillow to take a nap. Roc let me get some rest and I was glad about that. I was still puzzled why Monica hadn't called me back, but when I checked my phone, she had. She said that they were having a good time, and she'd see me tomorrow. The only reason she'd missed my call was because she couldn't hear her phone ringing, due to the loud arcade games at Incredible Pizza. I smiled, thinking of my daughter having fun, and fell asleep.

What seemed like hours later, I was awakened by a loud boom. I jumped from my sleep, noticing that Roc was lying next to me, asleep as well. His arm was around my waist and the room was partially dark. I looked at the alarm clock on the dresser, and it showed 9:45 P.M. Since Roc was still sleeping, I figured I was just hearing things.

My eyes searched the room for a while, then I lay back to watch the TV. A few seconds later, the booming sound happened again. This time it was constant and sounded like someone banging hard on the door. I shook Roc's shoulder to wake him.

"Roc, wake up. I . . . I think someone is knocking at your door."

He was groggy as ever and all he moaned was, "Huh?"

"Someone is at your door. Don't you hear that?"

Roc forced his tired eyes open, listening for a knock. He heard several, and that's when he threw the covers aside.

"Wait right here," he said, slowly getting out of bed. He turned on the lights, causing me to squint. Wearing nothing at all, he grabbed his housecoat, and then opened up a drawer. I noticed him put his gun in his pocket and then he made his way down the hallway.

"Who is it?" he yelled. "And why in the fuck you bangin' on my damn door like the police?"

I had already started to bite my nails, and being with Roc at his place was starting to become a problem. I had never spent the night with him in his territory. In the past, we always stayed at my house. There was a possibility that I would

resort to staying at my house only. I was trying
to give him the benefit of the doubt, but this was
getting ridiculous.

As I was in thought, I could hear a female's
voice yelling and screaming. Yes, Roc told me
to stay where I was, but I was never one to listen to his orders. I got out of bed, wearing his
white long T-shirt I'd changed into before taking
my nap. His white socks were on my feet and I
teased my hair to straighten it. I made my way
to the top of the stairs, looking down to see what
was up. The door was wide open. Roc stood on
one side, and his son's mother, Vanessa, was on
the porch. She looked up at me, causing Roc to
turn his head in my direction as well.

"Good-bye, Vanessa. If you don't stop all of
this clownin' and shit, you gon' regret it."

She tried to come inside, but Roc held up his
arm to block her from entering. "Nigga, move
your damn arm! Let me in! I see why yo' ass ain't
been answerin' your stupid-ass phone."

Roc slightly shoved her back, but she kept
charging forward to get inside. "I haven't answered my phone because I told you I don't fuck
with you no more. What's so hard for you to understand about that?"

Vanessa ignored Roc, and when she ducked
underneath his arm, she made progress to the

second step. Roc grabbed her waist and tossed her back out the door like a paper doll. I felt bad for her, and in no way was I going to stand by and let him go overboard with her.

"Roc," I said. He turned his head toward me. "Just come inside and close the door."

As his attention was on me, Vanessa lifted her foot like a punter in the NFL, kicking him right between his legs. When he doubled over and grabbed himself, she slapped the shit out of him. He was caught off guard and she ran inside again. This time, she almost made it up the stairs. She lunged out at me, but immediately went tumbling back down the steps. Roc grabbed her ankles, and she hit the steps so hard, I knew she had to have broken something. Roc reached for her hair, squeezing it tight and jerking her head.

"Bitch, didn't I tell you to exit? I can't be nice to yo' ass for nothin'! You just ain't satisfied unless I got my foot up yo' ass, are you?"

"Let me go, muthafucka! I hate yo' ass, Roc! I hate your fuckin' guts!"

Roc slammed her face into the wall, and I swear that every breath in my body left me. I could in no way watch things go down like this, so I hurried down the steps to pull him away from her.

"Is this what you want?" he said, turning her around and holding her in a headlock. As his grip was too tight, she couldn't say a word. "What's that?" he said, seething with anger. "I can't hear you. You was just talkin' all that shit, but yo' ass ain't sayin' nothin' now."

Tears were pouring down Vanessa's face and she couldn't open her mouth if she tried. I reached out, trying to remove Roc's arm from her neck.

"Don't touch me, Dez! Go back upstairs and stay the fuck out of this!"

I ignored Roc, still trying to loosen his grip. Finally he let Vanessa go, and her body was so weak that she dropped to the floor. I was so angry that I turned around and headed upstairs to go. With my back turned, Vanessa rushed up and grabbed the back of my hair, pulling me backward. Thank God for the banister, as she moved so quickly that I would have been on my butt. Roc grabbed her again, this time twisting her arm hard behind her back.

"I will break this muthafucka off! Let her fuckin' hair go."

The pain must have been too much for Vanessa to bear, because she let go of my hair in an instant.

I pointed my finger in her face, fuming. "Touch me again, and Roc won't be the only problem that you have. And trust me, he's not nothing compared to me," I spat. I kept it moving up the stairs and didn't even turn around to see what would happen next. If Vanessa thought that I was her problem, she was sadly mistaken. Her problem was with Roc; then again, so was mine. I went into the bedroom, closing the door behind me so I wouldn't have to listen to what was happening. I wondered why Vanessa wouldn't just leave, and if a man said that he didn't want to be bothered, then why force the situation? My mind went right to Latrel, and I wondered if he had ever been in a situation where a woman had hit on him like Vanessa had done to Roc. Would Latrel do what Roc did? I seriously doubted it, but his father and I had taught him to always defend himself. No matter what, I didn't like what was going down with Roc and Vanessa, and as soon as they settled their differences, I intended to leave.

About ten minutes later, the bedroom door flew open and Roc came inside. I was sitting against the headboard with my knees pressed close to my chest. Roc looked at me, and then went over to the dresser to put the gun back inside.

"Before your mouth starts goin', Dez, I don't want to hear it. You know nothin' about my situation with her, so keep your comments to yourself."

I got off the bed, and reached for my keys and purse on the nightstand. My flip-flops were already next to me, so I slid into them. I made my way toward the door, but stopped before exiting.

"Enjoy your evening, Roc. No, I don't know much detail about your relationship with Vanessa, but I do know this, a man should never hit a woman, but I guess you felt as if you had to do what was necessary. That's your decision to make, but through my eyes it makes you look really bad. I can't help the way I feel, even though she works the hell out of me."

His mouth dropped open. "You saw for yourself what she was doin' and you're damn right I'm goin' to always defend myself. That bitch has tried to shoot and stab me before. She gangsta like that and some women you have to handle in a different way. She'll be all right, and when you keep gettin' your head bumped enough, you'll eventually learn somethin'."

I couldn't help but to shake my head. "If you've continued in a relationship with a woman who has tried to shoot or stab you, then you're getting what you deserve. The wake-up call obviously came awhile back, but too bad you missed it. Trying to cut her off now may not work in your favor, and head bumping will get you nowhere but back in jail. I hope you know that."

Roc didn't respond, so I walked out the door. He shouted my name as I made my way down the hallway.

I turned with an attitude. "Yes."

"Being with me will not be easy," he said, now standing in the doorway to his bedroom. "What you see is what you get. I'm not goin' to sugarcoat nothin' and you need to decide if you're wit' me or not. I can't have no woman who thinks she can walk in and out of my life when she gets ready. I need one who knows my situation and accepts it. As you can see, much of this shit is beyond my control. I'm tryin' to get rid of the bad seeds, but they won't disappear as quickly as you want them to. Think about what I'm sayin' and get at me when you've come to grips with the way I do things."

"Do your bad seeds include Vanessa and being in the drug game? I just want to be sure that's what you're referring to."

"Exactly. Just don't expect everything to change overnight. In due time, they will. For now, all you need to know is I'm not sexually involved with Vanessa and I've had no part in sellin' drugs. I hope you're at least happy about that."

I shrugged, somewhat knowing that Roc was just saying what he did to please me. If anything, I had hoped being in prison had taught him a lesson. The verdict was still out, so, "Possibly happy," was all I could say. In no way did I want to leave Roc under these conditions, but what had happened today left a sour taste in my mouth. I closed the door behind me, and as I made my way to my car, I noticed my passenger's side window was cracked. "B.I.T." was spray-painted on my door. I let out a deep sigh, as the truth was now staring me in the face. Roc was home, and I had a feeling that it wasn't such a good thing after all.

Chapter 3

I talked to Roc every day for almost two weeks straight, but had not been back to his place. He hadn't come to mine either, but since we had planned to have a picnic, he was on his way over with his son. He was upset about what had happened to my car, but not as much as I was. He promised to give me the money to pay for the damages, but I knew where his money was coming from. According to Roc, he was no longer "hands on," but his condo and any money that he had was given to him by Ronnie. This concerned me, and I had plans to see what I could do to help him earn his own money. I had already contacted my insurance company to have my car taken care of. The window was fixed right away, but I had to wait another week for the paint job to get done. Until then, I drove around in a rental, and kept my car in the garage. What a stupid thing for a woman to do, and, at this point, I had very little sympathy for Vanessa. A fool she was, and along with her pulling my hair, I considered this strike number two for her. There was only so much one could tolerate, and my patience with her was wearing thin.

It was a Saturday afternoon, and I had put together some ham and cheese sandwiches, chips, fruit cups, and cupcakes for us to eat on our picnic at Forest Park. I made Chassidy and Li'l Roc some frozen Mickey Mouse Popsicles and hoped they wouldn't melt too quickly. For entertainment, I dusted off two fishing rods in my garage that Latrel and Reggie used to go fishing. I bought Chassidy a smaller one and picked up some bait while I was at the store. I figured we could do a little fishing, just to have some extra fun. It was about eighty-five degrees outside, so I dressed Chassidy in a pair of jean shorts and a pink T-shirt. Pink and white Nike tennis shoes covered her feet, and her hair was sleeked back into a neat ponytail, tied with a pink ribbon. I guess I was being biased, but she was quite adorable. I wore my blue jean stretch capris, a plum-colored T-shirt, and tennis shoes. My hair was also in a ponytail, because I wanted to be comfortable.

I stood in the kitchen, making sure I had everything packed and ready to go. All I was missing was the insect repellant, so I hurried to the closet to get it. Chassidy followed me, trying to keep up. She was such a happy child, and giggled as she chased me.

"Girl, you can't keep up with me," I teased. When the doorbell rang, I couldn't keep up with her. She rushed to the door, but I was right behind her. Roc had a new steel gray Lincoln Navigator, and I could see it parked in the driveway. I opened the door, inviting him and his son to come inside. The first thing he did was ease his arm around my waist and peck my lips.

"What's up, sexy? You know anytime a woman can dress down and still look good, she one bad mamma jamma."

His compliments always made me blush, and seeing him period genuinely excited me. He reached for Chassidy, picking her up and kissing her cheeks.

"Muah," he said. "Hey, beautiful. Girl, you know you lookin' more and more like yo' daddy every day."

I cut my eyes, as sometimes the truth was hard to admit. Li'l Roc was still standing by the door, so I reached out my hand to his.

"Hi," I politely said. He wouldn't smile at all, but did reach out to shake my hand. "You are so adorable. How old are you?"

"Five," he responded, but pouted right after.

"Are you okay?" I asked.

"Leave his knucklehead ass alone," Roc said. "I had to get in his shit in the car and now he got an attitude."

I closed the door. "Well, come on inside and let's go in the kitchen. I'm just about finished getting everything together and we can leave in about ten minutes."

Roc carried Chassidy in his arms, tickling her and making her laugh. Li'l Roc followed us, and when we got to the kitchen, I offered him a Popsicle. He declined, moving his head from side to side, still pouting.

Roc commented again. "When somebody offer you somethin', what are you supposed to say?"

"No, thank you," Li'l Roc replied, then slightly rolled his eyes. Roc put Chassidy down, then stepped up to Li'l Roc, poking at his chest. I definitely knew where that came from.

"You need to get yo' shit together. Do you remember what I told you in the car?"

Li'l Roc nodded and listened. "I meant what I said and I will not repeat myself again. Get it together, all right?"

Li'l Roc nodded again, this time without pouting. Roc pointed to Chassidy. "You know who that is right there?" Li'l Roc shrugged his shoulders. "That's your li'l sister, Chassidy. She got it goin' on like you and me, don't she?" He nodded again. "Always have her back, 'cause that's blood right there. The same blood runnin' through your veins runnin' through hers." Roc crossed his fingers. "Tight like this, okay?"

Li'l Roc crossed his fingers and repeated what Roc said. "Tight like this."

Roc rubbed the top of his son's head. "Now, that's what's up."

It appeared that everyone was back on the same page, so I gave Roc the picnic basket, blankets, and pillows to put in his truck. As we stood outside loading up, he looked at me like I was crazy with the fishing poles in my hands.

"Where in the hell are you goin' with those?"

"We're going fishing. Have you never been fishing before?"

"If I have, I can't remember. But I thought we were supposed to be havin' a picnic."

"We're doing that too, but we can also catch fish as well."

"Are you cookin' the fish later on tonight?"

"Nope."

"Then what's the purpose?"

"The purpose is to have fun with the kids and with you."

Roc cut his eyes at me, and after the kids were strapped into their safety seats, we left. Roc had no concern for our ears and he blasted the music as high as it could go. I looked back, seeing Li'l Roc bobbing his head and Chassidy, with a frown, covering her ears. Definitely, like mother, like daughter; like father, like son.

"Now, you already know what I'm going to say. I think you raise the volume on that thing just to irritate me."

Roc smiled and bobbed his head, ignoring my hint. A few minutes later, he turned down the volume.

"Before I forget, look in the glove compartment and get that envelope," he said.

I reached for the envelope in the glove compartment, noticing several hundred dollar bills inside.

"That's for your car. Sorry about that, but payback gon' be a muthafucka."

I put the envelope back into the glove compartment and closed it. "My car is already taken care of. Thanks, though, and I appreciate your kindness. I'm almost afraid to ask, but have you talked to her since then?"

"We don't talk anymore. All we do is cuss each other out. Yes, I've had the pleasure of cursin' her ass out because she came over again, tryin' to bring mo' noise. This time, I didn't open my door, so she had to handle her business on the other side."

"Well, that was a smart move. Just be careful and I know I don't have to tell you to watch your back. She has some serious issues, and if you've been dealing with that mess for . . . how many years?"

"Seven. And, yes, we have always had a rocky relationship, but don't ask me why. All love one minute, hate the next."

"I guess it be like that sometimes."

As much as I wanted to know about Roc's relationship with Vanessa, I really didn't care about it. I already knew what it consisted of, and the answer was a whole lot of disrespect. Shame on both of them for being in a battle for love for that damn long.

When we arrived at Forest Park, I could see a cozy spot from a distance. It was underneath a shaded tree on a slight hill. A few feet away was a pond where several people were already fishing. The kids had plenty of room to run around and play. I predicted we would have a decent time.

Roc carried most of our things to the designated spot and I held the kids' hands. He laid the blankets on the green grass and dropped the pillows on top. I blew up two huge balls for the kids, using an air pump. They couldn't wait to play with them, and when I suggested eating first, they refused. I sat on the blanket next to

Roc, who was already laid back on one of the pillows. A cool breeze was coming in, making it so relaxing.

"Aren't you going to eat something?" I asked Roc. I pulled out the ham and cheese sandwiches, showing them to him.

"What is that? Ham and cheese? No, thank you. Had enough of that shit in jail. What else you got in there?"

I pulled out the chips, fruit cups, and cupcakes. "Okay, which one?"

Roc turned to his side, resting on his elbow. He reached for the fruit cups and a small bag of Doritos.

"Thanks," he said with a smile. He looked so sexy in a dark blue wife beater, cargo shorts, and Jordans on his feet. I wasn't the only one who could dress so simply, yet look spectacular. All day I had wanted to kiss him, just to let him know that I wasn't bitter about what had happened at his place. I took the opportunity, and leaned in to give him a lengthy, juicy kiss. He reached up to the back of my head, holding it steady and softly rubbing my hair. My eyes closed, as kissing him always seemed so perfect. Chassidy interrupted our kiss when she came over and reached for a cupcake. I opened the package for her, and gave Li'l Roc a bag of chips he was reaching for. When

I asked if either of them wanted a Popsicle, both of them said no.

"Why doesn't anyone want a Popsicle? It's hot and I thought they would help to cool us down."

"Shit, then give me one," Roc said, looking down at his goods. "I definitely need somethin' to calm me down right about now."

He wasn't the only one, so I gave him one of the Popsicles and kept one for myself. The kids ran off to play again while Roc and I slurped on each other's Popsicles. "Remind me to thank you later," he said. "This pic-nookie was an excellent idea, and who would have thought I'd be havin' this much fun?"

The Popsicle juices were dripping from his lips, and you better believe I was there to suck them. He was working my lips and Popsicle too, and we couldn't help but laugh.

"You know if the kids weren't with us, I would lay you back on this blanket and fuck somethin' up. Feel how hard my dick is right now."

"I don't have to feel it. I can already see it through your shorts. Calm down, baby, and you know I'm going to take care of that real soon."

"Soon? Shit I was hopin' you'd take care of it for me now. Let me play with those titties, touch your pussy or somethin'. That will calm me down real quick."

I watched Chassidy and Li'l Roc continuing to play with their balls and chasing each other. They seemed to be having a good time, so I responded to Roc's suggestion. "Not out here, okay? There will be so much time left for that later."

Roc moved over, straddling his legs behind me as we both sat up. He wrapped his arms around my waist and nibbled on my ear.

"Be creative, Roc," he said, repeating those words I'd said before. "Work with what space—"

I turned my head to the side. "You are not going to let me forget what I said to you about being creative, are you?"

"Nope. And I'm goin' to live by those words, especially when we're together."

His hands eased up my shirt, touching my lace bra. My nipples had already become erect, and when he softly shaved his hands across them, I could feel my breasts tighten.

"See," Roc whispered in my ear. "This looks totally innocent, but brings great pleasure. Keep smilin' and lookin' at the kids playin' and they will pay us no mind."

I couldn't believe I was letting Roc massage my breasts and get me so aroused in public. There weren't too many people around, but it did feel pretty awkward. His touch felt good, too, so I couldn't complain about that.

Roc placed his lips on my earlobe and whispered in my ear, "Damn, these titties soft as hell. I wanna suck them, though. Can I?"

My body was tingling all over, but sucking my breasts would be going too far. "No, Roc. This is as far as we go and this is quite enough."

"Aww, you ain't no fun. All you gotta do is throw these covers over your head for a minute or two. We can pretend that we're wrestlin' or playin' around."

My eyes were still focused on the kids, but my mind was elsewhere. "No," I laughed. "Absolutely not. And is this your idea of a pic-nookie?"

Roc lowered his hands from my breasts, causing the tingling to go away. "Exactly. Now answer this question for me. Are you wet yet?"

I turned my head to the side as he rested his chin on my shoulder. "What? What's it to you?"

"I know you are, just by how hard those nipples were. Keep on grinnin' and watchin' the kids. Sit Indian style, and I'm gon' bend my knees. Pull up the blanket, and lay it across your lap."

"You got this all figured out, don't you?"

Roc didn't answer, just bent his knees and remained straddled behind me. I reached for the blanket, covering myself from the waist down. Roc touched my hips, and then eased his hands underneath the blanket. He popped the buttons

on my capris and his fingers dipped into my wetness. His touch always made me gasp, so I did.

"I knew you would like it," he whispered in my
ear. "Chill and . . . And how in the hell did you
get this wet so fast? Damn, baby, this shit feels
too good."

My eyes fluttered and all I could do was suck
in my bottom lip. "Please don't talk anymore.
You will make me jump on top of you soooo
quick and fuck your brains out."

"That's what I want you to do."

"But I can't," I whined.

"Then chill and just let me finish."

I took a few deep breaths, as Roc's fingers
were turning circles inside of me. I mean, he was
working it like a professional, flicking his fingers
fast and causing my insides to feel as if they were
being tickled. We could both hear what his actions were doing to my insides and my juices
were causing a stir.

"I love the sound of that," Roc whispered
again. "Don't you hear it?"

I nodded, squeezing my stomach tightly and
tightening my legs. I looked at the kids coming
our way and dropped my head. "Hurry, baby,
they're coming."

"So are you," Roc said, but my come didn't get
there fast enough. With the kids only a few feet

away, Roc pulled out, leaving me high and dry . . . well, actually, wet as ever.

Chassidy jumped into my lap and Roc stood up. "I'ma go over here to this bathroom," he said, smiling. "I'll be right back." He looked at Li'l Roc. "Man, do you need to go to the bathroom?"

Li'l Roc said no and stayed with me and Chassidy. They reached for the cupcakes, allowing me time to get up and button my capris. I felt very sticky between my legs, and when I got Roc home, I intended to make him pay for what he'd done.

Roc was in the bathroom for several minutes, and when he came back I didn't even have to ask what took him so long. "That was a good one," he whispered to me as I was trying to untangle the string on the fishing rod. "I let go of some mad-ass sperm and you should have seen it."

"Uh, thanks for sharing with your nasty self. You are so nasty and I can't believe I let you do that to me."

"That's 'cause you nasty too. Now, what's up with these fishin' rods?"

"I'm just trying to untangle this one. If you would get me some of that bait over there, I would appreciate it."

As Roc got the bait, I kept my eyes on Chassidy and Li'l Roc. He threw his ball hard at her face, causing her to fall on the ground. She hit the ground pretty hard, and that's what made her cry. I dropped my rod and went to go pick her up. Roc had seen what had happened as well, and he tore into Li'l Roc.

"Nigga, what's wrong with you?" Roc said, punching his chest. "Why you do yo' sister like that?"

I couldn't believe Roc's punch didn't cause Li'l Roc to shed one tear. It sounded off pretty loud to me, and calling him a nigga just . . . It just bothered the hell out of me.

"Speak when I'm talkin' to you, fool!" Roc demanded of his son.

Li'l Roc didn't say a word, just mean mugged his father as if he could tear him apart. That made Roc even madder and he grabbed him by his shirt.

I quickly put Chassidy down and touched Roc's shoulder. "Look. I know this is your child, but he didn't mean no harm. Kids have accidents all the time and it's no big deal. Please don't talk to your son like that. There is a better way to handle children when they get out of line. Chastising him by punching him is not the way."

"Fuck that. He needs to man up and take responsibility for his actions. I'm not raisin' no punk, Dez, so you can get that shit out of your head."

"There will come a time when he needs to man up, but you need to let a five-year-old be a five-year-old. Now, please let go of his shirt. You can do whatever it is that you want to do with your son, but not in my presence."

Roc let go of Li'l Roc's shirt. "You lucky today, but get your butt over there to your sister and apologize. And if you ever treat her like that again, I'ma put—"

I covered Roc's mouth, but he moved my hand away. "Put my foot up your ass!"

Li'l Roc apologized to Chassidy, but she couldn't care less. Yet again, I was pretty darn upset with Roc about his actions, but, for now, I left the situation alone. I told Li'l Roc and Chassidy to follow me down by the water, and showed them how to toss their rods into the water. At first, Roc was too mad to say anything, but after he realized that nobody was tripping but him, he finally got his act together. He helped Li'l Roc toss his rod, and the farther it went into the water, they gave each other high-fives. Chassidy could barely throw her rod, and after a while, all she did was chase the ducks that had come over to us. She was trying to pet them, and so was Li'l Roc. A few minutes later, Roc had a tug on his rod, and the two of them reeled in a fish. It was a mid-sized pan fish and was wobbling all over. Roc pulled it out of the water, watching it flop around in the grass. He and Li'l Roc both looked kind of scared of it.

"Now what?" Roc said, looking down at it.

"Touch it," I said. "Pick it up and touch it, before we throw it back in the water."

Roc frowned, but reached down to pick it up. The fish slipped out of his hand, causing me and Li'l Roc to laugh. I hurried to pick up the fish, inviting the kids to touch it. Li'l Roc hesitantly touched it, but said that it felt slimy.

"Yes, it does," I said, pointing out different parts of the fish. "These are his fins, his tail is right here, and these are scales. He's called a pan fish because he's just big enough for you to fry him in a pan. Can you see his eyes? What color are they?"

Li'l Roc moved closer, observing the fish and touching him again. "They look blue. Are we going to take him home to cook him?"

"No, I think we'd better put him back into the water. He really likes it there, but maybe we can try to catch another one that looks different. Great job on catching this one and thumbs up!"

I gave Li'l Roc a high-five and he was all smiles. I let him throw the fish back into the water and he did. He was anxious to catch another one, but, unfortunately for us, we stood in the hot sun for at least another hour and didn't catch a thing. Afterward, we played ball with the kids and lay out on the blanket, laughing and talking as if our lives had not missed one beat. Chassidy was getting antsy, so I suggested packing up and leaving.

The drive home was noisy as ever. The kids were talking and so were Roc and I. I really enjoyed my day with him, and looked forward to many more days like this to come. When we got back to my house, I cooked dinner, we watched a movie, the kids took showers, and then we called it a night. Chassidy had fallen asleep on Roc's lap, and wherever her *The Princess and the Frog* pillow lay, so did she. He carried her to her room, and I got the guestroom prepared for Li'l Roc. Latrel had so many action figures, video games, puzzles, etc. in his room in the basement, so I took Li'l Roc downstairs so he could gather some things to take to the upstairs guestroom with him. He picked up Latrel's Xbox and also got some games. He liked the big puzzle pieces of *Iron Man,* so I picked those up too. All kinds of books lined Latrel's bookshelves, so I picked up two books I figured Li'l Roc would like.

"Do you like to read?" I asked.

"No, I hate books."

"Why?"

"Because my teacher makes me read them at school."

"Then you must have a very, very smart teacher. She just wants you to be smart too, and I do as well. Reading books is so good for you and it's an excellent way to feed your brain. Your brain has to eat, you know. And when you feed it, wowww, so many wonderful things can happen to you. Remember that, okay?"

Li'l Roc nodded and we carried the items up to the guestroom. I could hear Roc talking to someone on his phone, so I let him handle his business with whomever and got Li'l Roc situated for bed.

"Now, you can watch the television and play with the puzzle tonight. Your dad can hook up the game for you tomorrow, but I want you to get some sleep. I hope you're comfortable. Do you like lights on or lights off?"

"Lights off!" he yelled, pulling the covers over his head.

"Well, okay." I smiled, turning the lights off on my way out.

"Miss Dez," he said.

"Yes."

"Thanks for being nice. My mama said you were a mean B."

I was stunned, but then again, no, I wasn't. "You're welcome. And I'm glad that you got a chance to see that I'm not mean."

He smiled and I walked down the hallway, shaking my head. How dare Vanessa say something like that to her son, with her dysfunctional self? What a poor excuse for a mother.

When I got to my room, Roc was sitting in my chair, laughing at what someone was saying on the other end of the phone. I went into my closet, stripped naked, and gathered my things for a shower. I tossed my nightgown over my shoulder and slipped into my house shoes. Leaving the closet, I eyeballed Roc and his eyes got wider. He licked his lips and tried to cut his conversation short.

"Uh, say, man . . . hold that thought." The person on the other end kept talking, and I watched Roc nod his head. I made my way to the bathroom and turned on the water in the shower. Wasting no more time, I got inside and started to lather myself. A few minutes later, Roc joined me. I had the pleasure of lathering his body, and the look of the white, sudsy soap against his black sexy body was priceless. I dropped the soap, pressing my body as close to his as I could. My arms rested on his shoulders, and before I said anything, I delivered a passionate kiss that locked our lips for minutes.

"Mmmm," Roc said, backing away from me. "Let's hurry this shit up so we can get to the bed."

"I say be creative and work with whatever space you have."

He smiled and rubbed his hands up and down on my backside. "Then I say bend that ass over and let's get this shit started."

After Roc strapped up with a condom, his wish was my command. We tore it up in the bathroom, but being in the shower didn't allow us the space we needed. The bedroom definitely did, and as Roc fucked me doggie style on the bed, I couldn't get enough. I threw myself back at him, as he tightly squeezed my hips. I massaged my own breasts and was on cloud nine feeling his hard, long meat slide in and out of me. His rhythm was perfect and the way he eased in from different angles was impressive. I felt defeated, and pulled on my hair.

"You . . . you got me, Roc. I am hooked on the way you do this pussy. You treat it so well and I loooove it!"

"I'm hooked like a muthafucka too. I crave for this shit, baby, every gotdamn day of my life! Nobody makes me feel like this. Nobody!"

I could feel Roc's dick thumping inside of me and I knew what was coming next. "Daaammmn, Dez, baby, why you fuckin' me like this."

"Ohhh, Roc, I'm there. Just . . . just keep at it, baby, and I will give you something special to remember."

I cut loose on Roc, coating his shaft and leaving his balls dripping wet. He held on tightly to my hips, and we both fell forward, completely out of breath. Slowly, he rolled over next to me, trying to gather himself.

I rested my head in my hand, looking over at him. "Do you think the kids heard us? We were pretty loud, you know. Maybe you should go check on Li'l Roc. I'm surprised you didn't go tuck him in."

"With your door closed, I doubt that they heard us. As for tuckin' him in, please. He don't need to be treated like no baby and those days are long gone. And if they did hear us, Li'l Roc knows what's up."

"What does that mean?"

"It means he knows what it sounds like when a woman and man are havin' sex. It also means stay put 'cause it ain't yo' business."

I reached over, rubbing his chest. "You know, I often wonder how the two of us are going to make this work. It's like we've come from two different worlds, trying to pull it together to create one that will make sense. Do you think it's possible for us to do it? I mean, the way you want to live your life is so different from the way I want to live mine. I'm forty-two years old, Roc, and even though I sometimes think this is just about us having fun,

there's so much more to it than that. I have very
strong feelings for you and there are times that I
feel as if I'm in love. Then I ask myself if I could
be serious, because this thing between us is complicated in many ways. Am I analyzing things too
much? Do you ever think or feel how I do?"

"All the time, ma, but I'm hopin' that these
feelings that we have for each other keep us together, no matter what. We gon' have to learn
to compromise on some things, especially you.
I'm usually down for whatever, but you the one
who set in your ways. Never will I make you feel
hoodwinked, bamboozled, or led astray. My shit
is out there for you to see, and you have to decide
what's up."

"Let's be real, Roc. You haven't been that open
and honest with me about everything. I'm left to
assume a lot, and not once have you said where
you would like for our relationship to stand. I
mean, what are we? Friends, companions, lovers
. . . What? I need to know, only because I want
to know what I can and cannot expect from you.
Does that make sense?"

"We can be whatever you want us to be."

"No, that's bullshit and you know it. I already
told you that I would never pursue a relationship
with a man who wasn't ready, but are you ready
to give me all that I may require?"

Roc was silent for a while, and I already knew this was a conversation he didn't want to have. "I would love to give you everything you require, but I got some loose ends to tie up. I planned on doin' so, and I can assure you that it will be taken care of soon."

"Loose ends meaning women? Just how many women are you seeing?"

"I'm not sexing nobody but you, but I still got some close friends here and there. It ain't nothin' serious about the shit and most of them fell off when I went to prison."

I sat up in bed, pulling the covers up over me. Roc followed suit and both of us sat against the headboard. "So, let me get this straight. For the record, you are only having sex with me?"

Roc turned to me with a very serious look on his face. "No one but you."

"Are you sure?"

"Positive."

"Why only me?"

"Why not you? I'm one hundred percent satisfied with how you put it on me, and I seek no one else to give me what only you can."

I shook my head, not even telling Roc that in no way did I believe him. If he was telling the truth, he was going to have to forgive me for giving him no credit. There was just something about him that made me not want to trust a word that he'd said. Then again, he was so into this thing with us that maybe I was wrong for feeling as I did. At this point, I wanted to pull my hair out for not being able to put my finger on the doubtful feeling I had inside. I don't know why I had such a skeptical feeling, but I knew my gut didn't lie.

Chapter 4

For the last month and a half, things had been progressing very well. Roc and I were spending an enormous amount of time together, especially with the kids. Latrel had been home twice, and he and Roc got along well. We went everywhere together and it was such a joy to see all of us on the same page. I had not been back to Roc's place to visit, but he had spent plenty of nights at my house. Maybe even more than he had been spending at his, and he often brought Li'l Roc with him. Latrel was overly thrilled about me and Roc getting back together. So thrilled that when I asked if he'd call Sherri to take her out again, he promised me that he would.

Another good thing that happened was that I'd gotten Roc a job in the mailroom where I worked. I wasn't worried about Greg working there because our so-called relationship was over. Roc didn't deliver the mail on my floor, and that was a good thing. In no way did I think it was a good idea to have him around twenty-four-seven, because he seemed like the kind of person who sometimes needed space. I did too, so whenever he didn't call for a couple of days, I was okay with it. As long as we didn't go weeks without speaking to each other, that was fine by me.

Mr. Anderson had been back from his business trip, and as usual, he had me running around the office like a chicken with its head cut off. I was standing in another VP's office, waiting on him to sign some papers that Mr. Anderson needed right away. Dressed in my silk purple ruffled blouse and hip-hugging gray skirt, I waited for Mr. Blevins to end a call. He held up one finger, nodding his head and whispering that he'd be with me in a minute. Just to give him privacy, I exited his office, taking a seat in a chair that was right outside of his door. I crossed my legs, looking at my bare legs and high-heeled black shoes. As soon as I looked up, I saw Greg coming my way. I did my best to avoid him by turning my head in the other direction as if I didn't see him. That, of course, didn't work.

"Hello there, Miss Thickety Thick," he said, checking me out. I hated to be called that, and it bothered me that he always referred to me as being thick. True to the fact or not, he didn't

have to always say it. I stood, just to address him
appropriately.

"Hi, Greg. How are you?"

"Sexy lady, I would be so much better if you
would agree to go out on another date with me. I
hope that's not asking too much."

I didn't want to hurt Greg's feelings, but he really wasn't my type. He wasn't a bad-looking man,
but he was a bit too thin for my taste. He was kind
of nerdy, too, and he was very much the opposite
of Roc. "Let me think about it, Greg. I am seeing
someone else right now, but it's nothing serious."

He swiped his forehead and smiled. "Whew,
I'm glad to hear that. I hope you call soon and
you know I'll be waiting."

I heard Mr. Blevins call for me, so I told Greg I
would talk to him later. When I walked back into
Mr. Blevins's office, he had the papers signed,
ready to give back to me.

"Sorry for your wait," he said. "Tell John I'll
see him around seven and do not be late."

"Will do." I smiled.

I returned to Mr. Anderson's office, and he had
his back turned while on the phone. He didn't
hear me come in, but I could hear him whispering
something over the phone. Now, as his administrative assistant, I knew what his phone calls

were all about. I knew what his so-called extended business trips were about too, but it wasn't my place to say one word. As he laughed at the caller, I cleared my throat. He quickly swung his chair around, abruptly ending his call. I handed the papers from Mr. Blevins to him.

"Mr. Blevins said he'd see you around seven and don't be late."

Mr. Anderson slapped his forehead. "Oops, I almost forgot about that. Thanks for reminding me." He looked at his watch. "Have you had lunch yet, or would you like to run across the street with me to get a bite to eat?"

"I'll pass. I'm trying to watch my weight a little, so I'm going to just grab something quick from the cafeteria. Thanks, though, and if you don't mind, I'm leaving in about five minutes. Is there anything else you would like for me to do before I go?"

"Nope. Just close my door on your way out. If I'm not back when you get here, I will see you tomorrow."

"Okay. Thanks again."

I left Mr. Anderson's office, closing the door behind me. He was really too nice to me, but at times could be a flirt. When I first started working for him, all he did was compliment me on how I looked and his stares made me uncomfortable. I didn't mind the compliments, but it was the way he said them that made the difference. One day, I pulled him aside, telling him how I felt and assuring him that I was in no way interested in married men. I didn't care much for dating much older men, either, so we got that conversation out of the way real quick. Since then, he chilled and we continued to get along just fine. He didn't say much about his daughter, Sherri, going on a date with Latrel, and I said nothing about it either.

I removed ten dollars from my purse and headed to the cafeteria to get something to eat. A couple of times I had been to the gym with Roc. Since I had been cutting back on eating so much, I felt myself losing a little weight. It wasn't much to brag about, and it wasn't like I had really been trying.

The cafeteria was crowded with some of my coworkers, as well as students. Normally, I sat with three other ladies from another department, Val, Bethany, and Emma. They were much older ladies, and I think Val was the only one who was in her forties like me. Emma waved so I could see them, and after I paid for my chicken salad and fruit, I went over to the table to take a seat. They all spoke and I spoke back.

"What's cooking with you, girlee?" Bethany asked. She was an older white woman who was nosey as hell. Val and Emma were black, but they were just as nosey.

"Nothing much. Mr. Anderson got me running all over the place today, and my feet are killing me," I joked.

"You know us admins can relate, but it's so much better working for a man than it is a woman. Jackie is a pain in the ass!" Val said.

We all laughed, only because her boss, Jackie, had a reputation for being a force to be reckoned with. Still, I disagreed that it was much easier working for a man, and we spent thirty minutes debating the issue.

Only a few times while I was in the cafeteria did I see Roc, and today I hadn't planned on it. Emma, however, nudged me and the other ladies to get our attention.

"Have you ladies seen or heard of the Mailroom Mandingo?" Bethany said.

I kind of, sort of, knew where this conversation was going, but I played clueless. "No, wha . . . who are you talking about?"

"The new chocolate hunk in the mailroom. Oh my God, Desa Rae, you have got to turn your head to see him. He is freaking gorgeous and hot as ever." Bethany fanned herself.

I was surprised by her actions, but Val and Emma agreed with her. "I can't believe you have not seen him, Desa Rae, and where in the heck have you been hiding?" Val asked.

I slowly turned around, just to look in the direction of the ladies' eyes. Yes, I did see Roc standing by a soda machine, debating what kind he wanted. How in the hell he made a simple mailroom uniform look so enticing, I didn't know. Pants were fitting his thighs in all the right places and the short-sleeved shirt clung to his muscular frame. The young woman behind him who was waiting to get her soda, her eyes were glued to his butt.

"Are you all talking about the young man at the soda machine?" I asked.

"Yes," Emma said. "What a piece of artistic work."

We all laughed and I couldn't help what I was about to do. I turned to the ladies. "He is fine, and see, I'm the kind of woman who when I see a man I want, I will go after him." I looked at Val. "Give me a pen and piece of paper."

Her mouth hung wide open. "Noooo," she whispered. "Are you going to confront him?"

"Yes, and I'm going to give him my number. Hopefully, he'll call me and we can indulge in some sweaty sex or something. Hurry, before he walks away."

The ladies sat almost speechless. "Wha . . . Well, he's already moved to another vending machine," Bethany said. "If you want to catch him, you'd better hurry."

Val hurried to give me a piece of paper and a pen from her purse. "I can't believe you're doing this. That's being a bit aggressive, don't you think? A woman should never approach a man, and I don't care how gorgeous he is."

"I beg to differ. My mother always told me to go after whatever it is in life that I wanted and never let a good opportunity pass you by."

The ladies sat in disbelief as I got up from the table, making my way over to the vending machines. By now, the other chick had kicked up a conversation with Roc, and she seemed to have his attention. Not for long. I crept up from behind, lightly tapping his shoulder. He turned, smiling to play it off.

"What's up?" he asked.

I held up the piece of paper and pen. "Nothing. I just wondered if I could get your sevens or possibly get you to come to my house and lay me tonight?"

The young woman he was speaking to, her eyes bugged and she pursed her lips. When Roc replied, "You can have anything you want," she walked away. He eased his arm around my waist, and when I looked over at the table where the ladies were sitting, their eyes were popping out of their heads and mouths were covered with their hands. I shrugged as if I were shocked by Roc's actions too.

"Why you playin'?" Roc asked. He pecked my lips and all I could do was laugh. I took his hand, asking him to follow me.

I didn't even notice Greg sitting close by until he spoke out. "It looks pretty serious to me."

I ignored Greg, but Roc stopped. "What you say?"

Greg repeated himself. "I said the relationship looks pretty serious to me. Only a few hours ago, Desa Rae said she wasn't in a serious relationship. Obviously, that wasn't true."

Roc looked puzzled, and I couldn't believe Greg was trying to put me on blast. "Greg, please. It is what it is, okay?"

He shrugged. "Whatever. Hey, your loss, not mine."

I moved forward, but Roc stopped me again. Luckily his voice wasn't that loud. "What in the hell was that all about? You fuckin' that nigga or what?"

"No. I'll tell you about it later. Right now, I want you to meet some of my coworkers." I stepped up to the table and couldn't decide who looked the most shocked.

"Girlee, wow, do you move fast?" Bethany said. "If I would have known it was that easy, I would have taken the initiative."

I decided to let the women off the hook. They'd heard me speak of Roc before, but no one knew he had been in prison. "Ladies, this is Chassidy's father, Roc. I know you all remember me mentioning him, right?"

The ladies' tongues were tied until Roc reached out, shaking their hands one by one.

"Oh, Desa Rae, you made us all look like fools," Val said. "But nice to meet you, Roc, and you are really a handsome young man."

"Appreciate the compliment," Roc said, blushing. "I do have to get back to the mailroom, but you ladies enjoy your lunch."

Everyone said good-bye to Roc, and I was surprised that, before he walked away, he gave me another peck on my lips. "See you later, baby," he said.

"No doubt," I said, watching him walk away.

"Desa Rae Jenkins," Emma said. "How . . . what . . . why . . . and where did you meet him? He is rather young, isn't he?"

I sat back at the table. "He's twenty-seven, but don't let his age fool you."

"I can sit here all day long and listen to you tell me how great the sex is, but I have a feeling that you will not spill the beans," Bethany said.

"Unfortunately not, but I will say this, age is just a number and a number don't mean jack."

The ladies laughed and we quickly changed the subject from bosses to men. Of course I was a little late getting back from lunch, and thank God Mr. Anderson had already checked out for the day.

Normally, Roc got off at 3:30 P.M., and I didn't get off until five. He went home and so did I. Sometimes, we'd meet up to get a bite to eat, and other times he'd meet me at my house. As I was driving home, my cell phone rang and it was him.

"What's the play for today?" he asked.

"Not sure. I'm not really hungry, but after I pick up Chassidy, I'm stopping at Monica's house to see her. I won't be long, but I should be home by eight. Are you coming over?"

"Nah, not tonight. I think I'm gon' just chill."

"Did you cash your check yet?"

"I dropped it in the bank. Never thought I'd see the day that I, Rocky Dawson, would be gettin' a paycheck, but anything for my Dez."

"I hope you're not working because of me. I hope you're working for yourself. You have to admit that it feels pretty good to make money the legit way, doesn't it?"

"Listen, I'm grateful, but I didn't mean it the way I said it. And if you think I'm supposed to be over here jumpin' up and down over a $960 check that I make every two weeks, I'm not that moved. Grateful, but not moved."

I had to slam on my brakes, almost hitting the car in front of me. I had jumped through hoops to get Roc that job in the mailroom, and with a police record like his, it damn sure wasn't easy. He was being ungrateful, and twelve dollars an hour was not bad at all. With the economy as bad as it was, millions of people would kick butt to hold his position. I couldn't even respond, so I didn't. I hung up on his butt, and when he called back, I didn't answer. No doubt, I'd pay for my actions later.

I picked up Chassidy from daycare and was on my way to Monica's house in Maryland Heights. When I got there, I was shocked to see Reggie's car in her driveway. I wondered what the hell was going on, and I couldn't wait to get out of my car to see what was up. I rang the doorbell, with Chassidy on my hip. Monica opened the door, whispering that Reggie had just come over and needed someone to talk to.

I went inside, whispering back at her, "What in the hell does he want?"

She shrugged. "He called out of the blue, looking for you. I told him you were on your way over here, and the next thing I knew, he just showed up."

I swallowed the lump in my throat, unprepared to see Reggie again. The last time we spoke, he chewed me out about Chassidy and ridiculed me for moving on with my life. I guessed since his second marriage had failed, maybe he was ready to talk like he had some sense. Monica's house wasn't the place to have this conversation, and how dare he just show up out of nowhere? I made my way to the kitchen, with Chassidy still on my hip. Reggie had his back turned, but his good-smelling cologne lit up the entire place. He was dressed in a brown suit with a peach shirt underneath. His wavy hair was perfectly lined and I could see his clean-cut beard from the side. He heard Chassidy's voice and quickly turned all the way around. Seeing me too, he stood up and grinned.

"Hello, Dee," he said, reaching out to hug me. I gave him a half hug and patted his back. Monica entered the kitchen, offering to take Chassidy into another room so we could talk.

"She may be a little hungry, Monica, so grab her veggie dips from my bag."

Monica got the veggie dips from my bag and left the room with Chassidy.

I sat across the table from Reggie, seriously wondering what the hell was up. He clinched his hands together, pausing before he finally said anything.

"You look really nice. Not that you ever didn't, but I guess I was a fool for not realizing a good thing when I had it," he said.

Reggie waited for me to respond, but I didn't. I folded my arms, and continued to listen.

"I . . . I just had this dying urge to see you. I stopped by the house a few times, but I could tell you had company. That's why I reached out to Monica. When she said you were coming over, I couldn't resist."

"Okay, so now that you've seen me, now what? I'm confused, Reggie, and what is this all about?"

"I want my life back. The life that I once shared with you and Latrel, I want it back. We were so happy together, and even though I didn't understand what it was that I was going through at the time, I now know that leaving you was one of the biggest mistakes of my life. I'm not asking you to drop everything right now for me, but I want you to think about it. Have you been on stable ground since we've been divorced? Can you honestly say that you have been happy with the person you're with? Roc is not the one, baby, and you know that he's not. All I'm asking for is another chance, and I have spent the last several months trying to figure out the best way to come to you about this. My life has been in shambles and I need a woman like you to help me piece it back together. You're the only woman capable of doing it and the only woman I have truly ever loved."

Reggie said a mouthful and I didn't even know where to start. Years ago, he left me high and dry with very little reasoning other than he'd fallen out of love. I went through hell without him, and he ripped our marriage apart, all for another piece of ass. There was a time that I would have given the world to hear him say what he'd just said to me, and even though Roc may not be the one for me, neither was Reggie. I was absolutely sure about that, and I did my best to spare his feelings, especially since my heart went out to him.

"I have very few words for you right now, Reggie. Obviously, you are going through something because of your failed marriage. I definitely know how that is, but traveling backward is not the solution to your problem. Besides, I'm not in love with you anymore. I care deeply for you and I wish that we could have a better relationship because of our son. You didn't seem to want that and all I can say is . . . is, honey, I have moved on. I may not be all complete yet, but one day I will be. I don't see you in my future in the way that you want us to be and I'm sorry to have to say that to you."

Reggie lowered his head, and rubbed his forehead. "I knew you were going to possibly say that, but just think about it before you—"

"There's nothing to think about. I'm sorry."

He sighed and rubbed his beard. "What's the story with you and Chassidy's so-called father? Are you in love with him? The two of you are like night and day, and I can't believe you're still dealing with him. Please don't continue in that relationship, for the sake of your daughter. In the end it will not be worth it."

"I haven't predicted our ending yet, and the verdict is still out on whether I'm in love with him. But whatever happens with us, I have very few regrets. He has given me a precious child, and, like you, there will always be a place in my heart for him. Now, I don't know what else to say to make you feel better, but you may want to try counseling like I did. It helped and I'm sure it can help you too."

Reggie sat silent for a while, and moments later he backed up from the table. He tossed his suit jacket over his shoulder and looked at me while shaking his head. "If you change your mind, you have my number to call me."

I said not one word and watched as Reggie made his way through the living room and left. Shortly after, Monica came in with her lips pursed.

"Now, he has some nerves," she said, taking her seat at the table. Chassidy was on her lap.

"How do you think I feel? I wanted to say something awful to him, but I felt bad for him. Reggie is only reaping what he sowed. Monica, you know I gave that man my all, and why in the hell would I even think about going back to him?"

"No, why would he think you would? I tell you, men are something else, and at forty-three years old, I am still trying to figure them out."

I threw my hand back. "Don't even waste your time trying. The things they do we will never understand."

"I agree. Meanwhile, what is up with you and the Rocster? I know things have been going well, but I'm concerned about you, Dee. I still haven't been able to swallow what happened at his place that day and I don't want you putting yourself in any more dangerous situations like that."

"I haven't been back over there since. Roc doesn't mention Vanessa or Ronnie around me, and I really couldn't tell you what's up with either of them. As long as they don't come to my house, we cool."

Monica got up from the table and asked if I wanted something to drink. I told her Pepsi would be fine and she got me one from the fridge. She also gave me a couple of my favorite Hershey's chocolates with almonds.

"Right on time," I said, opening one up. "Thank you."

Monica sat back down in the chair. "How's the job thing coming along? Does Roc like it?"

"I'm not sure yet. Today he said something over the phone that kind of pissed me off. I mentioned the job and he said, 'anything for you.' Then he said that $960 every two weeks wasn't much to rave about. I thought he was being very unappreciative and I hung up on him."

"That wasn't the appropriate thing to say, but he has probably made that kind of money in an hour on the streets. Give him time, and as long as he's trying, why are you upset with him?"

"Because I wish he would do this for him, not for me. I wish he would get that, but I don't think he does. I'm not mad at him. I was just taken aback by his comment. In an effort not to start an argument, I hung up."

Monica cut her eyes and pulled a twenty dollar bill from her purse. She laid it on the table. "I bet you twenty dollars the argument that you didn't want to have will find its way to you tonight. You can't treat him like that, and you already know that Roc ain't the kind of man who will sweep that under the rug."

I told Monica to keep her money. I knew more than anyone that she was right.

As soon as I pulled in the driveway, Roc was already at my house waiting for me. I had stayed at Monica's house until 9:00 P.M. and was pretty tired. When I got out of my car, he stepped up to me.

"Yo' battery on your phone went dead, right? Or, did you hang up on me, which one?"

Ironically, just as I was getting Chassidy out of her car seat, my cell phone rang. I was sure it was Monica, checking to make sure we safely made it home. I ignored Roc and the phone, making my way to the door with Chassidy asleep on my shoulder.

"Well, we damn sure know it wasn't the battery," he said.

I sighed, really not in the mood for an argument. "Would you mind unlocking the door for me, please? Chassidy is heavy and so is my purse."

Roc unlocked the door, then tried to take Chassidy from my arms.

"I got her. I'm going to go lay her down, and then you can yell at me all you want to, okay?"

"Hurry up then."

I carried Chassidy to her bedroom and Roc headed to mine. I tucked her in bed, kissed her cheek, and turned on her nightlight. When I got to my room, Roc was sitting in his favorite chair with his hands behind his head.

"First things first," he said. "Who the fuck is Greg?"

I blew Roc off, throwing my hand back at him. "Greg is a nobody. That's exactly who he is."

"Really? A nobody who came out and said what he did today. Did you tell him you weren't in a serious relationship?"

I was stunned that Roc was even going there, and could tell he was in the mood to argue. I stood, folding my arms, and defended my one-month relationship with Greg. "I dated him while you were in prison. We went on three dates, I wasn't feeling him at all, and I stop returning his phone calls. Anything else?"

Before he could respond, his cell phone rang. He looked to see who it was, then answered.

"What, muthafucka? I'm in the middle of somethin', nigga, and I told you I would call you back."
He paused, smiled, and then laughed. "Quit lyin',
fool. She did what?" He paused again, listening
and shaking his head. "All . . . all right. Let me hit
you back in a bit. Before I go, did you take care of
that for me?" He paused. "Cool. No doubt. In a
minute, all right?"

Roc hung up and walked over to the closet as
I was gathering my things to change clothes and
shower. "Okay, so you dated him a few times.
Did you up the pussy?"

If I spoke the truth, I suspected it would cause
a lot of problems tonight. It really wasn't his
business anyway, so I said what I felt like saying.
"No, I did not up the goods because, like I said
before, Greg is not my cup of tea. I was bored,
and being with him gave me a chance to get out
of the house, hopefully to have some fun. Unfortunately, that didn't happen. Now what?"

"Why did you hang up on me?"

"Because you were sounding ungrateful and I
didn't like it."

"So when you don't like what I have to say, you
hang up the fuckin' phone? Since when?"

I shrugged, making my way out of the closet.
Roc moved aside to let me pass by him.

"So we goin' out like that?" he said, reaching for his keys in his pocket. "That's cool and I'ma holla at you real soon, okay?"

Roc left the room, and moments later I heard the front door close. I was going to apologize for hanging up on him, but since he had left, I picked up the phone to call him. He answered right away.

"What?" he snapped.

"I'm sorry for hanging up on you, and maybe I should—"

He hung up on me, and when I called back, he had turned off his phone. I was too tired to deal with any drama, so I called it a night, hoping and praying that my little white lie wouldn't catch up with me. Not only that, I hoped I wouldn't regret getting Roc a job, especially working with someone I was involved with. While I made no promises to Roc about ever being there for him when he was in prison, something told me all of this would come back to haunt me.

Chapter 5

Roc was really trying to play me shady, and for the next week and a half, he did not pick up the phone to call me. I called him, though, only for him to either cut me short or tell me he was busy. While at work, he avoided me altogether. I tried to catch up with him a couple of times in the mailroom, and when I did, he pretended to be so busy. I couldn't believe all of this was going down over a stupid phone call and there had to be more to it. What? I didn't know, but I was sure time would tell.

On Thursday, we had just come out of a meeting and I was on my way to the bathroom. I had to go real bad, but was approached by Roc before I went inside.

"We need to talk," he said with a disturbing look on his face.

"I've been trying to for a week and a half now, but you've been avoiding me."

"Handle your business and meet me across the hall in the stairwell."

"Give me a minute," I said, going inside of the bathroom. I quickly used it, and as I washed my hands, I wondered what Roc wanted to talk about. Maybe it was something with his job, and I guessed it was no secret that he didn't like it that much. After drying my hands with a paper towel, I dropped it in the trash. I headed across the hallway and into the stairwell where Roc asked me to meet him. He was sitting back on the stairs, looking at me with a hard stare.

"What's going on?" I asked.

"You're a gotdamn liar, that's what's up."

His tone caught me off guard and my brows scrunched inward. "What are you talking about?"

"You know damn well what I'm talkin' about. You fucked that nigga, and you still been fuckin' his ass. He told me what was up, Dez, and why did you lie about the shit?"

I swallowed, wondering exactly what Greg had told Roc, if anything. "He told you what? And you believed him?"

Roc stood up, moving very close to me. "Are you callin' him a liar? I will go get that muthafucka right now, Dez, and have him repeat what he told me. Ain't no way in hell he knows what your bedroom looks like if he ain't been in it. Ain't no fuckin' way he knows how your pussy feels if he ain't had it! Ain't no cock-suckin' way he knows that you have a mole on your right thigh if he ain't hiked up your damn dress and seen it for himself. So tell me, baby. Who's the liar? You or him?"

I looked into Roc's fiery eyes, regretting what I had said the other day. I looked so guilty, and I really wasn't guilty of anything but a lie. There was no telling what Greg told Roc, and in no way was I in a position to defend myself. "Twice," I said, already knowing that he'd feel betrayed. Still, I didn't want to lie again. "I had sex with him two times, only when you were in prison. If he told you we have recently been intimate, that was a lie."

"Yeah, kind of like the one you told me." Roc sucked his teeth and put his hands into his pockets. "You know what? I thought you was about somethin'. You ain't shit, ma, and you just like these other fake-ass bitches out here. Then you always tryin' to judge me like yo' ass all that. You played me shady, baby, and you best believe there are consequences for that."

Deep down, yes, I was hurt because I felt as if this was on me. "I apologize for not telling you the truth, but please don't talk to me like that, or refer to me as one of your fake bitches. You're way out of line. The only reason I wasn't truthful with you about me and Greg is because I didn't want to argue with you that night. We had been getting along so well and I didn't want to go there with you."

Roc looked me over and threw his hand back at me. "To hell with you, ma. You ain't even worth my time. I don't believe shit you say, and whatever the hell was up with you and that nigga, you should have said that shit the other night. Regard-less."

I defensively crossed my arms in front of me. "And you have always been so on the up and up with me, right? Please don't stand there and pre-tend that you have been honest with me about every single thing, knowing you haven't."

Roc snickered and let go of the doorknob he had touched. "That's right. Play the blame game and throw that shit back at me. Blame me for your fuckups, baby, but that's the oldest damn trick in the book. Find a new plan and another play toy, too. To hell with this job, and do me a favor, ditch my number, and if you need any-thing for Chassidy, have Latrel call me."

Roc opened the door, but I couldn't allow us to go our separate ways over something so ridicu-lous. I reached for his arm, but he snatched away.

"Not now, not never. Touch my arm like that again and you will really see a side of me that you won't like."

I could see the anger in his eyes, so I let it be. Roc walked out the door, and even though I wanted to go after him, I didn't. I also wanted to go and confront Greg, but I didn't do that either. I headed back to my desk and tried my best to get some work done.

***

When Friday rolled around, I went to the mailroom to see if Roc had come into work. His boss said that Roc had called in sick. I figured that was good news since he at least called in, and hadn't told his boss that he quit. In no way did I want this to be permanent, so around noon, I asked Mr. Anderson if I could leave early. I told him I had many errands to run, but I was actually on my way to Roc's place so we could quickly resolve this matter.

I arrived at his place around 1:00 P.M., and when I rang the doorbell it took him awhile to answer. Finally, I could hear him coming down the stairs. He opened the door with no shirt on and his gray jockey shorts.

"I'm busy," he said.

"Do you have company? If you do, I'll leave."

He stared at me, then turned to make his way up the steps. I entered, locking the door behind me. I went up the steps and saw him lying back on the couch with his feet propped up on the armrest. He focused on the television, as if he were all into it. The room had a very smoky smell, and I couldn't tell if it was marijuana or smoke from the Black & Mild cigar that was lying in an ashtray. I sat on the loveseat that was across from him and placed my purse on the table.

"Can I please talk to you without you getting upset with me over something so ridiculous?"

Roc continued to look at the TV, pretending to ignore me. He had a toothpick in his mouth, dangling it around.

"I said I was sorry, and how dare you not forgive me after all of the things you've done to me in the past? I'm not here to play the blame game, but I did forgive you in the past for some of the things you've done. If my lie was so bad and you refuse to forgive me, fine. I made the mistake and I'll have to deal with it. But please don't quit your job and do not give up on your daughter. I'm not going to involve Latrel in our mess and you should always be there for her, no matter what."

Roc removed the toothpick, then looked over at me. "Are you finished? Let me know when you're done, so I can walk you out."

His eyes shifted back to the TV and the toothpick went back into his mouth. This was becoming so irritating for me, and I took a deep breath. I combed my feathery hair back with my fingers and gripped it in the back. "I'm not going to kiss your ass, Roc. If that's what you want me to do, I'm not. You can pretend that you have been so on the up and up with me all you want, but I know better. I know you've been over here tying up your so-called loose ends, and what about Vanessa? After all of those years together, now all of a sudden it's over? Please. Who do you think I am? I wasn't just born yesterday."

This time, Roc didn't even look at me when he spoke. "You finished yet?" He picked up his watch on the table, looking at it. "You don't have much time, so hurry up and say what else you gotta say."

Okay, if drama was what he wanted, then drama was what he was going to get. I stood up and snatched my purse up from the table. "Yes, I'm finished. And to hell with you, too, Roc. Don't call me, either, and as a matter of fact, I'm going to get my darn number changed."

"Sounds good to me," he said, sucking on the toothpick.

He sure as hell knew how to get underneath my skin, and his nonchalant attitude was doing more than that. I picked up a pillow from his loveseat and threw it at him. It bounced off his chest, and knocked his ashtray and watch on the floor. That surely got his attention and he jumped up from the couch. He held out his hands and stepped up to me.

"What you want, Dez? You want me to kick yo' ass, is that it?"

"No," I said, blinking away water that rushed to the brims of my eyes. "I want you to listen to me and understand that I have no desires for any man but you. We will always have some disagreements, but don't treat me like I mean noth-

ing to you. I need for you to man up and stop
acting so darn childish."

Roc sucked in his bottom lip, and when his
phone rang, he ignored it. "Good-bye, Dez. What
you need is a grown man, and obviously you've
found one in old boy at your job."

"Fine, forget it. You're not listening to me and
I'm wasting my time." I moved away from Roc,
slightly pushing him back so I could make room.
He reached for my wrist, squeezing it tightly.

"Watch where you're steppin', and if you think
a li'l crocodile tears are enough to move me, then
you got me all fucked up. I don't care nothin'
about no tears, or those fake cracks in your voice."

"Then what do you want from me, Roc? Do you
want me to get on my knees and beg for your for-
giveness? What? I'm confused." I stepped forward,
this time stepping on his feet. He pushed me back
on the loveseat, and, yes, I lost my balance.

"You may not know what I want," he said, removing his boxers. "But I damn sure know what
you want."

Roc used his foot to kick open a compartment
on his coffee table. He reached for a condom
package and put the condom on. He then pointed to his dick, which was hard as ever.

"This it, ain't it? Just like the others, this all
you want from Roc, don't you? When he ain't

around to give it to you, you take your ass else-where, right?"

I knew Roc was trying to compare me to Van-essa, but that was in no way the case. He was so wrong about me, but I let him get whatever it was off his chest. I sat up, but he lay over me so I couldn't move. All I could think about was the last time he forced himself on me, and I regret-ted that he was about to go there again.

"Please don't do this, Roc. Sex is not all I want from you and you know it."

"Then what do you want? You still haven't told me, and fuck all that talkin' and listenin' shit. What's really up?"

"I want whatever it is that you want. Now get off me. You're hurting me."

"So damn what? And since you won't keep it real with me, I'll tell you what I want. I want to know why you ain't told me that you love me. I've been home for four months, and you ain't said shit. I'm spendin' all my time with you, tryin' to do right by you, and all you've done is lie to me and complain. What's holdin' you back this time? Tell me so I can understand what the fuck is up. Is it Greg, Reggie, some other muthafucka, or what?"

I closed my eyes, taking a moment to think about Reggie. No, he wasn't holding me back; it

was all about Roc. "None of the above. I'm just
afraid, Roc, that's all."

"Afraid of what?" he said through gritted teeth.

"Afraid of being hurt again. I'm so afraid that
you're going to hurt me and leave me and Chassidy without you. I can't let my guard down, only
because I know how easy it is for you to choose
Ronnie over us. Vanessa doesn't even concern
me as much, but your dedication to Ronnie
scares me. I had fallen in love with you and you
just . . . just said to hell with me and your child,
and took the fall for him, choosing to go to prison. I was angry and it's so hard for me to believe
that you will never play us like that again. I don't
trust you, and it's difficult for me to tell you that
I love you, even when deep in my heart I know I
do."

There, I said it, and now he knew it. I tried to
fool myself into believing that this was just fun,
but I knew it was more than that. Roc had ownership of my heart and all I could do was hope
like hell that he wouldn't break it. He lifted himself off me, allowing me to sit up. He sat on the
table in front of me, rubbing his hands up and
down my thighs.

"Listen, I'm not goin' back to jail, so that decision will never have to be made again. You and

Ronnie on different levels, and in no way can I compare the love for him to the love I have for you. I do love you too, Dez, but holdin' back on me like you've been doin' makes me uneasy. In a relationship, I need a woman who is willin' to give her all. She needs to accept me for who I am and not try to change some of the things about me that will never change. I told you I'd meet you halfway, but I feel like I gotta go all the way with you. Then lyin' to me about some dumb shit ain't even cool. If it had been me, you'd be all over me, talkin' shit. I'm not thrilled about you havin' sex with that fool while I was in prison, but you made no promises to me whatsoever. As far as I knew, you'd moved on with your life, but I damn sure wish you would have been there for me."

I bit my nail, already admitting that he was right. "So, I guess this means I'm in trouble, huh?"

Roc cut his eyes, slightly grinning. "Hell, yeah, you in trouble. Big trouble, and I'm not gon' give you no dick, either. I told you that's what you wanted and you tryin' to play it down like that ain't it."

I pouted. "At the moment, I told you I didn't want the 'd' and I meant it. I do, however, need for you to hold me, touch me, make love to me, and give me a big ol' piece of the man I've fallen

in love with. I want this to work so badly, but
we've got to be open and honest with each other.
I can do it, but do you think you can handle that
for me too?"

"Yes," he quickly said. His cell phone rang,
and he picked it up from the table, seeing who
the caller was. "Hold that thought," he said
to me, then answered his phone. "BJ, make it
quick. What's the address?" Roc wrote down an
address on a piece of paper. "'Preciate it. Now,
don't call me back for the next hour." He looked
at my thighs. "Maybe two. Two or three hours,
and tell Ronnie I'm busy."

Roc ended his call, and for the next several
hours, we kept ourselves pretty busy. Being with
him felt so right, but there was still a big part of
me that was so afraid to give him my all. I had
to work hard at doing so, and maybe now that
everything was out in the open about our feelings for each other, it would be easier for me.
The only other concern I had was the constant
phone calls. Knowing that Ronnie was involved,
it always put up a red flag.

Chapter 6

Latrel was home for the weekend, and I was excited because he and Sherri had already been on one date and were due to go on another. I had invited her over for Saturday morning breakfast and she was on her way.

As for Roc, we were getting along so well that it was almost kind of scary. It had been a month since our unfortunate disagreement. He was back to work and I was very happy about that. He did, however, bring up the idea of Ronnie and me calling a truce, just to put him at ease. He told me that he expressed to Ronnie how important I was to him, and there was no way for him to keep the two most important people in his life away from one another. That conversation led to him asking me to go to the wedding and reception of his cousin, Andre. Ronnie would be in attendance, and even though I really didn't want to go, I agreed to do it for Roc. Loving him meant that I had to accept his family too, but it didn't mean that I had to put up with any nonsense. Hopefully, Ronnie wouldn't get out of line, and as long as he didn't say anything to me, I suspected it would be all good.

On Saturday morning, I had a packed house. Latrel was in the basement still asleep, Roc was in my bedroom, Chassidy was in her room, and Li'l Roc was in the guestroom. Monica had come over at 5:00 A.M. to help me with breakfast and Sherri was expected to show up at 8:00. I enjoyed having company and the house felt so lively. The smell of maple syrup was in the air, and I was standing in front of the stove, flipping buttermilk pancakes. Monica was setting the table, and we both had on white aprons as if we were working in a restaurant.

"I really do love the new dye that you put in your hair, Monica. The auburn looks pretty, and how did you get your hair to have so much body? Let me guess, Pantene shampoo and conditioner?"

Monica came up to me, moving her head from side to side so her hair could swing. "Uh, no, ma'am. Pantene is not for me. I'm a Dark & Lovely kind of gal. You should try it, but since your hair is always bouncing and behaving, I doubt that you will."

Monica swiped the back of my hair, trying to mess it up. I held up my spatula in defense. "Girl, you'd better back up before I cut you. You know I will hurt you for putting your hands on me."

Monica picked up a Jimmy Dean sausage and put it into her mouth. "You've been around Roc for too long. Put that darn spatula down and get back to flipping those pancakes before they burn."

"Don't blame that shit on me," Roc said, coming into the kitchen with white silk pajama pants on. They hung low on his waist and he was without a shirt. Yes, Monica was drooling, but she quickly closed her mouth and pretended to be occupied with setting the table.

Roc came up to me, kissed my cheek, and grabbed a sausage as well. "As I was saying . . . Dez was gangsta before I met her, so don't go blamin' me for bein' a bad influence."

"You got that right," Monica said. "I was just trying to make an excuse for her."

I threw my hand back at Monica and hoped she wouldn't get started on stories about our younger days. "Baby, why are you up so early? We won't be finished for at least another forty-five minutes."

Roc folded his arms while leaning against the counter next to me. "All I could smell was IHOP and I knew somethin' good was cookin'. Besides, I didn't feel that warm body next to mine and I couldn't get comfortable."

"I know how that is," I said, giving him a kiss.

"I'm gon' take a shower and put on some clothes. Hopefully breakfast will be ready when I get back. If not," he said, picking up another sausage, "you in trouble."

"I'll be sure to take my time. But if you and Monica keep eating up all of the sausage, I'm going to be standing here until noon, cooking."

Roc swayed his hand across my ass and squeezed it. "Umph, umph, umph," he said. "If only you knew what you do to me, especially in the mornin'."

He left the kitchen, shaking his head. Monica couldn't wait to add her two cents. "If you would like for me to finish up while you go get you a shot or two, I will be more than happy to take over."

I laughed at Monica trying to take the spatula from my hand. I bumped her with my hips, telling her to move aside. "Would you move, please? I've already had enough *shots* and don't need another one right now."

Monica leaned her backside against the counter, biting her nail and looking in the direction of my bedroom. "I don't see how you do it, Dee.

I would be in that room, right now, wearing him out! Girl, Roc is so handsome, and he really missed his calling as a model. That Polo guy better watch out! He'd better hope Mr. Roc never comes for his job."

We laughed and I couldn't agree more. "I told him the same thing, but he let a good opportunity pass him by."

"How are things going with Chassidy? Has she gotten any more bites from any modeling agencies?"

"Not in a while. I haven't had any recent pictures of her taken, but I'm going to soon, especially since the holidays are coming up. I'm going to make sure I take plenty of pictures."

"Good idea."

Monica helped me with breakfast and we were all done by 7:35 A.M. I woke up Chassidy and Li'l Roc, getting them both ready for breakfast. Roc had showered, but had lain across the bed and gone back to sleep. I figured he needed all of the rest he could get, especially since we had plans to go to his cousin's wedding at three. Latrel was going to watch Chassidy, and Roc was taking Li'l Roc to his grandmother's house. We had arranged to stay at a hotel for the night, only because the reception was there as well.

The doorbell rang and Latrel had gone to get it. Everyone was all seated at the table, with the exception of Roc. Sherri came in, looking very classy in her nicely fitted stretch jeans, stilettos, and silk shirt. Her hair was cut short and her makeup was on like a work of art. Latrel still didn't seem excited about her, as I had hoped, and in no way did I understand why. She was so polite, and had come in with a yellow flower and card in her hand.

"Good morning, Ms. Jenkins," she said, giving me a hug. "Thank you so much for inviting me over, and these are for you."

"Aww, that was so sweet of you," I said, hugging her back. She spoke to everyone around the table and I got up to get a vase for my flower. Latrel helped Sherri with her chair, and everyone was waiting on me to bless the food.

"Would you hurry it up?" Monica said. "These pancakes are stacked so high and they're about to fall over. Me and Li'l Roc hungry, shoot!"

Monica was sitting next to Li'l Roc and he laughed at her while kicking his feet underneath the table. Monica picked up her fork and started hitting it on the table, chanting, "Hurry." He did the same thing and so did Chassidy. Everyone laughed, and as soon as I put my flower into a vase, I blessed the food and we started to eat.

The kitchen was rather noisy, as everyone was talking and the television was on in the background. Li'l Roc and Chassidy liked to watch the cartoons, so they were tuned in. Monica was asking Sherri all kinds of questions, but she was sharp with her answers and truly impressed the heck out of me. I wasn't trying to jump the gun or anything, but I could really see someone like her as my daughter-in-law. Up until now I wasn't so sure, but her presence truly lit up the room. I noticed Latrel's demeanor too, and I could tell he was starting to let his guard down as well. He had mentioned another girl at school who he was dating, but hopefully he'd begin to see the light.

"So, Sherri," Monica said, cutting into her pancakes. "What do you think of our president? Obama is wonderful, isn't he?"

Sherri shrugged. "He's okay. He's kind of growing the deficit too fast for me and I hope he will manage to get all of this spending under control. Besides, I didn't vote for him. I voted for John McCain."

Monica damn near choked on her food and she kicked me underneath the table. "John McCain? You're a Republican?"

All of us had stopped eating, waiting for Sherri to answer. Now, I had nothing against Republicans, but *we* were all very progressive Democrats.

"Yes, I'm a Republican, but if we don't come up with a decent candidate in 2012 to defeat Obama, I'm not sure if I'll be voting at all."

I was trying hard to hold my peace, but *some* political talk was hard to ignore. This time I kicked Monica underneath the table and I could see steam coming from her ears. Latrel spoke up before either of us did.

"Time to change the subject," he suggested. "Everyone is entitled to their opinion, but no one can ignore or deny Obama's efforts to get this country back on track. We didn't get to this point overnight and he can't fix all of our problems overnight. Anyone expecting him to can, frankly, and no offense to Republicans, Sherri, but they can go to hell."

Monica smiled, but I held mine in. Latrel said exactly what I would have said, but I didn't want Sherri to feel uncomfortable because she had different views. I did change the subject, and when we started talking about reality TV shows, that had all of us cracking up. Even Latrel.

"I don't see how y'all watch that stuff," he said. "Most of it is fake and it is all for the ratings. The more outrageous those people are, the more people watch."

"That's the purpose," Monica said. "But them Kardashian sisters be working me. I be like . . . go somewhere and sit down, even though I can't get enough of them!"

We laughed, all agreeing again.

Breakfast lasted for about two hours, and Monica stayed in the kitchen with me to clean up. Everyone else was downstairs in the basement and the loud music was causing the floor to vibrate. I had gone in the bedroom to check on Roc, but he was still asleep. We'd had a long night, so I closed the door so he could get some rest.

"Latrel needs to turn that music down," I griped, making my way back into the kitchen. Monica was putting the dishes in the dishwasher and had already made progress on the messy kitchen.

"It is rather loud, and Miss Republican probably down there shielding her ears from the lyrics."

I hit Monica with a towel. "Be nice. Republican or not, she's still a nice young lady. She has a good family background, and the young lady is going to school to be a doctor. Thus far, she's the best thing Latrel has brought into this house, and I'm not going to complain."

"Well, I wonder if she's using any of that money Obama made available for college students, or if she's using those healthcare benefits that were extended to kids still in college under their parents' insurance plans."

"You got a point, okay? But let it go, Monica." I laughed. "Girl, let it go! I feel you, and I know none of it makes sense."

Unfortunately, Monica kept it going, this time putting her hand on her hip. "And then . . . she had the nerve to come in here with that flower, sucking up to you with a cheesy card. I wanted to throw up, and she blew it with me right then and there."

I covered my mouth and couldn't believe how upset Monica was about Sherri. When Roc came into the kitchen, she finally changed the subject.

"Did you get enough rest?" Monica asked. "I hope so, and I got you a full plate of pancakes, maple sausage, grits, cheese eggs, and biscuits right there on the table."

"Thanks," Roc said, smiling and taking a seat at the table. He now had on a pair of shorts and a white wife beater so Monica was able to contain herself a little better. She and I kept cleaning the kitchen, talking here and there as Roc ate his food. I didn't hear his cell phone ring, but his Bluetooth lit up, meaning that he had a call. I continued to talk to Monica while listening to him raise his voice at someone who was asking for money.

"It's the day of the gotdamn weddin' and those fools still beggin'? As much money as I've given up, this should have been my weddin'. You tell his ass I ain't got it. Fuck that. Niggas need to get they shit together." Roc paused, trying to eat his food and talk at the same time. All of the cursing was working me, but I had gotten used to it. "Look, I'm just a groomsman. Holla at the best man, or call Ronnie and ask him for it. I will predict that you'll be wastin' your time and he gon' say the same damn thing. A weddin' can go on without flowers."

Roc ended the call and Monica and I left the kitchen, leaving him at peace. We sat in the hearth room that was attached to the kitchen.

I wiped across my forehead, sitting on the sofa. "I am soooo tired. I don't know how I'm going to make it through this day. I at least need to get in one or two hours of sleep before the wedding."

Monica looked at her watch. "It's almost noon, and you don't have much time. I'm glad you found something nice to wear and I love the dress you picked out."

"I like it too, and I was a little bit worried because these hips of mine always get me in trouble. I've lost a few pounds, but if I start moving in the other direction, I'm going to have to have my clothes special made. With my waistline being smaller, it's hard to find clothes that fit me the right way."

"Yeah, that's a shame, too, because you do have a very nice shape. I know you may disagree, but you're blessed that everything is proportioned in the right places."

I'd heard that many, many times before; that's why I rarely complained about my weight. Roc seemed happy with it and that was a good thing. I watched as he put his plate in the sink, stretching his arms. Right after, Latrel, Sherri, and the kids came upstairs, and when Latrel put Chassidy down, she and Li'l Roc came over to me. I hugged them both, but couldn't help noticing Sherri staring at Roc and him staring at her. Latrel introduced the two of them and they both gave fake smiles. Li'l Roc got Roc's attention when he went over to him and tapped his leg.

"Daddy, what time am I going over to my granny's house?" he asked.

"In a li'l bit." Roc reached in his pocket and gave Li'l Roc his phone. "Call her to make sure she'll be at home."

Li'l Roc took the phone and went into another room to call her. Latrel and Roc kicked up a conversation, but Sherri couldn't keep her eyes off Roc. I couldn't keep my eyes off them, and Monica's eyes were on me.

"Yeah, like Prudential, she wants a piece of the Roc," Monica whispered. "She's got the hots for him, and how disrespectful for her to stand there looking at him like that."

"So I guess she's not allowed to look at a nice-looking man when she sees one, huh? Please give that young lady a break."

Monica sat back with her lips pursed and legs crossed. Sherri headed our way, informing me that she was about to leave.

"Thank you so much for inviting me over, Ms. Jenkins," she said, hugging me again. I stood up and thanked her for coming.

"You are welcome to come back anytime. Usually, Latrel comes home every other weekend, and I hope the two of you keep in touch."

She had her fingers crossed. "He did ask me to go on another date with him next week, so we'll see." She giggled, and after she told Monica and Roc good-bye, Latrel walked her to the door.

Time was moving fast, so Monica was on her way out and Latrel had offered to take Li'l Roc to his grandmother's house. He and Chassidy were going to see Reggie, and then he had plans to take her to the movies. I gave away plenty of kisses and hugs before sending everyone out of the door with a good-bye. I went into my bedroom, falling back on my comfortable bed and wanting to stay there. Roc climbed on top of me, pecking my neck.

"Mmmm," he mumbled. "I am so glad that everybody is gone. We still got a li'l time to shake somethin' up in here before we go, don't we?"

"Unfortunately not. As tired as I am, I would just lie here like a dead duck and let you do all of the work."

"That sounds like a plan to me, and just bein' inside of your pussy excites the hell out of me."

I slightly pushed Roc's chest back so I could look into his eyes. "Tonight, okay? You have all night to do whatever you wish, but please let me get at least an hour of sleep in before we go."

"That hour is going to make you more tired, but go for it. I'll let you get some rest and wake you up around one-thirty so you can get ready."

"Thanks, snookums."

Roc eased his way off of me and stood up. "Don't start that shit. You haven't called me that in a long time. That only means you want somethin' from me."

I laughed, as he was so right. I turned sideways, holding my head up with my hand. "I didn't want anything, but I did want to ask you something."

"What's up?" he asked, folding his arms in front of him.

"Did you know Sherri? I mean, there was just something about the way you looked at her and she looked at you."

Roc hesitated, then bent over on the bed to come face to face with me. "Remember that lie you told me about Greg? I'm not gon' do you like you did me, but, yes, I do know Sherri."

My stomach tightened, and I was almost afraid to ask how, but what the hell? "Do you mind telling me how you know her?"

Roc tapped the side of his temple with his finger. "Well, let's see. A few years back, I met her at a party and we got to know each other."

"As in sexually? She told Latrel she was a virgin, but I guess that was a lie."

"Ay, that's how women do it. Big lie. I owned and boned it several times, and she wasn't no virgin when I hit it, either."

Yes, I was starting to frown, even though this was before my time. "Why did the two of you stop seeing each other?"

"It was just a fuck thing and fuck things don't last for long. She wanted more, but I wasn't givin' more. She stopped callin' me and the rest is history."

"Truthfully, was it before or after you met me?"

"I don't always remember timelines, baby, but it was at least a year, maybe two before then. What difference does it make? Ain't nothin' poppin' with me and that chick."

I reached over to my phone on the nightstand, dialing Latrel's cell phone number. He answered right away.

"When is your next date with Sherri?"

"I told her next week, Mama, but I don't know—"

"Cancel it."

"What?" he laughed. "What did she do now? I guess Monica got through to you, huh?"

"No, she didn't. I jus' . . . I just don't think she would be good for you, that's all."

"Mama, now you know I don't like you getting in my business like this. And just because she's a Republican, it doesn't mean she's a bad person. Don't be like that, and you have always taught me not to judge people, even though you tend to do it a lot."

"I know, but forgive me. It's not because she's a Republican, it's because she was intimate with Roc before. Didn't she tell you she was a virgin? I don't want you to involve yourself with a woman who lies to you."

Roc was standing in front of me, shaking his head. "Ain't that about nothin'," he said. "You know you be killin' me."

I smiled at him and put my finger over my lip, asking him to be quiet.

"I can see why that would concern you," Latrel said. "But it doesn't concern me, especially if it happened a long time ago. Either way, the only reason I took Sherri out on those dates was because of you. She was decent, but in no way is she my type. I will soon show you my type, and I have been dating her for the past eight months. The only reason that I didn't tell you was because I didn't want to hear your comments about who I should or shouldn't be dating. Good-bye, Mama, and have a good time at the wedding."

I quickly sat up on the bed. "Eight months? Why didn't you say anything? Is she black, white . . . what? I hope she's . . . Well, you already know what I'm going to say, and make sure she is not a Republican. Please."

"I'm hanging up, Mama. I don't like to talk while I'm driving and if you want to put your precious cargo at risk of having an accident—"

"Bye, Latrel. I love you."

"Me too."

Latrel hung up, and as expected, Roc was still staring at me. "He's my son, Roc, and I couldn't let him make a big mistake like that one."

"Right, you're so right. I feel sorry for that man, and he will never find the woman of his dreams, waitin' on you to come around."

I pulled my shirt over my head, tossing it on the floor. "I guess he won't," I said. "And I guess that will only lead to me being in trouble again."

Roc winked at me, then jumped on the bed. "I knew you'd find a little time to fit me into your schedule. Lie back, baby, and swoop those pretty legs into position."

I did as I was told, and rubbed my hands on Roc's carved chest. "Do . . . Don't you think we fuck too much?" I said bluntly. "Every time I look up, there you are, looking down at me, smiling and stroking away."

"Then maybe you should turn around more often and let me get at your pussy from the back. Besides, I know you ain't complainin'."

I turned on my stomach, resting my head comfortably on a pillow. Roc straddled my legs, bending one of them so he could have easier access.

"Hike that ass up a bit so I can get at it like I want to."

I hiked up my ass, and he pulled my cheeks apart. When he entered me, I squeezed my eyes, and let out a deep sigh of relief. I thought about how good he made my insides feel, and confirmed that I wanted to feel him inside of me forever.

"Nooo complaints," I assured him. "And you could fuck me like this forever."

"That's what I thought and it's somethin' that I definitely know."

Cocky or confident, it didn't really matter. Roc was giving me what I really wanted and that was summed up as sexual satisfaction.

The sex session delayed us. By the time we got ready and arrived at Roc's cousin's church on Grand Boulevard, it was 3:45 P.M. The wedding hadn't even started yet, and since Roc was one of the groomsmen, that was a good thing. He drove like a bat out of hell getting there, only to be told that the minister hadn't shown up yet. I sat by myself in the crowded church that was filled with who I assumed to be many of Roc's relatives and friends. The church was beautifully decorated with turquoise, black, and white. I could tell someone had put a lot of money into the wedding, and I guessed the money for the flowers had come through. Beautiful lilies were everywhere, and each pew had a bundle of carnations with pearls. A big picture of the bride and groom was propped up on the stage on an easel, and the dim lighting made the sanctuary look even more elegant. The pianist started doing his thing, but for at least ten minutes, he seemed to be tuning the piano. I crossed my legs, looking down at my black silk and leather heels with pleats near my opened toes. The half-shoulder mustard-colored silk dress I wore tightened at my waist and hugged my curvaceous hips. It was knee-length level, but inched up a bit when I took my seat. My hair was pinned up, giving me a very classy look that kept others staring. Whenever someone smiled at me, I smiled back. One older lady in particular, she came over and stood next to me with her cane.

"Oooo, young lady, you're so very pretty," she said. "What gentleman in here do you belong to?"

I could only thank her and laugh. "Thank you for the compliment, and you are beautiful too. I'm here with Rocky Dawson. He's one of the groomsmen."

"You mean Roc?" The lady smiled. "Nobody calls him Rocky anymore, and he hates that name. I'm a longtime friend of the family, and we all go way, way back."

The lady stood next to me, going on and on about the Dawson family. I asked if she wanted to take a seat next to me, but she insisted that she was sitting elsewhere. Almost fifteen minutes later the pianist asked everyone to take their seats, and that's when the elderly woman walked away. By now, there was no place next to me to sit, and more people had crammed into the church.

The wedding got started, and instead of the groomsmen coming down the aisle, they all walked in at once and stood in front of the church. There were eight men total, all very handsome men, with the exception of Ronnie. Well, he was nice-looking too, but I couldn't stand him. To me, of course, Roc looked the best. The black tuxedo fit his body perfectly, and along with his fresh haircut and trimmed hair on his chin, my eyes stayed glued to him. I couldn't help that I was sitting in a church, thinking about what had transpired only a few hours ago. My mind was definitely in the gutter, and God would have to forgive me.

My attention turned to the bridesmaids coming in, and then to the flower girl and ring bearer. The bride was also pretty, but I wasn't going to say anything about her having on too much caked-on makeup. Whoever did her makeup needed to rethink his/her career. Other than that, she was perfect.

As the ceremony was in progress, I occasionally looked at Roc and he looked at me. We smiled at each other, but I also noticed his attention focused elsewhere. I followed the direction of his eyes, only to see Vanessa sitting in one of

the pews with another man next to her. I thought
I'd seen the man before, then I quickly realized it
was that goon Mississippi who was at Roc's place
that day. His dreads had been cut off, and even
though he looked a little better, he still wasn't all
that great looking to me. I wondered if Vanessa
was now seeing him, and I guessed as close as
they were sitting, it was obvious. I didn't know
how well that had gone over with Roc, but I really wanted to know how he felt about it. I suspected the day would get interesting.

The "I do's" were exchanged, so were the
rings, and the broom had been jumped over. The
wedding party was asked to stay to take photos,
and instead of waiting around, I left to go use
the bathroom, plus call to check on Latrel and
Chassidy. The hallways were so crowded that
you could barely move, and when I got to the
bathroom, a line was outside of the door. I dug
in my purse to get my phone, and I would be lying if I said I didn't hear the word "bitch" from
behind. I turned, seeing Vanessa standing only
a few feet away with three other women. To be
honest, she looked really nice in her lavender
sheer-like strapless dress with a small slit on the
thigh. Her long hair was pulled away from her
face, bumped up a bit, and clipped in the back.
All I did was cut my eyes at her, and started to

move in another direction. I was glad to see Roc exiting the sanctuary. He saw me and motioned for me to come his way.

"I want you to meet some people," he said. I made my way up to him and he eased his arm around my waist. He introduced me to several of his cousins, aunts, uncles, and some friends. He was all smiles, and seemed really proud to have me with him. I was kind of shocked by his reaction. More so by his arm that he never removed from my waist. People were taking many photos and I couldn't tell you how many times we had to stop and pose for the cameras. I had even posed in two pictures with Ronnie, and you best believe that he was on one end and I was on the other.

Everyone was starting to leave the church to make their way to the reception. I still needed to use the bathroom, so I interrupted Roc, talking to a couple of his friends.

"Say, honey," I said. "I'll be back, okay? I need to go to the restroom."

Roc held my hand, asking me to hold up a second. He exchanged a few more words with his friends, then they walked away. He then turned to face me, while wiggling his bowtie away from his neck.

"It's hotter than a mug in here," he said. "So, what did you think?"

"Think about what? The wedding?"

"Yes, the weddin' and my peeps. They ain't as bad as you thought they would be, are they?"

I smiled, thinking how surprised I was that he had some very nice and down-to-earth people in his family. I then reached out to help him remove the bowtie he seemed to have trouble with. It came loose and Roc placed it in his pocket. He wrapped his arms around me and I wrapped mine around him. "I think the wedding was beautiful, you looked so very, very handsome, and your family is everything I imagined them to be. Wonderful people."

Roc laughed. I swear his bright white teeth against his dark skin was a combination that set me on fire. "Quit lyin'. You are such a good liar, but you good."

He pecked my lips, only encouraging me to go for more. As we kissed, an older man interrupted us and held up his camera. He flashed it, making us laugh.

"Boy, you got yourself somethin' right there," he said, squeezing Roc's shoulder. "Good God Almighty, and if you can't handle all of that goodness, be sho' to let me know!"

"Will do, Cousin Freddy, but I'm positive I can handle it."

Freddy walked away, sucking in his lips and eyeballing me. I couldn't help but blush from his compliment.

"I really need to get to the bathroom," I said. Roc let go of my hand, and thank God the bathroom wasn't that crowded. After using it, I washed my hands while checking myself in the mirror. My lip gloss had gotten light, so I removed my tiny purse clutched underneath my arm to find my gloss. I must have forgotten it at home, so I snapped my purse back together and left the bathroom. No sooner had I walked out than I could see Vanessa, who had already made her way up to Roc. She was close to his face, pointing her finger and gritting her teeth. Several other people were standing around, and didn't she know how much she was embarrassing herself? Roc slapped her finger away from his face and that's when he saw me coming. He looked over Vanessa's shoulder at me.

"Are you ready to jet so we can go to the reception?" he said, trying to ignore her.

She quickly turned around with a mean mug on her face. I stepped around her, and stood next to Roc. She couldn't help herself from reaching up to hit him. This time, however, I grabbed her wrist, catching it in midair. Her eyes widened, as she couldn't believe I was protecting Roc.

"That will land you on this floor, and I don't think you want to catch a beat-down in no church. Take it up with Roc later, and if you don't, you will regret it."

She snatched her wrist away from me, and before any words could come out of her mouth, the man standing next to Roc pushed her backward. She almost fell, but charged forward again. This time, he squeezed her arm, ordering her to leave.

"Move out of my way, Steve! That bitch don't put her hands on me. She don't know me and I will kick her ass! I'm just tryin' to talk to Roc!"

"Wrong place," Roc said with a smirk. "Wrong time." He looked at Steve, who seemed to have control over her. So many people there were shaking their heads, and the whole scene was quite embarrassing. "Please do somethin' with her," Roc said to Steve. "Throw her ass in the river for all I care, but get her the fuck out of my face."

Vanessa called Roc all kinds of son of bitches, you muthafucka this and that. She was being pushed in one direction while we walked in another one. As soon as we walked out of the church doors, Mississippi was standing outside, talking to a gathering of other young men and several ladies. Roc was holding my hand, but I guess he couldn't help himself from saying something.

"Sippi, you need to go inside and calm your bitch down. She clownin', and if you care about her like yo' hatin' ass say you do, then go handle that."

Sippi pointed to his chest. "Nigga, you talkin' to me? I know you ain't talkin' to me."

Roc tried to let go of my hand, but I squeezed it. He snatched away, making his way up to Mississippi. I knew this day was too good to be true, and didn't somebody recognize that we were in a church? I called out Roc's name, but he ignored me. A few people had already started to move out. Many stayed to watch as Roc stood face to face with Mississippi with tightened fists.

"You damn right I'm talkin' to you, you fake-ass muthafucka. Now what, nigga? Yo' move."

Mississippi didn't have a move, especially since Ronnie and three of his henchmen walked up from behind him. He gripped Roc's shoulder, massaging it.

"Calm down, baby boy. There won't be no bloodshed today. G'on and take yo' pretty young thang to the reception and enjoy yourself. Sippi ain't mean no harm, did you?"

Roc hadn't moved, and he waited for Mississippi to respond. "Roc know he my boy, but he don't need to be comin' at me about some dumb shit over no trick."

"One who ain't even worth it, so we gon' leave this shit right here at the front door of the church," Ronnie said. "Squash this and let's move out. We got a party to go to."

Mississippi held up his fist for Roc to pound and squash it, but Roc cut his eyes and walked away. He took my hand, and, at a speedy pace, walked with me to his truck. Honestly, I didn't feel like going to the reception, and this ongoing drama with Roc was working my nerves. And then for Ronnie to suggest that they leave the drama at the church door—please. God was probably shaking His head at all of us. There was no denying that every time I attempted to be a part of Roc's circle, something tragic almost happened. I prayed for him and definitely for my safety.

Roc sped off the parking lot, only to be stopped by Ronnie, who stood in front of the truck, holding up his hand. He strutted around to the driver's side, and Roc lowered his window.

"You good?" he asked Roc.

"I'm fine. That fool was the one trippin', not me."

"I don't give a shit about him. All I care about is you. I don't want no shake, rattlin', and rollin' goin' on, so calm down and sleep on it."

Roc nodded, and before he rose his window, Ronnie looked over at me.

"Sup, Desa Rae? You lookin' lovely as ever. Glad you decided to come. When you and my Roc gon' tie the knot?"

Roc smiled and put his hand on the switch to raise the window. "Man, stop talkin' shit. You high, drunk, on crack, or what?"

I leaned forward to address Ronnie. "You look awesome too, Ronnie, and as for me and Roc tying the knot, not a chance in hell. I only use him for sex."

Ronnie laughed and backed away from the car. Roc looked disturbed by what I said, and I was bothered by what he'd said as well. That's why I responded the way I did. We couldn't get off the parking lot before he tried to tear into me.

"Not a chance in hell, huh? And all I'm good for is sex? You shot me down like I wasn't shit."

"I knew you were going to say that, but it was no worse than you saying Ronnie was high, drunk, on crack, or whatever if he thought we'd ever get married."

"I was just playin', and I told you that's how we talk."

"Well, I guess I'm learning from you, and, at the time, I couldn't think of a better response either."

I playfully shoved Roc's shoulder, and, just to irritate me, he blasted his music. I turned it down, feeling a need to ask him a few questions.

"Snookums, I don't really want to bring this up right now, but please tell me what is up with Vanessa. Why does she always carry on like that? Has she always been that way?"

"She's a crazy and deranged woman. She actin' like that cause I don't fuck with her no more. She didn't always act like that, but she definitely ain't got it all upstairs."

"Well, it's been awhile since you've been out of jail. Almost six months to be exact, and I don't understand why she doesn't accept the fact that you've moved on."

Roc stopped at the red light on Lindell Boulevard and looked over at me. "I don't know either. But since you showed her how gangsta you can be, next time you see her, why don't you ask her? I can't answer why she's a nutcase. Some people are just that way when they don't get what they want."

"Gangsta, no. I just don't have time for games, that's all." I touched the side of Roc's face. "Besides, I didn't want her messing up that handsome face. Not today anyway."

"No worries here. But I don't believe for one minute that you ain't got a li'l hood in you. It's there, and ain't no way you'd be messin' with me if it wasn't."

I threw my hand back at Roc, but he was on to something, because I did graduate from the one and only Charles Sumner High School. I did have my suspicions about why I thought Vanessa reacted the way she did. I couldn't believe any woman would constantly be carrying on the way she had been if she wasn't still someway or somehow involved with Roc. Maybe it was just me, but the next time I saw her, yes, I very well would ask.

The wedding reception was just as nice as the wedding was. It was in a ballroom at the Renaissance Hotel where we were staying the night. It was even more packed than the wedding was, and you would have sworn that Roc's cousin and his new wife were celebrities. I was having myself a good time. The people who sat at the table with me were funny, as well as entertaining. There was something about the way an older man cracked jokes, and the one next to me was on a roll. He was talking about everybody and their mama, including Roc and his bright white teeth. I even danced with the old man a few times, but when Roc cut in, the dance floor belonged to us. I still hadn't learned how to dance, but as long as Roc kept me close to him, I was perfectly fine.

"You feel it, don't you?" he said, pressing his hardness close to me.

"As a matter of fact, I do. In front of all of your relatives and friends, I feel how hard you are. I may have to bend over to give them something to watch."

He blushed. "Ooooo, you so nasty. But you know I love it, don't you?"

"I hope so. Now, how much longer are we going to be? My feet are killing me and I'm getting very tired."

"I'm gon' be awhile, but if you want to go upstairs to our room to get some rest, go right ahead. I'll be up later. Not too late, though."

That didn't sound like a bad idea, so I got the keycard from Roc and gave my good-byes to his family. I made my way to the elevator, on my way up. The door was about to close, but someone put his hand between the doors to make them open wide. It was Ronnie. He stepped onto the elevator with me.

"Going up?" he asked.

I nodded, feeling very uncomfortable being alone with him. We pushed the sixth floor button at the same time.

"I had a damn good time today," he said, sucking his teeth. "How 'bout you?"

"Great time," was all I said.

The elevator opened and he extended his hand, inviting me to exit first.

I walked down the hallway and Ronnie followed me. The keycard had door number 612 written on it, so I followed the arrows and made my way to it. When I found it, I stopped and Ronnie stopped behind me. I quickly turned.

"Is there something I can help you with, Ronnie?"

"Jus' . . . just open the door. I need to go inside and holla at you about a few thangs."

I folded my arms, and in no way was going inside of the room with him. "Whatever you have to say, you can say it out here."

"It's private, Desa Rae, and I'm not gon' hurt you. I just want to get at you about some things with Roc, particularly about him gettin' out of the game. I'm concerned about some things he's been bringin' on himself, as a permanent move like that can do more harm than good. I'm sure you understand."

I really didn't want to let Ronnie inside of the room with me, but I also didn't want to stand in the hallway discussing Roc. I told myself that if Ronnie tried anything stupid to kick him hard in his nuts and run!

I opened the door with the card and went inside. The suite was very nice, but I didn't have time to check it out like I wanted to because of Ronnie. He removed his suit jacket, then took a seat in one of the chairs by a window. I stood close by the bed with my arms folded.

He cleared his throat and rubbed his hands together. "Let's not pretend, Desa Rae. You don't like me and I damn sure ain't got no love for you. You've managed to get at my li'l nigga's heart and I'm not quite on board with that shit. I've thought about several schemes to get rid of you, and when anybody starts messin' around with my money, I gotta do what I gotta do. You know what I'm sayin'?"

"No, Ronnie, I don't know what you're saying. I don't understand how I'm messing with your money, and quite frankly, I haven't spent one dime of what belongs to you. As for your schemes to get rid of me, please let me know if that was a threat so I can get a restraining order against you and make the cops aware of this situation."

Ronnie chuckled and swiped his hand on top of his head. "Roc slippin', Desa Rae, and when you slip, eventually you fall. When you fall, you fall six feet under. He slippin' 'cause he ain't focused on what needs to be done. I've lost a lot of money in the last several months, and while you got him out here at a two-bit-ass job, makin' twelve or thirteen lousy dollars an hour, I'm losin' mo' money. While he busy over there playin' house with you and yo' gotdamn family, my family ain't gettin' takin' care of. Now, I'm bein' as nice as I can possibly be about this, but you and that baby girl need to quickly make way out of St. Louis. Tell that nigga somethin' came up, and you gotta go. If you don't, well, see, I would hate for somethin' tragic to happen." Ronnie shrugged. "Can't say who it will happen to, 'cause I don't know yet. But if you fall back, everything will be peaches and cream."

I stared at Ronnie and couldn't even respond. All kind of hate for him was running through me, and I had never felt like this for anyone in my life. I didn't even know fools like him existed, but sadly enough, they did. I went to the door and opened it.

"Please get out," I said. "You will have to do what you wish because I will never take orders from you."

Ronnie slowly stood up and stretched. With venom in his eyes, he walked to the door, looking me over. He reached his hand up, touching the side of my face. Before he could say anything, I smacked it away. He chuckled out loud and left. I slammed the door behind him, not sure if I would tell Roc about this incident.

Chapter 7

For whatever reason, I kept what Ronnie had said to me a secret. I hadn't said one word to Roc about the letters I'd been getting in the mail, threatening my life. All they said was:

You die, bitch! Your days are numbered!

The letters started after my confrontation with Ronnie. Someone was constantly calling my house and hanging up, and when a man ran into the back of my car the other day, I was quite shaken up. It seemed as if he just wasn't looking where he was going, and after the police came on the scene, everything checked out. Still, I was paranoid. I wanted to go to the police about this, but without any evidence against Ronnie, what could they really do? I intended to watch my back, and I did tell Roc to be very careful about his surroundings too. He assured me that he would. I did my best to make sure he spent plenty of days and nights with me, away from the drama that seemed to happen when he was on his turf. Roc seemed as if he had a new attitude about life, and he had not missed any more days at work. I was happy for him, and definitely happy about the way things were going between us.

Christmas was just around the corner, and for Thanksgiving I had dinner at my house. Everyone from the breakfast crew was there, with the exception of Sherri. Latrel had finally brought his girlfriend home to meet me, and I held off on making any comments. All I could say was I liked her, she seemed nice, and she was African American. At this point, I realized that it didn't even matter. As long as he was happy, I was. Until he intended to marry someone, I told Latrel he would never hear my mouth again.

Things were going so well that I had even started talking sensibly to Reggie again. He was in counseling and told me how much it was helping him. We hadn't laughed together in quite some time, and when he came over one day, apologizing again for what he'd done, I was okay. I was pleased that he'd realized his mistakes, but made it clear that we could never turn back the hands of time. He understood.

On Christmas morning, I got a call from Roc, telling me that he wasn't feeling well so he was staying at home. I was looking forward to our time together, and so was Chassidy. She wanted to give Li'l Roc his gift and I wanted to give him the ones I had bought him too.

"I hope you feel better," I said over the phone to Roc. "And if you come over, I promise to take care of you."

He let out a hacking cough, and asked me to hold while he spat. "I'm feelin' so miserable I can't even move. I'll get at you on the weekend, promise. Now let me talk to Chassidy so I can wish her a Merry Christmas."

I gave the phone to Chassidy, very disappointed that Roc wasn't coming over. While she talked to him, I turned to Latrel, who was coming up from the basement on his way over to Reggie's house.

"Where's Roc at?" Latrel asked.

"He's not feeling well today. Said he wasn't coming over until the weekend."

"I've been feeling a little under the weather too, but I took some Tylenol Cold & Flu last night. I feel much better."

I touched Latrel's forehead, just to see if he was running a fever. He wasn't. "Well, go ahead over to your father's house. Tell him I said hello and don't forget to get his presents underneath the tree."

"I won't. But since Roc isn't coming over, why don't you and Chassidy go over to Dad's house with me? It's not like you doing anything else."

"No, I don't think that's a good idea. Have fun and I'll see you later."

Chassidy gave the phone to me, and Roc had already hung up.

"Can Chassidy go with me then? I mean, it's Christmas, Mama, and she don't want to be cooped up in the house."

"We weren't going to be cooped up. I had planned on baking some Christmas cookies and chocolate cupcake bears."

"I don't want to leave you by yourself, but if you don't want to go with me, at least let her go."

Chassidy always loved going with Latrel, so I put on her clothes and told the two of them to have fun. It wasn't the first time I was alone on Christmas, and I suspected it wouldn't be the last. Besides, my house had gotten kind of messy, so I decided to spend my day cleaning.

Around noon, I was taking a break from vacuuming the floors and sat breathlessly at the kitchen table. I had a tall glass of ice-cold water in my hand, guzzling it down pretty quickly. The news had just come on, and at the top of the hour there was breaking news. Apparently, there was a murder in St. Louis and a police officer had been shot at as well. The person identified was a twenty-nine-year-old black man by the name of Craig M. Jackson. I somewhat ignored the story, because it disturbed me that so many black men were getting killed. It always made me think of Roc, and as the reporter wrapped up her story, she repeated the name. This time, she said that Mr. Jackson also went by the name of Mississippi, and if anyone had any information they were asked to call the number on the screen.

Almost immediately, my heart dropped to my stomach. I couldn't believe Mississippi was dead, and less than a month and a half ago, he and Roc stood outside of the church, arguing. I wondered if there was any connection and my gut was sending off signals that there was. I rushed to my bedroom to put on some clothes, and, yes, I wanted some answers. I didn't think Roc was capable of murder, but he damn sure knew something about this.

When I got to Roc's place, I started to use the key he had given me awhile back, but instead I knocked. I got no answer, so I knocked again. Finally, after knocking for at least five minutes, he opened the door. I immediately noticed a small bruise underneath his left eye and a scratch on his neck. No, he didn't look happy to see me and the cold stare in his eyes said so.

"Can I come in?" I asked.

He covered his face with his hand, wiping down it. "Dez, I'm tired. I was upstairs sleepin', tryin' to work off this cold."

"I won't be long."

Roc turned and headed up the stairs. He went back into his bedroom and got underneath the covers. The room was partially lit by the sun's rays coming through the window, but I turned on the light.

"What happened to your eye?" I asked.

"I ran into somethin'."

"And the scratch on your neck?"

"Somethin' bit me and I kept scratchin' it."

"Roc, stop lying. I thought we didn't go there with each other like that anymore."

He sat up in bed and put his hands behind his head. "Are you over here because I didn't come to your house for Christmas? I told you I wasn't feelin' well and nothin' else needs to be said."

"What happened to Mississippi?"

He cocked his head back. "Who?"

"Sippi. The one you got into it with at the wedding. The news reported that he was murdered. I thought you may know something about it."

Roc shrugged. "That's what that nigga get. No love lost here, and if I did know somethin' about it, so what? What you gon' do, call the police on me or somethin'? You runnin' up in here like you tryin' to get info for a reward."

"I don't know what I would do with the truth, but I want to know if you had anything to do with it."

Roc didn't answer. He reached for a Black & Mild cigar next to him and lit it. "So you don't know what you would do, huh? I feel you, ma, but just so you can sleep at night, no, you don't have a murderer lyin' in bed next to you and runnin' up in that pussy. I don't get down like that. Sippi had a whole lot of haters, as well as enemies. Ain't no tellin' who put two in his head, but it damn sure wasn't me." Roc defensively held out his hands. "Could have been anybody. Now, please, please can I get some rest? If it makes you feel better, I will stop by tomorrow. Promise."

Roc took a few more puffs from the Black & Mild, then put it out in the ashtray. I watched as he threw the covers back over his head, trying his best to ignore me. I really wasn't in the mood for this on Christmas Day, so I turned to leave. As I walked down the hallway, I stopped dead in my tracks. The news hadn't mentioned anything about Mississippi being shot twice in the head, and how would Roc know that? I turned, making my way back to his room, clearing my throat.

He snatched the covers off his head and sighed.

"I'm going to get out of your hair soon, but I wanted you to know that your cough is already sounding better. Let me know what kind of medicine you used, as it seems to work magic. Pertaining to Mississippi, I don't really care what happened to him, as I firmly believe you reap what you sow. But the news didn't mention that he was shot twice in the head. The only person who would know that is the killer, or *the one* who made the order to have it done. That's just something for you to think about while you're resting."

Roc held out his hands again, staring at me with a cold expression. "I said it wasn't me."

I left the room with nothing else to say. I knew Roc had something to do with it, but he would never tell. This secretive life he lived was killing me and there was so much about it that I didn't want to know, then again I did. I figured the truth behind all of it would hurt me, as well as, someday, Chassidy. I never wanted to sit her down and tell her what kind of man I suspected her father to be. A killer? I wasn't sure yet, but I prayed on my way out that it simply wasn't true.

I had gotten about two miles away from Roc's place when I saw a familiar face driving in the opposite direction on Grand Boulevard. It was

Vanessa. I didn't think she'd seen me. When I got to the light, I quickly made a U-turn just to see where she was going. She drove a white convertible BMW and I wasn't about to let it get out of sight. That thought was short-lived, as the light turned yellow and she rushed through it. I had to stop at the light and it seemed to take forever. I tapped my fingers on the steering wheel, already feeling the knot in my stomach tighten. I tried to loosen the knot by taking deep breaths, but the deeper my breaths got, the knot seemed to tighten more. The light changed, and Vanessa's BMW was out of my sight. That in no way mattered, and when I got to Roc's place, her car was already parked out front. She must have been inside, so I waited to see how long she'd stay. I couldn't believe that I was spying on Roc, but there were some things that I needed to know because he wasn't telling. *Do I stay out here?* I kept asking myself. *Or do I go to the door?* I sat in the car, debating with myself, and had also thought about just going home. That's what I should have done, but it didn't seem like much of an option. Before I knew it, I had been sitting in the car for about forty-five minutes. I had hoped that Vanessa would've come out by now, but she hadn't. I was so hurt inside, but my hurt wouldn't allow me to shed one tear, even though my throat felt as if it were burning, and my hands were starting to tremble. I took another deep breath, eventually saying, "Fuck it."

I got out of my car, making my way to the door. I fumbled around with my keys in search of the one Roc had given to me. I knew he had plenty of guns inside, and there was a possibility that I could get hurt. I figured Vanessa was the kind of woman who would protect her man at any cost, but I didn't care. I was numb and wasn't thinking clearly right now. I turned the lock, slowly pushing the door open. Immediately, I heard loud rap music playing, and it wasn't until I got midway up the stairs that I heard Vanessa moaning as if she were in tremendous pain. My entire body felt weak, and my legs felt as if I had been running a marathon. At that point, I knew I had all of the answers I needed. I wanted to turn around to leave, but this was an out-of-body experience that I had never felt before. I kept on moving up the stairs, and when I almost reached the top, I turned to my right. That's where all of the action was taking place. Roc was sitting up on the couch with no clothes on, leaning back and looking helpless. Vanessa's near-perfect naked body was straddled on top of him. Her back was facing him and she was giving him one hell of a ride. His head was dropped back and eyes were squeezed tight. So were hers. Seeing his dick plunge into her insides made me ill. His hands roamed her ass and he had the nerve to smack it. Then he eased his hand around to her clitoris, teasing hers like he often teased mine. She was near tears. All she could do was tell him how much she loved him. I'll be damned if he didn't respond, "Daammn, baby, I love how you do this shit! Keep on fuckin' me like this, and *nobody* makes me feel like you do!"

I'd heard it all before and could have fallen down the stairs as I quickly made my way out. As weak as my legs were, I almost did fall. I didn't care that I probably had their attention, and by the time I reached the porch, it was obvious that I did. Roc called after me, but I kept it moving. I hurried to my car, and he chased after me with a towel wrapped around his waist. Dick was still probably dripping wet from the festivities. As he crossed the street, a car almost hit him but swerved out of the way. The driver blew his horn, yelling profanities out of his window.

"Fuck you too," Roc said, running up to my car. He banged on the window, telling me to lower it. I looked in my side mirror making sure it was clear to pull off. It was, so I did.

I was a nervous wreck driving home. I kept smacking away my falling tears, fighting my pain. I don't know what it was about me that always tried to play the tough role, but this time, Roc had broken me down. I don't even think my divorce from Reggie had hurt this bad, only because at the age of forty-two, going on forty-three, I found myself in a very similar situation. The choices I had made had cost me dearly, but anyone could say what they wanted; I in no way deserved this. Bullshit came at any age, and some men would never stop bringing it. It was up to me to do better and I knew it. Sadly, I took a risk and in no way did it pay off.

As soon as I got home, I rushed inside and hurried to take off my clothes. I turned on my shower and got inside to let the warm water pour down on me. I had a sponge in my hand, scrubbing my skin hard, attempting to wash away the touch of Roc's hands. I knew the scrubbing was doing me no good, but I felt like the water was cleansing my mind, body, and soul. I closed my eyes, thinking of every single time he'd touched me, and couldn't get the thoughts of what I had just witnessed at his place out of my mind. Finally, the tears streamed down my face and I cried harder than I had ever cried before. I asked myself over and over again, *Where did I go wrong?* At the end of the day, I knew I had no one else to blame for this but myself. I'd let my guard down, and how in the hell did I allow myself to trust a man like him? That was one big mistake, and I should have seen this coming. He toyed with my feelings before he'd gone to prison, and this time was no different. He couldn't give up Vanessa if his life depended on it, and there was no telling who else was in the picture. Like in the past, I bet he'd been running from one woman to the next, pretending as if I was the one who had changed his life around. I hadn't changed nothing, and today proved to me that Roc was the same man that he'd been before. Damn! Why me?

I stayed in the shower until the water had turned cold. By now, my body was quivering and I was a complete mess. I was sitting on the seat in my shower with my head hung low and my hair dripping wet. My hands covered my face and I felt like I couldn't even move.

"You . . . you left the door open," Roc said. I heard the shower door slide open, but I didn't say a word. Right now I could have killed him. I often wondered what made Vanessa as angry as she was, and now a part of me understood her actions. Being screwed over and lied to by a man definitely wasn't any fun.

"Dez," Roc said, touching my hand and trying to move it away from my face. "I'm sorry. But can I tell you why I did what I did?"

I really didn't care, only because there was nothing he could say that would ever repair this kind of damage. I removed my hands from my face, trying to wipe my face clean. Roc squatted down beside the shower, trying to explain his actions.

"Maybe I should have told you this, but I've been upset with you for a while. Only because you didn't tell me that Ronnie approached you at the hotel, basically threatenin' my life and yours. I couldn't understand why you didn't say nothin' to me, but it bothered me that you didn't. As a woman who is supposed to love me, you need to have my back. When somebody—anybody—get at you with some shit like that, it is imperative for you to say somethin'. You made me feel as if I couldn't trust you, so I was like fuck it. I felt as if you wasn't givin' me your all, so I decided not to give you my all."

I still had nothing to say. Roc could sit next to me and explain his mess until he was blue in the face, and it wouldn't even matter. He knew damn well that he had never stopped seeing Vanessa. Whether I had told him about Ronnie or not, what happened today would have happened anyway. Roc reached for the faucet to turn off the water. He squatted next to me again.

"The truth about Vanessa, here it is. Yes, I was dippin' and dabbin' in that every blue moon. Nowhere near as much as you think, only because I wanted to do right by you. When I found out that you neglected to tell me about your conversation with Ronnie, I went back to the woman I felt safe with. Vanessa would lay her life on the line for me, Dez, and anytime Ronnie has said some shit that affected me, she's told me. Even so, I didn't want to be with her. I wanted to be with the woman who was helpin' me grow into a better man and encouragin' me to live a better life. The one who captured my muthafuckin' heart like no one had ever done before. I'm so sorry for what your eyes witnessed today, but I did it because I was hurtin' inside too."

Roc waited for a response, but I still didn't have one. Obviously, he was with the right woman if she was willing to lay her life on the line for him, because I wasn't willing to do so. I closed my eyes again, rubbing my forehead and hoping that he would leave.

He stood up, placing his hands into his pockets. "Lastly, I wasn't the one who killed Mississippi, but, yes, I do know who it was. He owed someone close to me a lot of money, and shit happens when you don't pay up. The bruise underneath my eye and the scratch on my neck was from Vanessa. She was upset because I told her I was spendin' Christmas with you and Chassidy. I didn't want to come over because I knew you'd question me about my marks. When Vanessa came to my place, I was upset with you, again, about not knowin' what you would do with information about Mississippi. It's shit like that, Dez, where you leave me with too many unanswered questions about you. If this is a wrap, so be it."

Roc left the bathroom, and I wasn't sure if he had left. When I heard the front door shut, I figured he had.

Chapter 8

I stood in the foyer, reading another letter that had been mailed to me. The words were a little different this time.

Yous a dead Bitch it said with a smiley face sticker. I tore up the letter and threw it in the trash. A part of me felt as if the letters were coming from Ronnie, but could a man as old as he was act so darn childish? I wasn't sure, and the thought of the letters coming from Vanessa had crossed my mind as well.

While in the kitchen, I gazed out at the backyard, watching Latrel and Chassidy make a snowman. Seeing them together always pleased my heart and I had to do whatever was necessary to protect them. In this case, calling the police to report the letters wasn't an option, and I didn't want to involve them because I'd have to mention Roc. I'd never had a gun in the house, but a few weeks ago I'd gone to get one. If I had to use it, I would do it in a heartbeat. Ronnie didn't seem like the kind of man that I could take lightly, and I was starting to worry more about his threats. Maybe it was a good thing that Roc and I weren't seeing each other anymore, but the letter that came today proved that someone wasn't backing down. No doubt, Ronnie hated me with a passion, and to be honest, the feeling was very mutual.

As soon as I took a sip from my coffee, the phone rang. I picked up, but no one answered.

"Hello," I said again. No reply. "You know, I could get my number changed, but I won't. Whoever this is, you don't scare me. Show your damn face, you coward. And when you do, you'd better believe I'll have something waiting for your ass."

I slammed down the phone. Even though I was afraid, I would never show it. I just took a deep breath, hoping that this matter would quickly resolve itself.

Like in the past, Roc called to say he would give me time to get my thoughts together and not pressure me about what I ultimately decided to do. Time was in no way what I needed, because I already knew that our relationship was a done deal. It was hard for me to swallow, and I knew that I still had to deal with Roc because of Chassidy. I also had to see him from time to time at work, and, by now, I had expected him to give up on his job. In no way did he need to be working, and it was obvious that there was still some moving and shaking going on behind the scenes. With him keeping his job, I figured he was just trying to prove something to me.

The new year had swooped in so fast, and, if you blinked, you missed the month of January. My birthday was in March, and I couldn't believe that I would be turning forty-three. I didn't quite feel it yet, and didn't look it, either. That was a good thing.

In August of this year, Latrel would finally be a senior. He wouldn't graduate until the following year, but time had definitely gotten away from me. He was still playing basketball, but he seemed to focus more on his engineering degree. His visits home had slacked up a bit, simply because he was starting to spend more time with his girlfriend. I was a little upset about that, but Latrel had a life to live and I had to accept that. Reggie had been griping about how much time Latrel had been spending with his girlfriend too. When he told me Latrel had mentioned getting married, I was stunned.

"Married?" I said over the phone, talking to Reggie. "Are you serious?"

"Very. I'm just warning you. I have a feeling about this one. There is something in our son's eyes that I'm seeing and I know what that means. He's in love with Angelique, and I would put some money on it."

"I think he's in love too, but I don't know about this marriage thing. It's too soon. He hasn't even known her for a year yet, has he?"

"He's known her for a while, but they started dating a while ago. I didn't call to get you uptight, and like I said, I just wanted to warn you."

I thanked Reggie for the heads-up, and eyeballed the phone after I ended our call. I picked it up to call Latrel, then decided to put it back down. *What's gon' be is gon' be,* I kept telling myself. I didn't know why I seemed so frustrated about this, but I guessed I just didn't want Latrel to make the many mistakes that his father and I had made.

It was back to work for me on Monday. When I got to my desk, there was a note on my computer. The note was from Roc, asking me if he could stop by after work to see Chassidy. It had been a little over three weeks since I'd had a conversation with him about her. Even though I debated in my mind what to do, I didn't want to keep them apart. I immediately called Roc's cell phone and he answered.

"Yes," I said. "That will be fine."

"I can come over?"

"Roc, you are welcome to come and see your daughter anytime you wish. She misses you too, and I would never prevent you from being a part of her life."

"'Preciate it. I'm leavin' work early today because I gotta go handle some business. I'll see y'all around six, no later than seven."

"Sure."

I kept myself busy at work just so I wouldn't think about my situation with Roc and Chassidy. I had a feeling that he was going to use her to get to me, and I had to make sure he could never slip through the cracks. A part of me still felt a little vulnerable, but that didn't stop me from cutting off my connections with Roc. Regardless, we had to make peace with this situation and realize that it wasn't about us anymore, it was about our daughter.

Around 6:30 P.M., the doorbell rang and I made my way to the door. Chassidy and I had been in the kitchen finishing dinner, where I had some fried pork chops, string beans, and mashed potatoes. I opened the door and Roc came inside with a teddy bear and card in his hand.

"Before you chew me out, the teddy bear ain't for you. It's for Chassidy, all right?"

I smiled, inviting Roc inside. He went into the kitchen, giving Chassidy her teddy bear and opening her card so he could read it to her. I started to clean up the kitchen, and before I had finished, Roc had taken Chassidy to her room so they could have some alone time. This situation felt so awkward. In the past we could always sit around each other, laughing, joking, and having fun. I certainly didn't want to give Roc the wrong idea about us, and, for now, things had to be left as they were.

Roc played with Chassidy for a while. They watched TV in the den together; he helped her put together a puzzle, and chased her around the house with a hand puppet. I was lying across my bed, reading a book, when she came running in the room screaming because Roc was trying to scare her with Oscar the Grouch.

"Roc, don't scare her with that thing," I said.

"She's not scared. We just playin'." Roc stood at the end of the bed and Chassidy jumped into his arms. It was getting late, so he carried her to her room, telling me that he was going to tuck her in.

Fifteen minutes later, he came back into my room and stood in the doorway. "I just wanted to let you know that I'm leavin'. Thanks for let-tin' me stop by, and I figure maybe I can make arrangements with you to drop by on Tuesdays and Thursdays, if that's okay with you. I know how you feel about her comin' to my place, and since things ain't always smooth on my home front, I'd rather come over here to spend time with her."

"You know I'm not going to argue about that, and Tuesdays and Thursdays sound fine."

Roc hesitated, then walked farther into the room with his hands in his pockets. "Are you ready to talk to me yet about what happened and about what you've decided to do? I'm real inter-ested in what you got to say."

I lowered my book and took off my reading glasses. "There's no need for us to talk about what happened. It's over and done with. You already know what I've decided. I'm not going to continue to play this back and forth game with you. It gets tiresome, and, for an old lady like me, it's played out."

Roc snickered and moved closer. "What you got planned for your birthday, *old lady?* Can I take you out to dinner or somethin'?"

"No, but thank you. I'll be right here on my birthday, and if it falls on a Tuesday or Thursday, maybe I'll see you then."

"It's on a Tuesday. Enjoy your book and I'll see you tomorrow at work. Remember tomorrow is Tuesday, so I'm comin' back this way again."

Every single Tuesday and Thursday, Roc had showed up to spend time with Chassidy. Sometimes, I would leave and go to Schlafly Library or the Galleria, just to give them some time alone together. No doubt, he'd kept his word about spending time with her and about keeping his job. Sometimes, he brought Li'l Roc with him to visit, and the farthest they would go was to some of the playgrounds in my neighborhood or to the grocery store to buy junk. I had become more relaxed with the situation and was glad that Roc hadn't suggested doing more than what he was already doing.

The day of my birthday, Mr. Anderson had ordered me a cake and many of my coworkers had come to my desk to get a piece. Monica had sent me some flowers, and so had Latrel and also Reggie. Needless to say, my desk was full of love and I felt pretty darn special. I packed up everything around 3:00 P.M., leaving for the day. I picked up Chassidy early from daycare and headed home to cook dinner. Since it was Tuesday, I knew Roc was coming over and I suspected that he would bring Li'l Roc with him. We had spoken earlier and I mentioned that I had plenty of cake left. Arriving at his normal time, Roc got there around 6:30. Li'l Roc was with him and he couldn't wait to tear into the cake I had placed on the table. I told him and Chassidy to have at it, and what did I say that for? Cake was everywhere, leaving me with one big mess to clean up. As I walked over to the sink to get a rag, Roc asked me to follow him into the den. I was still able to keep my eyes on the kids, so I went to the den to see what he wanted. He gave me two boxes and a card.

"Here," he said. "This is what Li'l Roc picked out for you. He would have given it to you, but, as you can see, he's too busy with that cake."

I opened the card first, reading what Li'l Roc had written in his own handwriting:

Happy Birthday Miss Dez. I love you very much and thank you for being like a 2nd mama to me. Sometimes I wish you were my 1st mama but I know you can't be. Thanks for my little sister 2 and you are a wonderful family.

I closed the card where he had written the names of me and Chassidy on the images of the woman and little girl on the card. My eyes watered, but I held back my tears. I swallowed the lump in my throat and opened the box, which contained a cross with diamonds. I was so touched, and stood up to go give Li'l Roc a hug and kiss.

"Wait a sec," Roc said. "Can you open my gift before you go back into the kitchen?"

"I told you not to do anything for me, Roc. And I don't want you spending your money on me, either."

"I didn't spend that much money on you, so just chill, all right?"

At his request, I opened the other box, and couldn't help but smile when I saw my favorite sundress inside. I knew he had to go to hell and back to find one exactly like the one he'd torn, and his efforts impressed me.

"Thank you," I said, looking up at him.

"Are you goin' to wear it for me tonight? I hope so."

I had no response and ignored his question while I opened the envelope inside of the box. There was a beautiful card, along with a cashier's check for $12,000. I held it in my hand, wondering what it was for.

"I've been saving my checks for Chassidy's education. That's my hard-earned money, so I don't want you trippin' with me about it. Every dime that I make will be for her, all right?"

I was speechless, and this was a very tough situation. I loved and appreciated so much about him, but then there was a side of him that I could in no way cope with. Roc stepped up closer to me and reached into his pocket. My heart dropped, as I thought he was going to pull out a ring. Instead, he pulled out a piece of folded paper. He unfolded it, then let out a deep sigh.

"You'd better not laugh at me. And if you do, I'm never doin' this shit again."

I didn't know what the note said, but in no way would I laugh at something he'd written. "Go ahead," I said, watching him look over the paper. "Read it."

He cleared his throat. "What is Black love and what does it really mean to me? For years, I thought that Black love represented drama and disrespect. In order to get somewhere as a black couple, there had to be pain or no gain. My partner didn't have to show love, 'cause she didn't know love. And if we ever had to go to blows with each other, then that just meant we were angry because we couldn't bear to be without each other. Yeah, that's what I thought, but for all of these years, I have been wrong about Black love. Dead wrong. Now, I know better, 'cause true Black love is alive in me. I feel love like I have never felt it before, and it's so energetic that it takes over my mind, body, and soul. It makes me laugh when I want to cry, it makes me strive harder when I want to give up, it causes me to be real with myself, as that is sometimes so difficult for me to do. Even in my darkest hours when I feel hopeless, or if I don't want to go on, the feeling of Black love picks me up and lets me know that I must move forward. Yeah, I finally get it, but I hope Black love don't give up on me, because I will never give up on it."

Roc folded the paper and seemed embarrassed to look at me. "That was nice," I said with tears in my eyes. "I have to ask, but did you write that? I mean, you just don't seem like the type of person who—"

"Yes, I wrote it. I know it was corny and everythang, but I just wanted to share with you my thoughts that I often write on paper. I did a lot of writin' when I was locked up, too, and these are my real thoughts, ma. I wanted to take this opportunity on your B-day to share that with you, even though we got some serious problems in this relationship."

"Thanks for sharing, your words were beautiful. I really don't know what else to say, but I will never give up on Black love either."

I stood up, giving Roc a hug. He squeezed me tight and kissed my cheek. "You've had your back turned, but when you turn around, please do not be mad at me."

I quickly turned my head and more cake was everywhere. Li'l Roc and Chassidy's mouths were full and their hands had cake squeezed all in between them.

"Why didn't you say anything?" I said, rushing into the kitchen to clean up the mess.

"I was lookin' down at my paper. I just looked up and saw them." Roc followed me into the kitchen. "Man, you know better," he said to Li'l Roc. "Get down from that chair and go wash your hands."

"Don't blame them," I said to Roc. "You're the one who should have been watching them."

I squeezed the cake with my hand, smashing it into Roc's face. He tried to move back, but I caught him off guard. It was smeared all on his cheek and Li'l Roc and Chassidy were laughing. I was too.

"Oh, so you think that shit is funny, huh, birthday girl? I got somethin' for that ass."

Roc picked up the entire cake and started following me around the kitchen. "I'm sorry," I laughed. "Please, put that cake down. If you throw that at me, Roc, that mess will be everywhere. You'll have to clean it up and . . ."

I tried to run out of the kitchen, but I wasn't fast enough. Roc pushed the cake forward, but when I held up my arm, it flipped backward and most of it got on him. The sheet that the cake was on hit the floor and we had one gigantic mess. Roc was still trying to get after me, and as I circled the kitchen island, I laughed when he slipped and fell hard. Before he could say anything, the light on his Bluetooth flashed and he hit the button. He then swiped his cake-filled hands together, rubbing them on his jeans.

"Speak," he said with a smile on his face. Seconds later, his smile vanished quickly. "What?" he yelled. "Nigga, I can't understand a word you're sayin'." Roc paused to listen, then hurried off the floor. "All right," he snapped. "Calm the fuck down! I'm on my way."

He looked at me. "I gotta go. I'll be back to get Li'l Roc later, and I promise I'll be back."

Roc rushed to the door and I rushed after him. "Wha . . . what happened?" I asked.

He yanked open the front door, staring at me for a few seconds with a confused look on his face. "Somebody shot Ronnie."

Roc rushed out, and it wasn't long before I saw his truck speeding down the street.

I slowly closed the door, feeling bad for Roc but unsure about my feelings for Ronnie. Yes, I hated him with a passion, but did I really want the man to die? There were times that I wanted to kill him myself, but those were just thoughts of the anger I felt inside. Hopefully, he was in the hospital and the situation wasn't that serious. I said a quick prayer by the door, and went into the kitchen to clean up the mess.

It was getting late, and after I cleaned the kitchen, I tucked the kids in bed, spending a little more time in the guestroom to thank Li'l Roc for my birthday present. I also read him a story. He had fallen asleep on me and when I looked at the clock it showed 1:00 A.M. I yawned, leaving the guestroom and making my way into my bedroom. Worried, I called Roc's cell phone, but got no answer. I left a message for him to call me back.

I hadn't found anything to wear for work tomorrow, so I went through my closet and picked out a skirt and blouse. I laid them across my chair, dropping the shoes that I wanted to wear on the floor. For whatever reason, I couldn't get Ronnie off my mind. Was it a possibility that my enemy was killed on my birthday? Well, you know that old saying: be careful what you wish for, right? I surely wanted to take back my wishes, only because I knew the loss of Ronnie would be devastating for Roc. I looked up, praying and reneging on what I had said about the man, now wishing him well. I had no idea what losing Ronnie could do to Roc, and the thought of it made me nervous. I cleared my head, quickly changing my clothes so I could get some sleep.

At 3:45 A.M., I heard the doorbell ring. I had just gone to sleep, so I pulled the covers back and rushed out of bed. I could see Roc's truck in the driveway, so I immediately opened the door. He came in so fast that it scared me to death. So much blood was on his shirt, and he staggered inside, appearing to be in much pain. I touched his chest, fearing that he'd been shot, and trying to help him keep his balance.

"Have . . . have you been shot?" I yelled in a panic, still touching all over his bloodstained shirt. "Oh my God, Roc, what happened?"

He staggered into the living room, falling back on the couch. His arm dropped on his forehead and he squeezed his eyes tightly together. His entire face was wet from tears and his breathing was very fast. "He died, Dez. Ronnie died on meee!"

I had never, ever seen Roc like this, nor had I ever witnessed any man crying so hard. My hands trembled as I reached out to touch his body that wouldn't stop shaking.

"It'll be okay, honey. I'm so sorry. Really I am."

Roc wailed out loud, tightening his fist and slamming it into the couch. I really did not know what to say or do to help him. Putting my arms around him only caused him to push me away.

"Just leave me the fuck alone," he cried. "Back up and give me some gotdamn breathin' room!"

I backed away from Roc, giving him the space he requested. Seconds later, Li'l Roc came into the living room after hearing Roc's loud voice.

"Why you crying, Daddy?" he asked tearfully.

Roc didn't respond. He just kept on sobbing and pounding his fist while screaming, "Damn."

I took Li'l Roc's hand and he looked up at me. "What's wrong with my Daddy, Miss Dez?"

"He lost someone very special to him," I said. I continued to hold Li'l Roc's hand, walking him back to the guestroom so he could get back in bed. "Give your dad time to cool off and he'll tell you about what happened soon."

Li'l Roc looked up at me again. "Did Ronnie get killed? Was it Uncle Ronnie?"

In no way did I want to answer Li'l Roc's question. I wasn't sure about his relationship with Ronnie, and the last thing I wanted was to bring a child to more tears. "I'm not sure. But get some sleep for me, okay?"

I noticed Li'l Roc wipe a tear, as he must have shed a few for his father. I had done so as well, and after I tucked Li'l Roc back in, I stood outside of the door to gather myself. I took several deep breaths, then made my way back into the living room where Roc was. He was sitting on the floor with his knees bent, shielding his face with one hand. With his back resting against the couch, I got on the floor and sat next to him. I put my arms around him and laid my head on his shoulder.

"Don't worry. You'll get through this and I will do whatever it takes to make sure you do. If you need me for anything, I'm here."

Roc leaned forward, removing my arms from around him and making sure my head left his shoulder. He squeezed his stomach and continued to break down on me.

"This shit hurts, ma. Losing that muthafucka hurts. He's all I had, Dez. Now what the fuck I'm gon' do?"

Roc rocked back and forth while I rubbed his back. He had me to depend on, but with us limitations had been put in place. I knew that the love he had for Ronnie in no way compared to what he felt for me. All I could say to him was, "You still have to live for you and you have so much to live for. Your children need you, just like you needed Ronnie. Don't give up, and I love you so much."

Roc stayed in the living room and I tried to find out who killed Ronnie and why, but got no answer. I didn't press the issue and didn't leave his side until morning. I was too tired to go to work, so I called in sick. I also called Roc's boss, telling him that Roc had a loss and wouldn't be in for a few days.

Ronnie's funeral was scheduled for Saturday, and I had barely talked to Roc since he left on Wednesday afternoon. When I asked if he knew who had killed Ronnie, he said no and refused to talk about it. Our phone calls were short and he seemed to be so out of it. He invited me to attend the funeral with him, but, to be honest, a big part of me didn't want to be there. I knew how much Ronnie disliked me, and I felt as if going to his funeral would be very disrespectful on my behalf. In no way was I happy about what had happened to him, and I truly wished that this whole situation had turned out differently. But I just couldn't relay those words to Roc. He needed me, and if the shoe were on the other foot, I know he would have been there for me.

I told Roc that I would meet him at the funeral, and, ironically, it was at the same church as the wedding. When I pulled into the parking lot, as expected, the funeral was packed. I was very nervous, and had anticipated sitting in the far back, out of the way. With all of the people standing around, I wasn't sure if I'd see Roc. I just hoped he knew I was there to support him. I walked into the church, dressed in my black linen short-sleeved dress that had a waist-length jacket to go with it. Pearls were around my neck and adorned my wrist as well. My hair was pinned up again and I wore very little makeup. My black heels made me tall, but even so, I hiked myself up on the tips of my toes, looking over the many people in front of me to see if I could find Roc. I didn't see him so I made my way into the sanctuary, taking a seat in the far back. Ronnie's shiny black and chrome casket was already up front and on both sides of the church were pictures of him. I swallowed again, feeling so uncomfortable. I couldn't understand why I continued to put myself in these kinds of situations, but a lot of it was because of Roc.

My eyes wandered around, looking at the hundreds of people piled into the church. The middle section was for the family, so the ushers started to bring in chairs. Moments later, I looked to my right and saw Roc standing next to me.

"Why you didn't let me know you were here?" he said with a very saddened look on his face. His eyes were red, and puffy underneath.

"I figured you would know I was here."

He reached out for my hand. "Come out here with me. The family ain't comin' in until last."

I wasn't family, but instead of saying it, I took Roc's hand. We made our way through the crowd, where people were rubbing his shoulder, telling him everything would be all right, and giving lots of hugs. That made Roc very emotional, and every time we stopped to talk to someone, he squeezed my hand. I figured he thought I was going to let go, but I didn't.

The funeral was under way, and the long line of family members proceeded to go into the church. Roc and I were seated in the very first pew. I kept praying for God to give me strength so I could pass it on to Roc. His legs were trembling and his eyes were glued to Ronnie's casket. Every few seconds, he'd let out a deep breath and sit back. Then he'd let out another and lean forward. He was very fidgety and I reached for his hand to calm him. I held on tight, occasionally rubbing his back and patting his leg.

Midway through the funeral, it was pure, deep torture. The cries in the church were getting louder, the singing choked me up, and one person after another stood up to tell how Ronnie had caused such an impact on their lives.

"Y'all just don't know," a young man stood in front of the church saying. He was crying his heart out. He pointed to Ronnie's casket. "That man right there, he took care of everybody. You could ask him for anything, and he would do it, no questions asked. We lost a hero, but I'm gon' be thankful that I got a chance to know who the real man was."

So many people in the church vouched and hollered, "Amen."

Roc tightened his fist and whispered, "Say that shit, man, say that shit again." He rolled up Ronnie's obituary, tapping it against his hand. At one point, he seemed to calm down, and reached his arm back to rest it on top of the pew. I looked up at him, but it was almost as if I were looking through him. This was a different Roc sitting next to me. A much colder one.

According to the obituary, it was now time to view the body. This was the part that I hated so much. With us being rather close, there was no way for me to avoid it. I prayed, yet again, for strength. The funeral directors opened the casket, and all I could picture in my mind was Roc lying there. From a short distance, I could see Ronnie laid out in his black pinstriped suit and burgundy accessories. Roc was staring at him again, and it wasn't long before the people in the church erupted with more hollering and screaming.

"Jesus Christ," one lady shouted, covering her mouth and damn near fainting. I had never seen so many men cry in my life, and another man dropped to his knees in front of the casket.

"Why you leave us like this, man? Why?" he screamed. "You was supposed to be a soldier!" The ushers had to carry the man out, and, one by one, some of the visitors kissed Ronnie, placed items in his casket, or fell all over it in tears. Shouts of pain rang out, and when Roc dropped down to one knee, I stood up behind him. Several men came to his aid, trying to hold him up. Eventually, they had to carry him out of the church as well. I followed, wiping my tears and hoping that this torture would all be over with soon.

Nearly two hours later, it was. We were now at the gravesite at St. Peter's Cemetery on Lucas and Hunt, where Ronnie was soon to be put into the ground. I stood, holding Roc's hand, looking at all of the people there to pay their last respects. Yes, Ronnie may have been hated by some, but he was still loved by many. The proof was in the pudding, and now he was in the hands of a man who he would have to answer to for the good, bad, or maybe ugly. I said one last prayer for him and made my way with Roc back to his truck. He plopped down in the driver's seat, looking dazed. Another man was riding in the passenger's side, and he got into Roc's truck.

"Are you coming over?" I asked, standing beside Roc's truck. "I'll cook you some dinner."

"Nah, I'm goin' home."

I touched the side of his handsome face, rubbing it. "Okay. If you need anything, call me. Take care, baby."

Roc shut the door and I made my way to my car. I could see Vanessa staring at me from afar, and at a time like this, she had the nerve to confront me.

"I see you're not ready to give up on Roc just yet, huh?" she said.

I sighed and quickly turned to face her. "Vanessa, please stop with the childish games. If Roc is your man, so be it. Why are you constantly approaching me with your nonsense? I know why. Because you know, like I do, that all we are to Roc is some pussy. He doesn't know how to love you, nor does he love me. The only person he has ever loved is now gone, so stop wasting your time with this. Because no matter what you do, Roc is going to be the man you've known him to be for all of these years. Too bad you haven't figured out what kind of man you have on your hands. I have, and that's what you're so afraid of. So stop fighting with him, and instead figure him out. Then you can decide how you wish to proceed in your relationship with him, and in no way will what you decide affect me. That's just a little something I think you should know."

She pursed her lips and put her hands on her hips. "Roc does love me and he can get pussy anywhere. No matter what, he always comes back to me, and that's just something I think *you* should know."

I reached for the door handle on my car, as this chick just wasn't getting it. "Don't chalk it up as love, Vanessa, as it can always be mistaken for convenience. His security blanket you may be, but after a while a blanket gets worn and tired and gets thrown away. I regret to inform you that, personally, I think your days are numbered. Simply because a woman doesn't have to keep fighting for what's hers, she only fights for what's not. Obviously, Roc is not yours."

I got in my car, because this wasn't the time or place for the kind of action I knew she wanted. I couldn't help but to wonder where things would go from here now that Ronnie was gone. Would Roc now become the Head Negro In Charge, or was this the right time for him to move away from the bullshit and be done with it? Just from observing and noticing all of the people coming up to him, along with Vanessa and her continuous mess, I wasn't so sure.

Chapter 9

I guess it didn't take long for my question to be answered, and, just for the record, Roc had been fired from his job. His boss had come to me this morning, telling me that Roc had taken too many days off and failed to call in to say why. I knew he hadn't been coming to work, and every time I spoke to him, he said that he needed more time to get himself together. Basically, he didn't feel like working, so he wasn't coming in. His Tuesday and Thursday visits had come to a halt, and the last time I'd seen him was at the cemetery that day. In no way did I want to pressure him, and when he asked for space, I gave it to him.

Besides, on my end, I had an even bigger fish to fry. My weight had been fluctuating and the stress I had been under was causing me to eat more. Since I hadn't been working out with Roc, I had packed on seven pounds and wasn't too happy about it. My self-esteem had plummeted, and I just couldn't get out of this funk I was in. In addition to that, Latrel had finally broken the news to me, telling me that he wanted to get married. I was livid, because he hadn't even finished college yet. He still had one year to go, but he refused to wait.

"What is the rush?" I asked, talking to him over the phone while I was on the treadmill at Gold's Gym. This weight was coming off of me, and the last thing I needed was to feel uncomfortable about how I looked.

"There is no rush. I've known her for a while and I'm in love. We feel now is the right time to do it, and before we go back to school in August, we will be married. Either you're on board or not, Mama. It's going to happen and I'm not going to argue with you about this. Just be happy for me, all right?"

"I'm trying to be, Latrel, but I don't understand why you can't just finish school first. That would make so much more sense. Give this relationship *thingy* a little more time."

"I'm not on your time, I'm on my time. Angelique agreed to marry me and I'm not going to wait to do it."

"She's pregnant, isn't she? Why don't you just come out and say it, Latrel?"

"I would tell you if she was, but she's not. Look, I'm not getting anywhere with this conversation. I'll be home next weekend and we can talk more about it. I have to get to class, so bye, Mama."

He hung up, leaving me fuming inside. In no way was I against him getting married, but Latrel needed to wait. He was moving way too fast, and just two years ago he was claiming to be in love with someone else. It reminded me so much of the situation Reggie had put himself in. I was concerned about Latrel following that path. I called Reggie at work, ready to chew him out for . . . nothing.

"Would you please talk to your son?"

"I have, Dee, but it's his life and we have got to let go. I know how hard this is for you, but, baby, it is his choice. We got married right after college, and if he wants to do it a year sooner, so be it. Why are you stressing yourself over this?"

I started to walk faster on the treadmill. "I don't know. I guess . . . I guess I'm just afraid of losing him."

"You will not be losing him. As I see it, you're gaining a lot. You'll finally have a daughter-in-law to go shopping with and to chat with over the phone. She'll—"

"Ughhh. I don't need anyone to go shopping with and chat with over the phone. I have Monica for that and no one will take her place."

Reggie laughed, trying to convince me that this was the right move for Latrel. I wasn't buying it, and when I called Monica to vent, she told me the same thing. I guess it was time for me to get on board, but then again, maybe not.

The weeks had flown by, and I was so sure that Roc would have made some time for Chassidy, but he hadn't. Basically, he had cut her off and I didn't like it one bit. I was very upset with him, and even though I figured he was probably still going through a hard time, his approach was wrong. She had been asking about him and I really didn't have a legitimate answer as to why he had stopped calling and coming over.

Friday after work, I decided to go get my answer. I remembered the turmoil that going to his place brought me the last time I paid him an unexpected visit, but I was prepared to deal with whatever. He wasn't my man and this was all about how he intended to move forward with his daughter. I wanted what was in her best interest, and if Roc had decided not to be a part of her life anymore, I needed to know that.

When I arrived at his place, I knocked, getting no answer. I rang the doorbell; no one came. I waited, and, yes, I contemplated using my key. That would be such a bold move, and if the shoe were on the other foot, I would have a fit. Still, that didn't stop me from putting my key in the door and going inside. Just like the last time, the music was up very loud. This time, however, I called Roc's name to let him know that I was inside.

"Roc, are you in here? It's me, Dez."

I got no answer as I made my way up the steps, fearing to look into the living room and witness what I'd seen before. This time, the living room was empty, but it was a mess. Clothes were everywhere. Smoked blunts were in an ashtray, and empty beer cans, as well as liquor bottles, were all over. It looked like somebody had been partying and partying hard. I checked the dining room and the kitchen, but they both were empty. Two of the kitchen chairs were tilted back on the floor, and empty bags from London & Sons Wing House were on the table. I picked up the chairs, placing them back underneath the table. Afterward, I turned, making my way down the hallway to his bedroom. I felt very uneasy. As I slowly walked, the floor squeaked loudly. Seconds later, I heard Roc's voice coming from his bedroom.

"If you make another move, I swear I'll kill you."

I stopped in my tracks with an increased heart rate. "Roc, it's me. Dez."

I got no response, but as I inched my way to the door, I peeked into his bedroom. He was sitting up in bed. His gun was aimed in my direction, and when he saw me, he dropped it into his lap. The room was partially dark, because he had put up some curtains to cover the window. I turned on the light, and just like the rest of his place, everything was a mess.

"What's going on, Roc?" I asked, walking farther into the room. The smell of marijuana nearly burned my nose and it was very strong. Roc's eyes were bloodshot, and I had never seen the hair on his head, as well as his facial hair, look so scruffy.

He scratched his head and I could hear how dry his hair was. "Ain't nothin' goin' on. Just chillin', that's all."

I sat on the bed in front of him, looking around at his messy room. "It looks like something has been going on. Did you have a party?"

"Nope. And if I had, I would have invited you."

"Don't do me any favors." I chuckled. He didn't laugh, and all he did was clear his throat.

"I . . . I'm not going to stay long, but I stopped by because you haven't called or come by to see Chassidy. She misses you, Roc, and I do too. Have you given up on your daughter? I know things haven't been going well with us, but I at least thought you'd still see about your daughter."

Roc sat back on the bed, resting against the headboard. "Yep. I've given up on everything. Ain't no place in this world for a man like me, so I'm here in my own space, doin' my own thing."

"So, in other words, you're hiding out? From what? Me? Chassidy? Who?"

"I'm not hidin' out. I just don't want to be out there right now. I like right where I am and this shit is peaceful, ma."

"Well, I definitely don't want to interrupt your peace. I know how it is when you feel the need to be alone. I was the same way when I lost my mother, so I can understand how you feel." I touched the side of his face and rubbed it. "Just know that I'm here for you, and don't give up on life, okay? Chassidy and I really miss you and I want you to be well."

He said not a word, just glared at me in a trance. I stood up, willing to leave Roc at peace. When it came to healing, people were on their own time and they dealt with the loss of a loved one how they wanted to. I figured Roc would come around, so I wasn't too worried. I gave him a hug and he barely hugged me back. Needing no answer as to why, I made my way to the door. I reached for the light, turning it back off.

"Dez," Roc said, halting my steps.

"Yes." I turned to see what he wanted.

"I . . . I did it all for you. For you and Chassidy. I just wanted to let you know that."

My brows scrunched inward. "Did what for us? What did you do for us?"

I saw a tear roll down his face and he swiped it away. I moved closer, asking the same question. Roc looked into my eyes, sucking his teeth.

"He was gon' kill you, baby." He spoke tearfully. "You and my daughter, and I . . . I couldn't let him do it. I couldn't, Dez, and I had to make a decision. He was days away from doin' it, and when I found out about the letters and phone calls from my boy Ned, I . . . I had to take action."

It felt as if cement had been poured over me. I couldn't move. I opened my mouth, but no words came out. Roc lowered his head and squeezed his forehead.

"Please forgive me, but I can't be around you and Chassidy anymore. It hurts too bad and it reminds me of what I had done to him."

I looked at the gun in Roc's lap, realizing that he must have been over here contemplating suicide. What a messed up situation to be in, and there was no doubt in my mind that Ronnie was coming for me. This was so very tragic and I never thought or believed that it would have resulted in this. I slowly sat down on the bed, moving the gun away from Roc's lap. He began to tell me how he had Ronnie set up, and the paranoia he'd felt from doing so. He even let me listen to a tape that was given to him by Ned, where Ronnie clearly had planned to do away with me and Chassidy the day after my birthday. I was to be blown away at the front door, and directions were given to do away with anyone else in the house and make sure the little girl, Chassidy, didn't live. I was stunned that any man could be so cruel, but then again, I wasn't. This was one time that I had passed the correct judgment on a person, and it pleased my heart, more than anything, knowing that Ronnie was now in hell.

I could see the pain Roc was in for making such a difficult decision. I put my arms around him, thanking him repeatedly for basically choosing our lives over Ronnie. "Please don't be so hard on yourself," I said tearfully. "I am so grateful to you for what you did, and one day you will realize that you did the right thing. Thank you, baby, thank you. I love you so much, and you don't know how much Chassidy and I need you."

I had a tight hold on Roc, but his hold on me wasn't so tight. He begged me not to tell anyone the truth and did his best to convince me that him not being in Chassidy's life was a good thing. According to him, there was no way for him to be the father he needed to be to her, and if anyone ever found out the truth about what had happened to Ronnie, we could all lose our lives. In no way did he want that to happen, so he asked me to please understand why it had to be this way. Of course, I disagreed.

"I will give you all the space and time you need, but you're not going to do this to us again, Roc. You promised me that you wouldn't give up on us and I'm going to hold you to that promise. I will never repeat a word of this to anyone, and at the end of the day, you made a choice that saved the lives of two people who didn't deserve to die. I know it hurts, but it was a brave thing to do."

"Maybe so, but I'm not feelin' it right now. I . . . I really don't want to talk about this anymore. All we're goin' to do is disagree about Chassidy and I have to do what I feel in my heart is best. Chassidy will one day get it. She's so young right now, and by the time she turns ten, she won't even remember who I am."

The thought of what he said choked me up even more. How could he continue to easily walk in and out of our lives like this? My mouth hung open and my throat ached from the thought. "How can you say that? Every child needs their parents, and if anybody knows that it should be you. How dare you sit there and give up on her like that? I guess this is so easy for you, as it wouldn't be the first time you've done it. Chassidy loves you and she has gotten to know—"

"What about you?" Roc asked. "Do you *really* still love me too, Dez? Ain't this got somethin' to do with you? This not all about Chassidy, so let's be real. What about us getting back together? You ended this shit with me over some pussy. Pussy that don't mean shit to me no more."

I looked down, fumbling with my nails. "I . . . I love you, but I can't be with a man I don't trust. You make this so hard for me and I don't want to keep being with a man who hurts me all the time. I appreciate all that you've done, but it's not enough."

He quickly fired back. "Not enough! I had Ronnie killed." He paused, unable to say it again.

"I know," I said, standing up and squeezing my forehead. I was so confused and debated with myself about what to do, as well as say. "I just don't know about us being together, Roc, and that's a separate issue. Give me time, and I'll deal with it as it comes. Meanwhile, I hope you think about what you're saying about your child. Focus on being there for her, and I can't tell you how much she needs you. She will always need you and that's never going to change."

"I have thought long and hard about Chassidy. This is best for everyone, and even though you may not see it now, you will soon. Now, please. I got a headache right now and I need my peace. Lock the door on your way out."

I couldn't believe what Roc was saying and I threw up my hands in defeat. "Fine," I said, picking up my keys so I could go. I wasn't going to sit there and beg Roc to be a father to his child. Like so many other mothers, I could easily do this by myself. I should have known that it would come to this. Stupid me, and there I was again having hope and faith about this situation turning out differently. I abruptly walked down the hallway, hoping that Roc would call my name to stop me. He didn't. Then, something else hit me. My thoughts were sometimes late, but accurate. I went back into his bedroom.

"You're telling me all of this because you're leaving St. Louis, aren't you?" I asked.

He didn't hesitate one bit. "Yes."

"When?"

"Soon."

"How soon? Days, weeks, months. . . ."

"Days."

I stood, shaking my head, feeling the huge lump in my throat that wouldn't go away even when I swallowed. "And you weren't even going to tell me, were you?"

"No, because I knew you wouldn't understand."

I was stunned, angry, disgusted . . . all at the same time. This in no way made sense to me, but it clearly confirmed that Roc had love for no one. I reached into my purse, pulling out something that I knew would come in handy. I read Roc's own words back to him, hoping that he would reconsider. "What is Black love and what does it really mean to me? For years, I thought that Black love represented drama and disrespect. In order to get somewhere as a black couple, there had to be pain or no gain. My partner didn't have to show love, 'cause she didn't know love. And if we ever had to go to blows with each other, then that just meant we were angry because we couldn't bear to be without each other. Yeah, that's what I thought, but for all of these years, I have been wrong about Black love. Dead wrong." I looked up at him, just to make sure he was paying attention to me. He was. "Now, I know

better, 'cause true Black love is alive in me. I
feel love like I have never felt it before, and it's
so energetic that it takes over my mind, body,
and soul. It makes me laugh when I want to cry,
it makes me strive harder when I want to give
up, it causes me to be real with myself, as that is
sometimes so difficult for me to do. Even in my
darkest hours when I feel hopeless, or if I don't
want to go on, the feeling of Black love picks me
up and lets me know that I must move forward.
Yeah, I finally get it, but I hope Black love don't
give up on me, because I will *never give up on
it.*"

I tore the paper in shreds, watching each piece
slowly drop to the floor. "Like everything else, I
guess that was a bunch of bullshit too. Good-bye,
Roc. Have a nice life."

Chapter 10

For the next several months, my life remained Roc free. He stuck to his guns, and it was confirmed by a very credible source that Roc had moved out of his condo and had left St. Louis. I felt dissed all over again, but I kept it moving. Like the last time, I threw myself into work, focused on my children, lost weight again, and put the past behind me. There was nothing that I could do to change the past. I had regretted that I hadn't made better choices, for me, and for my daughter as well. Because of me, she would not know the man she often called her father. She would be left with a very vague memory of him. I was so sure she would one day wonder what she, herself, had done wrong to cause him to abandon her. In no way was this her fault, and I would someday tell her that all of this was on me. No matter how I looked at it, or tried to spin it, it was on me for making bad choices.

Latrel's wedding was the following day, and, by now, he had my full support. I had completely changed my attitude. If I couldn't get this thing called Black love right, I was counting on him. He truly loved Angelique and I was looking forward to her becoming a part of our family. I liked her mother and father a lot, and even though they were divorced like me and Reggie, they still got along well.

The day of the wedding, Monica picked me up early so we could go to Forest Park, where the wedding was taking place. I wanted to be sure everything was in order. Angelique wanted an outdoor wedding, but, unfortunately for all of us, light rain was in the forecast. The sun was shining bright for now, but I wasn't sure how long it would last. I prayed for God to hold off the rain for as long as He could, or just long enough for Latrel and Angelique to say, "I do."

When we got to Forest Park, everything seemed to be in place. The chairs had already been set up. The gazebo sat up front, decorated with many beautiful red and white flowers. Angelique had wanted a horse and carriage to bring her in, and I checked with the wedding planner just to make sure it was a go. She said it was. After tying a few big ribbons and bows around several of the trees that would show in the pictures, Monica and I left to go get ready. We both got ready at my house and Latrel and Reggie got ready at his place.

"I can't believe you are finally letting your son go," Monica said, pulling Chassidy's dress over her head. "And I just knew you'd request to be his best man, instead of Austin."

I threw my hand back at her, continuing to look in the mirror while glossing my lips. "I haven't let him go and I will never let him go. I may play second fiddle for a while, but Angelique knows who the real boss lady is."

We laughed.

"I'm sure she does, and I must say that I'm glad she's a Democrat," Monica gloated.

"Uh, sorry to bust your bubble, but she's not."

Monica cocked her head back. "Then what is she? Latrel needs to call this mess off right now, 'cause he don't need to be marrying no woman who belong to a Tea Party."

I reached over, patting Monica on her back and whispering. "She's registered as an Independent, so calm down, okay? And as far as I know, she doesn't belong to no Tea Party."

She playfully rolled her neck in circles. "And just how do you know all of this?"

I put my hand on my hip, twitching my finger from side to side. "Because I already did my homework. Spent hours on the Internet, Googling her name and finding out everything that I could possibly find out about her. She did have a racy picture posted on her Facebook page, but everything else checked out."

"Ooooo," Monica laughed. "You are so, so bad. I saw that picture too. Did you see that she had a judgment filed against her for not paying her credit card bill?"

My eyes widened. "Don't you tell me that, girl. Did you check her out too?"

"I sure did," Monica confirmed with a serious look on her face. "As soon as you told me Latrel was getting married to her, I got busy. She's pretty clean, but not paying your bills may not be a good sign."

"Are you sure it was her?"

"Let's go check and make sure."

We laughed, running over to my computer and checking the information Monica had found. "See, right there," Monica said, pointing to the information given for a person name Angelique S. Branson who owed $7,385 in credit card debt.

"Umph," I said with my hands on my hip. "Scroll down." Monica scrolled down, but I immediately realized that Angelique's middle name was Lashay.

"Monica, that's the wrong person. Her middle name is Lashay."

"Is it?"

"Yes," I said, walking away from the computer, playfully swiping my forehead. "I'm glad about that, and I damn sure didn't want my son paying for no big bill that she'd made way before his time."

"I know what you mean, but shame on us." Monica laughed. "Both of our asses were in big debt when we got out of college. If I recall, Reggie did have to pay for those Visa credit cards you racked up on, didn't he?"

"If you won't tell, I won't tell." I snickered. "Now get your shoes on so we can get the heck out of here. You're going to have me late for my own son's wedding. You know I wouldn't miss this for the world!"

The wedding was in progress and Angelique's father had just given her away. She stepped up to Latrel, who looked handsome as ever, tightening her arm with his. Monica sat next to me and Reggie sat behind us. He had brought another woman with him, and all I did was say hello. Monica saw me already getting emotional, so she slipped me some of the Kleenex she'd al-

ready had in her hand. I dabbed my watery eyes,
pleased by how happy Latrel looked, and smiling at Chassidy, who was the flower girl and just
couldn't keep still. She was swaying from side to
side, and every chance she got, she waved at me.
I waved back and several people laughed. Then,
all of a sudden, the lady who was sitting to my
right moved and I looked up, only to see Roc take
her seat. He was razor sharp. Dressed in a black
single-breasted tailored suit that traced his sexy
frame. Two diamond-studded earrings were in
his ears and his hair was trimmed to perfection.
Minimal hair suited his chin, and I would have
loved to see him on the cover of *GQ* magazine.
I swear he could give Lance Gross a run for his
money, and Roc would come through slightly on
top.

"Glad I didn't miss too much," he said, sitting
next to me. I watched him wave at Chassidy, and
she smiled, waving back. She was about to run
over to us, but I whispered for her to stay where
she was. Roc smiled. "Latrel would have killed
me if I didn't make it." He looked over at Monica.
"Hey, Monica. What's up?"

No doubt, we were both shocked to see Roc,
and Monica could barely get the word "hello" out
of her mouth.

Roc cleared his throat, crossing one leg over the other. I looked at the sparkling diamond watch on his wrist and two diamond rings on his finger, wondering what he'd been up to. My mind quickly got back to the wedding and it remained my focus for quite some time.

As the wedding vows were being exchanged, everyone was taking peeks up at the cloudy sky. The dark clouds were slowly moving in, so the minister decided to hurry it up. Angelique and Latrel exchanged wedding rings, and after it was all said and done, they laid a big kiss on each other. The rain held off for as long as it could, and it had started to drizzle. I was glad, only because it helped to cover up the few tears that had fallen down my face.

"That was so beautiful," Monica whispered. "Shame on us for underestimating Angelique."

"No. Shame on you."

The minister shouted, "I give to you Mr. and Mrs. Latrel R. Jenkins."

Everyone stood and applauded as they ran down the middle aisle, shielding themselves from the rain that was picking up. Latrel paused for a moment, mouthing that he loved me and nodding his head at Roc. I blew a kiss to him, sealed with approval.

Giving the wedding party time to leave, I held my tiny purse over my head, trying not to let the rain damage my hair too bad. The carriage and horse had brought Angelique to the wedding, but she and Latrel, along with the wedding party, were leaving in limousines. They rushed to the limousines, getting ready to take the short drive over to the reception that was at a nearby indoor banquet room. After everyone got into the limousines, the guests started to leave. By now, the rain was coming down pretty hard so everyone was rushing.

"I'll see you in the car," Monica said, squinting from the rain. She looked at Roc. "Are you coming too?"

"It depends. But I need to talk to Dez for a minute."

"Okay, but don't be long." Monica gave me a quick hug, then ran off to the car.

I continued to hold my purse over my head, but it did me no good. My hair was getting flat and I could feel my heels sinking in the ground. As for Roc, he was completely drenched. He reached out his hand to move my hair away from my face, gazing at me with his lowered, hooded eyes.

"You look so sexy," he said, blinking his wet eyelids. "Damn, you're gorgeous."

"Too bad being beautiful has never stopped me from getting hurt. What's going on, Roc?"

"I'ma make this quick, but, uh, I just wanted to tell you that I moved, but not too far. I live in Kansas City, Missouri now, and I wondered if you and Chassidy would consider movin' there with me? I'm ready, baby. I am so ready to do this shit with you. I got my shit together, got a job, and lookin' forward to startin' a new life with you. I want you as my wife, and the sooner, the better. Tell me what you're thinkin'. Can we do this shit or what?"

I lowered my head, knowing deep inside that I still loved him so much. I had been miserable without him, but had done my best to ignore the void in my heart. I felt like we had been to hell and back, but the time had come for us to stand still. I slowly moved my head from side to side. "I'm sorry, baby, but your timing couldn't be more off. I believe that people come into your life for a reason, season, or a lifetime, and your season is over. Obviously, you were never meant to be my lifetime, and the way you continue to walk in and out of my life shows it. If I allow you to, you will continue to come and go as you please, but not anymore, Roc. You hurt me too bad this time, and I can't let you do it again. The one thing I regret is letting you back in. I could have prevented all of this from happening to me twice. I soooo wish things could have turned out differently between us, but the ball was always in your court, never mine. I truly wish you well, and take care of yourself."

I reached out, just to give Roc a hug. He didn't hug me back, but that was perfectly okay with me. I ran off, shielding myself from the rain with my hand, and intending not to look back.

"Black love," Roc shouted. "No matter what, you can't fight it! It's there, Dez, and it's always gon' be between you and me."

I turned, just to get one last glimpse at his handsome self standing in the rain. I had to respond. "You're so right about Black love, Roc," I shouted back. "It's out there and I'm not giving up because one . . . two men didn't get it right. Keep the faith, and I hope you don't give up on true Black love either!"

I hurried to open the door to Monica's car, and hopped in on the passenger's side. My eyes connected with Roc's as he continued to stand motionless in the rain. While it may not have worked out between us, I was so serious about not giving up on love. No matter what age a man was, or I was for that matter, Black love was still out there and I was determined to find it.

Monica pulled away from the curb and I let out a deep sigh. I was pained that my season with Roc was over, but eager to see what my lifetime had in store for me. After this much experience with relationships, I felt ready to meet my soul mate. It wasn't Reggie, and unfortunately, it wasn't Roc either.

Tell Me About It!

By

Nikki-Michelle

(for Sam and Michelle)

Chaper 1

My life has always been mundane and for the most part, I have been okay with that. Mundane has kept me free from most of the dramas of life, women, and men. I have no man and no desire to have one. I have been that way for the last four years. The last man I dated was so busy lying that even he didn't know when he was telling the truth. It wasn't like he did a lot of lying about cheating, not to say that he wasn't, but it was other simple things that irked my nerves. Like, why lie about your grades in school or why lie about why you haven't taken your car to the shop to get it fixed yet? Simple stuff like that irked me.

I liked to stay to myself mostly because that meant no worries of trust and people issues, but it seemed as of late the drama followed me to work. *Come on five o'clock.* I kept chanting that inside of my head all day! I was tired, sleepy, and cranky as hell. I had to do way more work than I was being paid to do and the slackers that worked with me annoyed me too. I had been in the same cubicle for four years at this simple entry level position at Atlanta's top marketing and advertising firm. B&G Marketing and Advertising had almost been run into the ground by the former executives and CEO. With all of the sex scandals and sexual harassment lawsuits being thrown at the company left and right, it's a wonder we are still standing.

"You okay over there Chyanne?" Justin asked when I answered my earpiece.

We were working on some research and analytics for this contract that the company had just acquired. We had landed a major deal with a big production company in Atlanta to do all of their marketing and advertising so it was imperative that we get this done on time. There were seven floors in this building, not including the basement. And the whole sixth and seventh floors had been fired. All the old executives were out. They didn't leave one.

I nodded. "Yeah, I'm good."

"You sure, girl? Because you are as quiet as a damn mouse."

He laughed and swung his invisible hair. Justin was as gay as gay would ever get. Let him tell it, he was more woman than me and that was no easy feat since I was what America considered full figured. A big girl some called it. My thirty-six double-D's made me curse them at times and my thighs touched when I walked, but they were not overlapping each other. I was a size sixteen and could squeeze my big ass, and I mean that literally, into a fourteen. Hell just last month I had lost myself and was pushing a size eighteen. I quickly threw away juice and everything that wasn't chicken or fish. I mean don't get me wrong, I had no problem with being super thick, but I didn't want the diabetes and high blood pressure that ran in my family either. I was deathly afraid of being taken out of here like that. So no, I didn't have washboard abs, but damn it, I made my clothes look good!

"Yeah. Just trying to get this report done," I answered.

"You know why everyone is walking on eggshells around here today, right?"

Justin was also a gossip queen.

"No."

"Bitch, I swear! You are so clueless sometimes," he fussed. "We could have a hurricane in this bitch and your ass wouldn't notice."

I giggled a bit. "Shut up and tell me!"

"Well, today is the day that the new CEO makes his debut on the first floor."

I turned to look at Justin and he made a dramatic effect, nodding his head and turning his lips down. His cubicle was right across from mine. The new CEO had been here for weeks cleaning house.

"Oh really?"

"Yes Ma'am. That's why that sour pussy bitch Lola has been prancing around here all morning. How much do you want to bet she has already sucked his dick?"

"Are they firing people down here too?"

"Seems like it girl! You know that girl Andrea right?"

"Yeah."

"Well she just filed another sexual harassment claim against the company and John's old white ass."

"Damn! His old cripple dick was getting with and at everybody huh?"

"Yes Ma'am! But bitch let me tell you, that new CEO is sexy as fuck. You hear me?"

I kept typing and laughing, while Justin kept talking. "Girl that thang came down here early this morning before you got in and I almost dropped down and sucked his dick for fun."

"Ewww Justin! Really? Save me the graphics will you?"

He laughed a little. "Girl that fucker is fine! You hear me and he's a brother."

"If he's a brother and he's that fine then he's probably down low gay. You know how they do."

I expected Justin to agree but I heard his line click. When I went to glance over at him, my eyes stopped at the waist and blue suit pants of someone standing directly in front of my cubicle. I got annoyed and looked up into hazel brown eyes. He had a bald head with a smooth baby face. Dimples were easy to see, evenly placed on each side of his cheeks. He had thick eyebrows with long curly lashes that gave his eyes an exotic appeal. He stood in a wide legged stance with his arms folded across his chest. His expression showed something that I couldn't read. I removed my earpiece and looked back up at him.

"Chyanne, is it?" He asked. I could tell he was from New York. His accent was thick.

I nodded. "Yes, it is."

"Is there anything you want to ask me about my personal life?"

Everything and person in the place was quiet. Even the clocks seemed to have stopped ticking.

"No sir, there isn't."

I assumed this was the CEO.

"You sure? Because you could have fooled me."

"I said I didn't," I snapped.

The way his eyebrows lifted told me I had touched a nerve with my tone of voice.

Before walking off he said to me, "Before you leave today, I need to see you in my office."

His whole demeanor, attitude, and accent grated my nerves. Even the way he strutted over to the elevator worked me. He must have come in from the stairs because he sure didn't come off the elevators or I would have seen him. Justin cut his eyes over at me and mouthed the words 'I'm sorry'. I shrugged and went back to my report. I was a little antsy for the rest of the day. It was well known around here that I didn't take any mess or hold my tongue, but the proof was in the pudding. Out of the five degrees I have, a Master's in business and a BA in marketing is what got me this job, and yet here I was in an entry level position. I finished all of my reports at around 4:00 P.M. and since I was set to leave at five, I packed up my belongings and headed to the elevator. Hell if he was going to fire me, it was going to be on their time. I could see a few people eyeballing me, wondering if they could have my hours once I was gone. I stepped onto the elevator and rode it up to the seventh floor. I caught my reflection and saw my fro was all over the place. I had one of those wild manes that would make Angela Davis's fro look like a baby fro. I ran my hand threw it to try and give it a better look. That didn't help. Oh well.

I gave myself the once over. I had on all black everything; black cropped dress shirt, black wide legged dress pants, and black six inch caged Chanel booties. I could feel my phone vibrating in my purse. It was probably April. She was my best friend. Had been for the last five years. I'd call her back later. After I find out if I still had a job or not. The elevator stopped with a ding and I stepped off onto the seventh floor. I made no qualms in speaking to anyone. Even when the guard asked me who I was there to see, I kept walking right past him.

I rounded the corner and walked down the long corridor. I could see Lola in his office. Mr. McHale's office was big enough to house a small family. The only thing that wasn't made of glass was his big cherry oak wood door. He had the blinds pulled up. Smart move. Guess he didn't want any trouble. Judging by the way Lola was acting, she had probably already sucked his dick like Justin said. Lola annoyed me too. She was light, bright, and darn near white. She had a honey blonde weave with a Kelly Rowland body and a Kim Kardashian outlook on life. By the time I made it to his office, she was coming out and heading back to her desk. The rude trick didn't even speak. She cut her fake honey golden eyes at me and shook her head with a smirk that said she knew something I didn't know. I ignored her and without knocking walked right into the CEO's office. He stopped what he was doing, quirked an eyebrow, and tilted his head. I could tell he was either surprised that I had come early or surprised that I had walked right in.

"Have a seat Chyanne," he said to me.

Like hell I was. If he was going to fire me, I was not going to sit down for it. I watched as he turned and put some papers away in a file cabinet behind him. When he turned back around to see me still standing by the door, he stopped mid stride and looked at me. I watched as he calmly pulled his big black desk chair back and sat down.

"Will you please have a seat? This shouldn't take long," he said to me.

"If it won't take long there is no need for me to sit."

He frowned a bit and this time the expression on his face showed annoyance. I could care less. He inhaled and exhaled before brushing his fingers across his lips. He had full lips. Thick lips. My eyes were drawn to his lips.

"Look, I understand what you all had to deal with before I got here, but that's not the case with me. So if you would, please, have a seat."

I switched my purse from one hand to the other and made my way over to the black cushioned wing back chair in front of his desk.

"Good! Now first things first. You're fired."

I closed my eyes and sucked in my bottom lip to keep from snapping.

He kept going. "Now tell me why a woman with three degrees, a Master's in Marketing, a BA in business, and Associates in accounting, is still in entry level after four years?"

I looked at Lola as she pranced through the doors with bright red pants that looked like they were painted on. They were so tight I could see all that she had been blessed with. She handed him a file and switched back out. He told her thank you and turned his attention back to me right after moving his eyes from her assets. That woman had a gap so big in between her legs that I could fly a 747 through it.

"Care to answer my question," he asked me as he put the file on the desk and clasped his hands together. He licked his lips and stared at me.

"I don't know. Maybe it's because I don't lay on my back for positions," I shrugged for dramatic effect. "You know how it is."

He smiled and leaned back in his seat. "Well I was firing you from one position to offer you another but since you don't fuck your way up the corporate ladder I guess I can keep my offer."

I looked at this man to see if he was serious. The fact that I couldn't read his face pissed me off. For some reason the way he looked at me unsettled me. I felt my blood pressure spike. This was the point where I should have turned back around or quit or resigned or something, but I stayed there after he smirked and told me he was joking. I took the position he was offering and prepared myself for a new break in my career.

Chapter 2

"I am beginning to hate dating in Atlanta!"

That was April. We were sitting at the bar in Club Miami and once again the boyfriend she had been seeing for about two years turned out to be a lying, cheating, blah blah blah. This was beginning to be the norm for her and I always asked her why did she just have to have a man? Because as soon as one threw her away like a used tampon she was out looking for another. April was thirty-five with three teenage boys. One was a senior in high school and the two twins were freshmen. So when she called me once again I became the dutiful friend. I pulled on some high waist wide legged black slacks with a black ruffled blouse that tapered to my waist and pushed my breasts up a little more. Slid my feet in my black and gray platform six inch heels and pulled my fro back into a puff ponytail. We both hopped in my car and here we were.

I sipped from my Ciroc and lime. "Girl please. You'll be right back at it tomorrow."

"Not this time. Do you know he had the nerve to tell me phone sex is not cheating?"

I laughed. "Well, technically it isn't."

April looked at me. She was a light skinned thick chick from Louisiana, with about five feet six a short spiked platinum blonde pixie hair cut. Her chocolate brown eyes gave me a look that said she wasn't in a playing mood and I don't care what she said. The fact that we were in a bar only a few hours after her break up meant she was on the prowl again. The short denim skirt with the five inch heels and half shirt said the same thing.

"Well that may be the case, but the fact that the bitch could tell me about my brand new Egyptian cotton sheets closed the deal," she said, sipping from her drink and looking around the club.

The music was too loud. Some fool was scream-ing through the speakers talking about "Oh let's do it!" This was one of the reasons I didn't like coming out. The only time I hit any club was when April was going through one of her moments. Other than that she and whoever she was dating were inseparable. I was an afterthought.

"Damn! He had the girl in your house?"

"Yeah, some young ass bitch. She's about your age. Young and fucking dumb," she spat.

I was about to ask her was that a shot at me. She always had some something snide to say at or about me. But it seemed like the only one dumb here was the thirty-five year old woman sitting across from me who couldn't keep a man. But I would shut up for now. We sat quiet for a while and I zoned out. My mind had drifted off to work. For three weeks now I had been in a new position at work. Aric, that's what he insisted on being called, had promoted me to his executive assistant. This pissed a lot of people off including Lola who had been demoted to my old job.

We had been working all kinds of late hours trying to get the company back on track. I would like to think that we were doing a pretty bang up job. We had contracts coming back in left and right. Aric had other executives following his lead and I guess more assistants were following mine. For a while it was just me and Aric on the seventh floor after five. I had become so accustomed to staying late that I had started to bring a change of clothes after the work day to be more relaxed in. Last night was the night that stuck out in my mind. Aric and I had papers scattered all across his office floor trying to figure out which contracts were more important than the

next. We had been at it since four o'clock that
afternoon with no end in sight. We had even ordered Chinese because it was apparent that the
night would be later than the rest.

We had a bid to pitch to this company that
specialized in mineral makeup and everything
had to be packaged and ready for him to present in the morning. That's the thing about Aric,
he was very hands on. So there we were in the
middle of his office floor. He had kicked his
shoes off and his dress shirt hung open, showing his white wife beater. I found myself staring
at his chest and arms. It had become so obvious
that Aric was well defined with muscle. His arms
were thick and sinewy. I also noticed that he had
a Kemetian tattoo that circled his right arm and
he wore thin black framed reading glasses. When
he inhaled and exhaled I could see the muscles
in his stomach through his wife beater give a
little ripple. I caught myself and looked away.
Everything was going as planned until the food
came and we started getting personal with our
questions.

"You don't have a man you need to be getting
home to Chyanne," he asked me before he put a
spoonful of shrimp fried rice into his mouth. He
watched me as I examined the way he licked his
lips and chewed his food.

"No, and even if I did, he would have to understand that sometimes I will have to work late."

"Yeah, but you have been in here with me at least ten days straight. Don't you think that would be a problem?"

I swallowed my sweet and sour chicken before answering. "No. Which is probably why I don't have a man."

He chuckled. We sat in silence and ate a bit before I said something else to him.

"What about you? You have a girl or a wife somewhere?"

For a second and only a second his eyes clouded over and he shook his head. "Naw. Women are complicated. I fuck and keep it moving."

His bluntness caught me off guard. So much so that I damn near choked.

He continued and laughed at me. "I don't have time for a relationship or marriage. Now casual sex, a date here and there, I can do. Anything else is for the birds."

"Well, okay then," was all I could answer with.

"What? You have never had casual sex Chyanne?"

"No. Not planning on it either. I view it all as a big waste of time." I took a sip of my Pepsi and moved to sit on the sofa behind me. My thick thighs and the floor were not getting along. Aric put one last spoonful of rice in his mouth and stretched out on the floor. I watched as his long body stretched and was totally thrown for a loop when he adjusted his manhood like I wasn't even in the room. My mouth was hanging open and I didn't even know it.

"Are you going to tell me why you feel it is a waste of time or is what you are staring at that fascinating to you?"

I didn't even lie. "Well, I just feel that it would be. So that's why I have never had casual sex and yes your ah . . . yes, it is impressive."

He laughed a bit. "Nothing sexier than an honest woman. As for casual sex, you either don't know what you are missing until you try it or you can't miss what you have never had."

"I'll take your word for it. Besides there are too many diseases out here to catch. Not to mention people get crazy after they have sex," I said as I closed my tray and stood to pick up the mess I had made. Good thing I had brought a black velour jump suit to change into. I could move around freely.

He laughed. "Especially good sex. Good sex is enough to drive most people nuts, especially women. You all get too emotional and attached."

"I wouldn't know about all of that. Are you done," I asked him before picking up his plate.

He hadn't even touched his soda. I didn't realize I was standing directly over him until he quickly stood. If I had been his height we would have been standing chest to chest. That's how close we were. I felt him looking down at me and I couldn't bring myself to look up. Standing at five-seven, my head came up just about to his shoulders. I could feel the lump from his pants on my stomach. This was the place I didn't want to find myself in. I didn't want to have anything but a professional relationship with my boss, but my heart beat faster and my breathing deepened. I knew I should have stopped the conversation we were having a long time ago. I had let it get too personal. Taking his hand and placing it under my chin, he brought his eyes to meet mine. He was smiling. Pretty white teeth he had.

"You're very beautiful Chyanne. Anybody ever tell you that?"

I swallowed the lump in my throat. The cologne he had on took my senses away. "Yes."

He was still smiling a charming yet seductive smile. I watched as his eyes roamed over my face. He licked his thick lips and brought them closer to mine . . . just a bit.

"I could kiss you right now." As he talked his lips brushed up against mine and created a spark and current so strong that I started to shake a little. Whatever he was doing to me I could feel it in my bones.

"I have been watching you. The way you carry yourself. Most full figured women aren't as comfortable with themselves as you are." He ran his fingers through my fro. "There is something wild and uninhibited about you, yet there is this sweet innocence that has got me curious about you."

Both his hands caressed my face as his lips came closer to mine. His hands were warm and strong. I dropped the plates in my hand when his tongue traced my bottom lip then my top. I didn't know what to do. One part of me was screaming for me to run. The other part told me to stand right there. I inhaled and grabbed onto both his wrists when he finally brought his lips to molest mine. His lips were soft and plush. His tongue was kind of coarse and velvety. He took his time with the kiss like he was trying to decode my DNA with this kiss. I didn't even realize I was holding my breath until he released me from our dance of tongues. When it was all said and done, he left me in the middle of his office as he walked away and out of his office. I didn't know what to do or what to say so I started to clean things up. We ended up leaving the office about an hour later. Nothing was said about the kiss though. Nothing was said today either. He acted like it didn't even happen so I did the same.

April brought my attention back to the present. "By the way, what's up with you and the new boss?"

I looked at her while she sipped her drink. "What do you mean?"

She was busy bobbing her head to Wale talking about pretty girls. "I mean he promoted you and now you are always at the office working late. I have seen the man and he is finger licking fine."

That annoyed me. What she said, it annoyed me. I turned my head to people watch before asking. "When did you see him?"

"Oh, the other day. I came up there to do lunch with Justin and Mr. CEO was coming off the elevator into the lobby. Sexy motherfucker. I need me one of him. And he has money too? Shit yeah. Need me one of him. Is he single?"

For some reason her saying that made me angry. I took a big swallow to finish off my drink and shrugged. "I don't know if he is single or not and there is nothing going on with us. Just work."

"Well, something needs to be going on. Shit if you don't want him, I will take him. He seems more of my type anyway."

"What does that mean?"

"I mean he just does. You don't think so?" she asked. "I may strike up a conversation if I run into him again and with the way he gave me the once over, he'd go for it and I will give it to him!"

She turned around on her stool and ordered another drink. I stared at her long and hard. I would have probably started some mess by asking her what the hell she meant by that whole he's more of her type thing again, but two brothers walked up to us and asked us to dance. Of course April immediately went for the tall mocha colored one who looked like he bathed in money. He had dark chocolate eyes with pencil thin locks that sat just above his shoulders, smooth skin, and I could tell he either visited the dentist frequently or he had brand new teeth. He had on a nice pair of dirty denim jeans that fit him loosely with a crisp white button down shirt and a black blazer. He had on a nice pair of casual white and black loafers with his attire.

April stuck her hand out to shake his and put on her mega watt hoochie-flirt smile. "Hello. I am April and this is my friend Chyanne."

He shook her hand and smiled while his chubby friend who looked like a Cedric the Entertainer reject was slobbering out of the mouth looking at her thighs. He was standing there in what looked like a three-piece baby blue suit. I shook my head and chuckled under my breath.

"Hello, my name is Jamie and this is Jamaal. We came over here to see if we could get you ladies to join us for a dance or two?"

April was off of the bar stool before he could get the words out of his mouth. "We were just about to take it to the floor anyway." She turned to me. "Chyanne, this is his friend Jamaal . . . ."

"Actually," Jamie cut her off. "Jamaal came over to dance with you and I came over to keep your friend company."

"Oh," was all April could get out. Jamie removed his hand from hers and held it out for me to take. I shook his hand.

"Nice to meet you, but actually I am not in the mood to dance so if you want to go ahead and dance with my girl, that's cool," I said.

"No. I am not a dancer. I can chill right here with you until they get back," he laughed and winked at me. April looked back at us like she was at a loss for words. Jamaal took her now vacant hand and was grinning like a Cheshire cat as he led her onto the dance floor. Jamie and I sat there and kept a pretty descent conversation going. He was a bookstore owner who was feeling the weight of the economy crashing around him. He owned five bookstores throughout Georgia and was in the process of shutting down one. He was thirty-two and single and had one child who he had joint custody of. He had his own place and liked to think he was drama, debt, and STD free. He was a cool dude, but I was ready to leave.

About twenty-minutes later April came storming back over and snatched up her clutch.

"Girl, let's get the hell out of here," she snapped.

"Fine with me. Nice to meet you Jamie," I said before hopping off of the bar stool and shaking his hand.

"You too, Chyanne. Can I call you sometimes or maybe you can call me," he said, handing me a business card. I slid it into my purse and told him I would, knowing I really had no intentions to do so. I just wanted to get out of there and go home to my bed. It took us about another fifteen to twenty minutes to get through the crowded club. Once outside the wind had its way with my fro. I folded my arms together tightly to try and keep from shivering. I knew April was about to freeze to death. It was warm when we left the house and now this September wind was cutting deep. Nights like this I was glad I had meat on my bones. We were so stiff walking to my car. April's arms were stiff by her side and she had her head down to shield her face from the wind. It was blowing directly at us.

"Damn!" That was me. I said that as soon as my derriere hit the seat in my 650i BMW Coupe. It was black. My favorite color. "Dang! It's cold. . . ."

"You didn't have to play me like that in there," April snapped.

"What?"

I cranked the car and turned the heat on. I watched as she folded her arms and snapped her neck around at me.

"Oh, *you can dance with my friend if you want*. What the fuck? I don't need you pushing niggas off on me like I am some charity case!"

"April, what are you talking about? All I did was tell Jamie that if you two wanted to dance . . . ."

"That's the thing. I don't need you to *tell* nobody shit for me!"

"Oh, wow! Okay. But whatever."

I put the car in reverse and pulled out onto Peachtree Street.

"Don't whatever me and put me off. That shit was embarrassing!"

"Well now you know how I feel when you do it. You are always pushing somebody's raggedy friend off on me."

"So what? There's a difference between me and you. You always sit your ass there and keep the bar company. Nobody ever asks you to dance anyway."

I didn't say anything after that. I had to hold back my anger and bite my tongue so I wouldn't say something that I would regret. I put my foot

on the gas and got her home quick. I almost
jumped out of the car and whipped her butt for
slamming my door. She was more upset because
the one she had laid eyes on first didn't have eyes
for her, and that really bothered me. I mean, as
friends, there should be no competition for men
between us. I didn't hear from April for the rest
of the weekend. Not like I cared. I was tired of
dealing with her mess anyway.

Chapter 3

Monday rolled around and I found myself in a board meeting with Aric. Good thing I had done those PowerPoint presentations and spreadsheets because I ended up running around that boardroom and office like a chicken with its head cut off. Making copies of this, faxing that, and filing this. I found myself watching Aric way more than I should have been. He was working the all black pinstriped Armani suit. He had taken the suit jacket off and laid it on the back of his chair. The vest to match his pants and the white shirt, the black tie, and the wing tipped dress shoes all worked well on him. The thick New York accent washed over me at times and the way he said my name was working on me from the inside out. I needed to get it together. This man had messed me up with one kiss and I had absolutely no explanation for it. *It was one kiss Chyanne! Get it together. The man has barely said two words to you that had nothing to do with business.* I came back to my senses as the last of the executives were leaving and Aric clapped his big hands together.

"We are in the money baby," he said. Excitement was laced in his voice. He smiled as he bit down on his bottom lip and sat on the edge of the long conference table. I smiled and kept picking up the contracts that had been signed.

"Love when we have days like this," he continued. "I need you to get those faxed down to accounting as soon as possible though."

I shrugged. "I'll just walk them down. I have to hand deliver some things to production that I want to make sure get into the right hands anyway."

I picked up the last folder and was getting ready to walk past him when he grabbed my arm and pulled me close to him. I stood directly in between his legs as he took his hand and placed it under my chin lifting my face to his. With his glasses on his hazel brown eyes had an extra sparkle. He brought his lips to mine and gave my top lip a gentle suck before placing his lips fully against mine, letting our tongues touch just once before pulling back and letting his thumb brush across my lips. I could feel my clit swell against my boy shorts and my most delicate part felt like it had a heart beat. My body felt like it was about to float from beneath me and I didn't know what to make of that kiss. My breathing had deepened so much so that you could clearly see my chest rise and fall. I couldn't figure this man out and it was threatening to drive me mad. What is it about him that made him such a mystery?

"Why don't you have dinner with me tonight Chyanne? Me and you. You like the Cheesecake Factory?"

I nodded and he got up with his body placed right next to mine, chilling me. He walked over and gently snatched his suit jacket from the back of the chair and once again he left me standing there. Just me, my thoughts, and my wet underwear.

We never made it to dinner. April called me right after that to go to the school and pick up her boys. She would never make it from her job in time and she didn't want them to be taken to juvie hall. Apparently Jonathan, the eldest who was seventeen, was about to get jumped and the twins, Aaron and Aaden, weren't having it so it turned into a five on three brawl with April's sons being the victors. By the time I made it to the school it was two-thirty and the twins were sitting in the principal's office looking smug.

"Sexy Chy. Mom sent you to get us," Aaron called out to me. That was his name for me. I don't know why he did that.

"Yes, Aaron. What the hell happened?" I asked when I saw the bruises and cuts on their faces.

"You know how it is Auntie Chyanne," Aaden answered. "Niggas thought they were about to jump Jo-Jo and that aint happening. You dig?"

I cringed at his vernacular and looked around for Jo-Jo. "Where's Jo-Jo?"

"Coaches got the team doctor checking him," Aaron answered. Even though he and Aaden looked exactly alike, they were as different as night and day. "You know he has to play next week for the homecoming game. Are you coming Sexy Chy?"

I nodded. "I plan on it. Where do I need to go to sign you guys out?"

They both pointed to the double doors. "Go through there and ask shawty at the desk."

Aaden and I were going to have to have a talk about his language. Both of those boys looked like their father who resembled Morris Chestnut, but ten times better. Jo-Jo looked like April. I got up and made my way through the double doors as Jo-Jo was coming toward me. I almost fainted looking at the big bruise across his torso. He was holding an ice pack to his eye and what was left of his shirt in his hand.

"Dang Jo-Jo! What the hell," I said before I could stop myself. The whole office turned to look at me.

"Stop tripping Chyanne. I'm all right," he said with that dimpled smile plastered across his light, bright face. His hazel and green eyes stared at me with a sparkle. He walked over to me and hugged me. He towered over me. I could see he had a fan club. Some little big booty and big chesty girl walked over to him, handing him some water and a towel.

"You need anything else Jo-Jo," she asked him. It was clear she was infatuated.

"Naw baby girl. This is good." He kissed her forehead and she giggled before walking off. I didn't know what to say, especially when another group of young girls called the other a fat bitch and mumbled about what he wanted with her.

"Come on, Jo-Jo. Let me sign ya'll out."

I shook my head as I walked with them to check them out. April was known to act a fool when they got in trouble at school. We walked over to the front desk with Jo-Jo's arm casually thrown across my shoulders.

"You know your mother is going to act a fool right?" I asked looking up at him.

He shrugged. "Well what she want? Me to get my ass kicked?"

I cocked my head back, shocked by his choice of words.

"Sorry Chyanne. But I am not taking no as—I ain't getting beat up for nobody!"

"Did you have to get Aaron and Aaden in it?"

"Those two damn fools—"

I snapped my head around at him again.

He shamefully dropped his head. "Sorry. They came out of nowhere. One minute I was slanging niggas off of me and the next I see these two fools slamming niggas."

"Must y'all use the N word like that," I snapped.

"Sorry Chyanne. I've been working on that though. Ever since you showed us that DVD about the march on Selma and those other DVD's on Emett Till and what not."

I nodded. "Good."

I asked the principal's assistant to get me started on checking them out and waited for her to get me the proper paperwork. Aaron and Aaden came in and they along with Jo-Jo gave colorful commentary to me on the fight. I had to admit, I was happy they helped their brother and ended up winning with the odds against them. Come to find out, some little boy was mad because he thought Jo-Jo was talking to his girlfriend. I shook my head. Something stupid but they had to defend themselves.

"Come on," I said to them once the process was over. I swear it was like Jo-Jo was a celebrity. Everybody was waving and speaking to him like he was the star of a show. Being on the football team and the star wide receiver had its perks I suppose. Hell he didn't even get suspended. We stopped at McDonalds and picked them up some food for now and I took them home with me until April got off. I know she was pissed because of the way she was snapping when I called her and told her they were home with me.

"You should have let those bad motherfuckers starve," she snapped and yelled. "They get on my nerves! Their daddy needs to come and get them. I am sick of this mess Chy! Sick of going through this shit with them!"

I shut up and let her vent. Truth is, I didn't think the boys were that bad. They just needed April to listen to them and be there for them more. I helped them all with their homework until I heard April's car door slam. The laughter going on at my dining room table immediately ceased. April banged on my door. I looked at the boys and their eyes immediately focused on their homework.

"It'll be okay."

That's all I could say. I opened the door and April almost knocked me down, going right for Jo-Jo. She hit him so hard across his already bruised face that it brought tears to my eyes.

"April, why you hit him?"

She ignored me.

"You think I send your fucking ass to school to get into fights Jo-Jo?"

Jo-Jo had backed into the corner in my dining room.

"They started it Mama." Aaron said.

She reached over and smacked him too. "You shut the fuck up! I aint talking to you!" Aaden got up and moved before her hand could connect with him, but she caught him anyway. He got what his brothers got.

"I am sick of ya'll! Ya'll hear me? Every damn day it's something! I have to work all of these fucking hours and pay for shit for y'all and you ungrateful fools want to be in school fighting and acting like idiots? And I should whoop your ass Jo-Jo! You don't cause enough problems so now you want to drag them into your mess!"

I could tell by the look on Jo-Jo's face that he'd just about had it. And so had I. I had seen this mess too much for my liking. So many times April had gone after Jo-Jo in anger, especially after their father left. April's face was red and twisted with anger. All three of her sons towered over her, but right now she looked way bigger than them.

"Mama, I'm tired of you putting your hands on me," Jo-Jo said through staggered breaths and tears. Before I knew what happened, April had balled her fist up and went at Jo-Jo like he was a grown man. I jumped over my sofa and rushed over as fast as I could.

"Who the fuck you think you talking to," she yelled at him. Jo-Jo shielded his face and just stood there, but I could see that he was at his breaking point when he balled his lips and his fist. He came out of the corner and pushed April away from him. She stumbled back, but didn't fall. April picked up the vase from the table and I grabbed Jo-Jo before she could hit him. The vase crashed against my wall. Aaron and Aaden were yelling and crying for her to stop. She followed me and tried to swing over and around me to get to him.

"April stop!!!" I screamed at her because if she hit me in my head again I was going to turn around and whoop her behind. I managed to shield Jo-Jo until I got him to my bedroom and pulled the door closed.

"Chyanne get the fuck out of my way! He put his hands on me with all that I do for him. I am going to kill him!"

I stood in front of my door with my hands on the knob. April tried to get past me and I pushed her back.

"Back up April. That's your child in there—"

"Exactly! Now move out of my way—"

"Mama please . . . ." Aaron pleaded. Aaden had tears in his eyes as he stood beside his twin. "Wasn't his fault Mama. They were trying to jump him. He had to fight back Mama. He had to."

This scene broke my heart. I could feel tears burning my eyelids. April stood there with this wild look in her eyes before she looked over at her other two sons.

"Get your shit and let's go! You can keep his ass over here. Nobody I clothe and feed is going to put his hands on me," she said and pushed her way past Aaron and Aaden.

They stood there looking at me and my closed bedroom door. I don't know what the look on their faces read. Don't know if it read help, I want to stay with you, or what.

"I said let's go!"

They went to the table and grabbed their book bags quickly making their way out of the door. She slammed my door on the way out. I dropped my head and went to lock my front door when I heard her pulling out of my driveway. I started to clean my kitchen and picked up the glass from the vase that she broke. My whole front room and dining room was done in black and snow white. I shook my head and looked at the juice that had spilled on my all white carpet. I left Jo-Jo in my room until he was ready to come out. It took him a full thirty minutes to decide to do that. By then I was done scrubbing my carpet with Shout, baking soda, and Oxy-Clean. He stood in the entry way leading to the front room and the dining room looking broken.

"Why she don't like me Chyanne," he asked. It was times like this that I hated April. She had broken his spirit so many times. And when he was like this he was a big kid. He wasn't the mature young man who was in all advanced classes. He was a kid. A little boy who wasn't quite sure his mother loved him. Hell, I wasn't so sure. I do know that she made them all pay for their father's mistake. For him leaving her, she made them pay. Tears rolled down his handsome face.

"She does Jo-Jo. Your mom just has a lot on her shoulders. She loves you."

I patted the sofa beside me so he could sit down. We sat quiet for a while. We both watched Smackdown on my forty-seven inch flat screen.

"I talked to Daddy," he said.

My eyes got wide and I asked, "Say what now?" I turned the volume down and looked at him.

"I talked to daddy. Me and The Twin Towers." That's what he called his little brothers who were almost bigger and taller than him. "He came to the school last week and this week. Gave us all a thousand dollars."

"Did you tell your mom?"

He shook his head. "Daddy doesn't want us to." He stared straight ahead at the TV. "We have been talking to him since he left."

"Really? Why don't you guys tell April?"

"Because then she would be mad and we would not be able to see him no more. He wants us to come and live with him."

I slightly turned toward him and propped one leg under the other on the sofa.

"Oh, wow! Where does he live?"

"Alpharetta Country Club."

"For real? Jonathan is doing it like that now?"

He smiled and looked at me while he nodded. "He came to get us last Saturday and took us to his crib while mama was at work. He's got a fiancée. She's pretty. Nothing on Mama though. They have a big ass crib Chyanne."

"Language Jo-Jo."

"Sorry. Daddy said they gave him his old job back and then promoted him to VP so he got a fat check."

I nodded. I was happy for Jonathan because I believe that was one of the reasons he and April had so many problems. He had lost his job at the architectural firm because of the economy and I was so glad he got that back and then some. Jo-Jo stayed with me the whole weekend. Aaron and Aaden came over every day and set up the PS3 or the 360 in my front room with him. Those boys loved each other. I even got in on some of the butt kicking action on Madden 2011. Aaron and Aaden shocked me with the way they joked on each other's girlfriends. Aaron said he liked them like me, thicker than a snicker and he told Aaden that the skinny chicks he dated needed to eat a couple of biscuits with gravy. I laughed so hard at those two. Jonathon called me to come over and see Jo-Jo. I didn't want to get in the middle of that so I made other arrangements. I gave Jo-Jo the keys to my car, told him to be careful and he and his brothers met their dad somewhere. I had no idea what I would tell April.

Chapter 4

The next couple of weeks were a blur. Jo-Jo went back home the following Monday after he and April's altercation. He told me he had talked to her and she said it was okay for him to come back home. I was happy about that. October was here so fast that I didn't even realize it. It had been raining and thunder storming like we were in Seattle. Work had been crazy. With the extensive media coverage on our old executives it was a wonder we could still even get clients, but they were coming left and right. I don't know what Aric was doing or saying but it was working. Although we hadn't shared one of those kisses again, the late night hours didn't let up and the flirting was undeniable. So was the sexual tension. I had been trying to stay my distance. You know, keep it professional since I seemed to lose my good sense whenever he came close to me. I didn't know what it was about him that made me forget all about that rule I had of never mixing business with pleasure.

I looked at the clock as I pushed the send button on the e-mail I was sending out to the whole office for Aric. It was just an e-mail he asked me to send out every week thanking everyone for their hard work. This e-mail included numbers for everyone's bonus too, which I was happy about because we hadn't gotten one in two years. He had already told me that we wouldn't be working late today so as soon as five o'clock hit I was out of there.

My phone buzzed. "Chyanne let me see you in my office for a minute."

That thick New York accent had a lot of women drooling and their panties dripping wet. There was something else mixed with it that I couldn't place.

"Sure," I answered before logging off my computer. "Do you mind if I step into the restroom first?"

"Not at all."

I clicked off the phone and quickly went to the restroom to handle my business. I gave myself the once over in the mirror. The black high waist pencil skirt and black and white collared button down shirt showed off all of my assets and then some. Truth be told I looked like a school teacher who dressed way too sexy. I laughed at myself. Even though the only skin I showed was what the skirt left of my calves, my breasts, hips, and backside would not be denied. The Spanx did a good job of pulling in all of the extra meat on my bones. I hated a muffin top look. Nothing was worse than seeing a plus-sized sister in tight fitting clothes with no extra support. My black and white head band still had my fro sitting nice and pretty and the band kept my hair out of my face. I washed my hands and then looked at my black CL pumps to make sure there wasn't a scuff on them. I was a shoe whore . . . sue me.

I made my way back to Aric's office and waited for him to end a phone call before he addressed me. He must have been talking to an old friend because of the casual conversation he had going on. I looked around his big office. A small family could live in here comfortably. Books lined the wall on a floor to ceiling bookshelf. The big window behind and on both sides of his desk kept the sun, when it was out, shining in. I sat on the burgundy Tudor style sofa after I added some water to the few plants he had. I turned around to look at him just as he bit into a peach. The way he bit down into that thing made his lips enclose around it and suck on it. That gesture made my core bud start to jump. Juice from the fruit slid down his mouth and chin. What he didn't catch with the paper napkin he had in his hand and he licked it away with his tongue. Once he hung up the phone he looked at me. I watched as he stretched his tall body before he came to join me on the couch. He smelled so damn good. He took his glasses off and stretched his arms wide as his head fell back on the sofa.

"Are you busy tonight," he asked. "Around eight?"

"No. Why? You need me to stay?"

He shook his head. "No. I was on the phone with a friend from college and business associate of mine. His bosses are having a little get together with some other business associates and he asked me to come. Think you could join me?"

"Yeah, I guess. Sure."

"Damn," he said as he sat up, leaned on his legs and looked at me as he clasped his hands together. "You don't have to sound so excited about it."

I giggled a bit and waved my hand. "No. I didn't mean it like that. It's just that I was thinking about if I had anything to wear," I lied.

"I am sure whatever it is you decide to wear you will look good in it. Should I pick you up at about seven?"

I nodded. "Sounds good."

I looked at the clock on his wall. He stood and so did I. "Oh yeah, if you don't mind, ask a friend of yours to join you. My friend is new in town and needs someone to talk to."

"I'm sure that won't be a problem."

"Good," he said, watching me as I left his office.

As soon as I got to my desk I called April. She was the only friend I had, so of course she was the one I would ask. I called her at work, but she wasn't there, so I called her cell.

"Yeah. What's up," she answered.

I hadn't talked to her since that incident in my dining room. "Hey. You busy?"

"On lunch."

I could hear noise in her background. "Well, I was calling to see if you wanted to go to this social event Aric invited me to tonight."

"Hold on."

I could tell she was walking away from the noise. "What time is it?"

"Well he said he would be by to pick me up at around seven."

"So we're riding with him?"

I figured she had decided she was going already.

"Yeah."

"OK. I'll be at your place around six-thirty."

"OK and it's like a business social type thing, dress accordingly."

She was quiet a second. "Bitch, I know what to wear to a business gathering," she laughed. "Anyway. Got to get ready to go back to work, but I will see you at six thirty and you're the one who needs to be trying to figure out what to wear."

Before I could respond, she hung up. That's just how April was. I guess calling me the "b" word was her favorite pastime since she had been doing it since we had become friends. I let what she said slide. Although she laughed, what she said grated my nerves. I left work early and did a little shopping. First thing I did was stop by a hair salon and got a four strand French braid so my fro wouldn't be all over the place. I must say that I was pleased with the outcome. I didn't visit the salon that much so that was a treat. I stopped by Simplicity Spa to hook up a manicure and a pedicure. I had no choice but to rush into Lenoxx Mall and ran inside of Neiman Marcus to pick up a nice evening wear gown. I didn't want anything extravagant but I wanted to be cute. So I spent way more than I should have on a black one shoulder draped Charmeuse dress that came past my knees and contoured to my body. The pair of silver Jimmy Choo six inch stiletto heels with diamond studs on the cuff that strapped around the ankle were costly too.

By the time I was done, it was five o'clock. I rushed into my house, and couldn't remember the last time I had rushed so fast to get ready for a date. I jumped in the shower so quick it was like the water barely touched me. I moisturized my skin with honey and vanilla body cream from Bath & Body Works. I quickly got dressed and hurried to the door when the doorbell rang to let April in. I must admit that she looked stunning. The bold red dress that flared over her hips and ass, stopped mid-thigh, left me speechless. The silver strap up stilettos only enhanced what God had already blessed her with. Her short hair style was freshly done and her makeup brought out the glow in her butterscotch skin complexion. The dress hugged her extra small waist and drew attention to her forty inch hips. Her C-cups were almost spilling out of the top of the dress that tied around her neck and made a V on her chest, leaving most of her back exposed.

"Damn, girl! I said we were going to a business social not the Velvet Room," I exclaimed.

She only looked at me and rolled her eyes before walking in past me.

"Whatever! Are you driving or are we being picked up?"

I looked her over once again and I felt underdressed. "You look good though," I complimented her.

"Thank you. So you driving?"

I shook my head. "No. I told you Mr. McHale is picking us up."

She smiled. "So you're back to calling him Mr. McHale now?"

I shrugged while looking in my mirror on the wall behind my loveseat and putting my diamond earrings in my ears.

"He insists that everyone calls him Aric, but I want to keep it professional."

"Yeah sure he does and I bet you do."

April made her way to my kitchen. I heard her pull my fridge open.

"So are you and Mr. Man getting y'all grown folk on?"

I frowned at her when she rounded the corner with a bottle of my Dasani water in her hand. "No. I don't mix business with pleasure."

"Bitch please! As fine as that man is I would be sucking and fucking every chance I got."

I didn't get a chance to answer. The headlights turning into my driveway let me know Aric was here.

"Speaking of the devil," April crooned. The way she smiled and the seductive look that laced her eyes gave me a sinking feeling in the pit of my stomach. I didn't know why I was tripping. All this man had ever done was kiss me twice and he hadn't said a word about us hooking up. My doorbell rang and it was like I was stuck where I was. Aric made me nervous like that. I watched as April opened my door like it was her house. I noticed the surprise register on his face and then I saw the way his eyes gave her a once over and a once over again. His face clearly showed that he liked what he saw. April's slow and easy smile clearly gave off the vibe that she approved of his approving of her. My hand went to my hair and then back down to my side. I felt my hair to make sure my edges were still lying down. You know just making sure my natural look was holding up.

Aric held his hand out for April to shake. "Hello, April. Nice to see you again," he greeted.

She bypassed his outstretched hand and went in for a hug with a giggle. "No need for all of the business and polite stuff. Save that for Chyanne. How are you this evening?"

He embraced her and I looked away.

"I'm doing fine. Thank you. You look great by the way."

She pulled away from his hold and playfully tapped him on the shoulder with another giggle. "Thank you. You know, you are not looking too bad yourself. You are making that suit look good."

He gave a chuckle. "Thank you."

April finally moved and let him in the door. He had to kind of crouch down so his head wouldn't hit the door frame. Looking at him left me speechless. I mean I had seen him done up in business suits and all at work, but he was killing this all black Armani suit. It was so well tailored to fit him that nobody else could come close to pulling that look off. The wide legged pants were cuffed to fit his tall frame perfectly. I stood there like a deaf mute until he looked over at me. When he finally did a slow and easy smile crept over his face. His pearly white teeth added even more sexiness to his smile.

"Good evening Chyanne. Wow! You look beautiful," he said, walking over to me.

"Thank you," I said to him as he grabbed me into a tight embrace. He smelled so good. Like Ivory soap mixed with a masculine fragrance. He pulled away slowly from the hug and when I thought he would kiss me my heart rate sped up. He didn't kiss me although his eyes lingered on my lips. I ran my tongue across them out of nervousness.

"You look very handsome tonight as well."

"Not as good as you do," he whispered to me so only I could hear.

I smiled. "Let me get my purse and keys."

"Do you need for me to stay with you while you lock up," he asked.

I shook my head and smiled. "No, I got it."

Truth be told, I needed to get myself together. I quickly went to my room and grabbed my purse, BlackBerry, and keys. Aric and April had already stepped out to his truck. I walked out to hear the end of whatever conversation they were having.

"We'll talk," I heard him say to her.

With the way she was standing close to him it made me wonder what he meant by that statement. He was standing on the passenger side of his cream colored Cadillac Escalade with the door open. When she walked around him her breast brushed across his chest. He smiled at her and looked over at me. I don't know why she felt that she automatically got to ride in the front beside him. I don't know if it was in my walk or what, but when he opened the back door for me I didn't even look at him. I am sure my attitude was visible. He tried to take my hand and help me up, but I snatched it away from him.

"You okay?" he asked me.

I looked at him. He didn't have his glasses on and his light eyes shone at me. "Yeah. Shut the door."

I didn't give him a chance to say anything else. I reached over and slammed the door shut for him.

"Damn, Chyanne," April laughed.

With steam coming from my ears, I watched Aric walk around to get into the truck.

"You ain't mad, are you?" April teased me as he slid into the truck.

Something in her voice struck a nerve, but I let it go. Aric put the car in reverse and turned to back out. I don't know how he backed out without hitting anything because his eyes stayed on me the whole time. I couldn't look at him for as long as he looked at me so I turned my head in another direction.

We ended up at the Intercontinental Buckhead in one of their ballrooms with Atlanta's business elite. So much business power in one room made for a boring night for me. After we found our table, Aric introduced us to his friend and business associate Gabriel. Gabriel was a sexy dark chocolate brother that should have been a carnal sin. He and Aric were the same height. Aric had a thicker build than Gabriel and a sexier smile but that didn't take away Gabriel's appeal. The brother had a nice head of neatly done locks that swayed around his shoulders and his accent was a killer. He had that deep

Southern baritone that would make a woman drop all of her clothes in a matter of seconds. His goatee was perfectly aligned and his eyes made his smile more enticing.

"Hello, April," he said as he stood to greet her. She always got the greeting first and it wasn't lost on anyone that his eyes roamed over her body from head to toe then toe to head again before he even looked at me. As usual she gave a tight hug and returned the greeting.

"Nice meeting you, Gabriel," she crooned. "Chyanne never told me she worked with brothers who looked like this."

All three of them chuckled and laughed. I didn't. Gabriel took his eyes off of April long enough to turn to me.

"You must be Chyanne," he said with a smile.

"Yes I am," I said extending my hand to him. He bypassed my hand and pulled me into an embrace that made me feel some type of way. For whatever reason, I glanced over at Aric. He sipped his drink and looked away for a quick second. His smile had disappeared.

"I've heard a lot about you," he said pulling away. "I guess Aric is happy he finally found a competent assistant."

I smiled. "That's always a good thing and I hope everything is all good that he has told you about me."

Gabriel chuckled and handed his glass to a passing waitress. "All good, but he didn't tell me how beautiful you are. Guess he wants to keep you all to himself."

I didn't know what to say to that. I just laughed a bit. "With as much work that is on my desk he has me for at least . . . another ten years."

He said, "You could always come and work for me. I know how to treat my employees and with one that is as good as Aric says you are I could use you in more ways than one."

I took a quick sip of my drink and looked at April as we all took a seat at the table. She only chuckled and moved her tongue around in her mouth before sipping on her wine and giving me a side eye. Before I could think of anything to say Aric spoke up because I really didn't know how to respond.

"That's too bad now isn't it? She's not going anywhere. As a matter of fact when we get back to the office on Monday I'm going to need that in writing. This Negro is trying to take you from me. Not going to happen. Besides nobody will do her like I do. It would do you good to remember that Chyanne," he laughed.

I was glad he laughed because if I didn't know any better I would think they were serious. Especially when Gabriel looked me up and down, smirked, and made a 'hmph' sound under his breath. He folded his arms across his chest and looked at Aric, then at me.

"Chyanne, everything is not always what it seems and if ever you get tired of this asshole, look me up," Gabriel finished.

I smiled. "I will keep that in mind," I said. I needed to get away for a second so I excused myself. "Excuse me. I need to visit the ladies room."

April stood as well. "I'm going to go and keep Chyanne company. You guys behave until we return."

Gabriel and Aric stood when we stood. I assumed they didn't sit back down until we had walked away. I observed as men drooled over April. She had what we liked to call the pony walk and when you threw in the stilettos she had on, it made her all the more enticing. This was a mess. My body and my nerves were jittery and shot to hell. For whatever reason, I didn't know why. I made it to the ladies room, staring at myself and tossing cold water in my face. April was standing at the counter with her arms folded looking at me.

"What," I asked her.

The smirk on her face let me know this would not be good. What I should have done was left right then and there, but I didn't.

"Why didn't you tell me Jonathan called you?"

"When?"

"When Jo-Jo was at your place?"

I exhaled and shrugged. "I didn't think it was a big deal. He called and asked to speak to the boys. I thought it would be okay."

"Why in the fuck did you think I would be okay with that bastard talking to my kids?"

"Because they are his kids too, April. All he did was—"

"And you let Jo-Jo take your car to take Aaron and Aaden to see him. Why?"

Other women in the bathroom were looking at us on the sly.

"Because they asked. What's the big freaking deal April? Jonathan has a right to see his children. Just because he doesn't want anything to do with you doesn't mean he doesn't love his kids. You need to stop trying to make them choose between you and their father. He doesn't want you anymore! So what? He has moved on. Why don't you?"

I knew I had said too much before the words left my mouth. April stood to her full height and I did the same. Hell, if she was going to swing then I wasn't backing down. People were looking at us. They all had stopped doing what they had come in the bathroom to do to watch us.

Over the years April and I had been through a lot. I was with her when her mom died. With her when Jonathan started coming home later and later. I was her shoulder to cry on. I stayed with her when she drank herself sick. I was with her when she and Jonathan lost the last child they conceived together. Now we had come to this and I didn't know why. We had been friends for five years. Met when we were in Georgia State together. She ended up having to quit for a while because Jonathan lost his job. Her whole attitude had changed when Jonathan actually left, but I just thought it was because she was hurt. Now I didn't know what the problem was but I was done trying to figure it out. She put her hands on her hips, clucked her tongue to the roof of her mouth, and looked me up and down before snatching the bathroom door open and walking out with the same smug smirk that she had been carrying all night

I rushed behind her. "Look, April, I'm sorry," I apologized as I tried to grab her arm and she turned and snatched away. She looked at me, the look in her eyes cold.

"It's cool," was all she said before she sashayed off. I rushed behind her and then remembered I had left my clutch in the bathroom on the sink. I quickly turned around and slammed right into somebody that was built like a brick wall. I stumbled and almost fell back. He caught me by my arm.

"Excuse me," I said. "I am so sorry."

"Chyanne?"

I finally looked up and into the face of a man who looked familiar.

He said, "It's me, Jamie. Do you remember me from a few weeks ago? We met at Club Miami."

I nodded. "Oh, yeah. I am so sorry about running into you, but let me go and get my purse. I left it in the restroom and I will be right back."

He nodded and I went into the restroom to get my purse. Thank God it was lying where I had left it. I walked back out into the lobby and Jamie was nowhere to be seen so I walked back in the direction of the table where we were all sitting. I stopped in my tracks when I spotted Aric with his arms wrapped around April and they were dancing to a slow song the live band was playing. He was looking down at her and smiling and she was so close to him she may as well have been his skin. My heart dropped when she brushed her fingers across his lips and all he did was run his tongue across his lips in return. I was so caught up in what was going on in front of me that when someone tapped my shoulders from behind I nearly jumped out of my skin.

I turned around and Jamie had an amused look on his face with his hands up like I was sticking him up. "My bad! I'm sorry!" He laughed when I smiled.

"You just scared whatever hell I had in me away," I joked.

"I am truly sorry but I came over to ask if you would like to dance. I don't know what the hell they are playing, but I think we can keep up," he smiled.

He looked different tonight. Maybe it was because his locks were pulled back nice and neat and the black suit he was wearing complimented his physique. His dark eyes held a sparkle that pulled me in and his smile was enough to charm me into the dance he asked me for. I let him lead me to the dance floor and when he pulled me close to him for some reason I laid my head on his chest and relaxed.

"So what brings you here, Ms. Chyanne? I didn't think of you as the uptight type," he said.

I lifted my head and looked up at him. "What does that mean?"

"I mean look around you." He shrugged gazing down at me with a smile on his face. "Look at all of these boring business men and women and listen to this music."

I laughed. "Hey my boss isn't boring and what does that make you since you are here?"

His head fell back a bit and he laughed before looking back down at me. "Good question. Who's your boss by the way?"

"Aric McHale . . ."

"Oh the brother who took over at B&G?"

I nodded. "That's him."

"Well I heard about what they used to do over there. You good?"

I nodded. "Oh, yeah. Aric is the best. I haven't had any problems."

"Well you can always call me if you do."

Before I could respond Aric and April were right in my view, Aric's eyes were planted on me. I looked away for a second and then back at him. He kept his eyes locked with mine.

When he mouthed the words '*I want you*' to me my heart rate increased and coochie started to leap around against my lace boy shorts. I could feel myself get so moist that I wanted to cross my legs to stave off the feeling. Jamie was saying something to me but I couldn't register it especially when Aric blew a kiss at me from where he was standing. I stopped dancing for a second and was lost.

"You okay," Jamie stopped to ask me. Luckily the music was ending.

"Yes. A little dizzy."

"Where's your table?"

"Over by the balcony, but I'm sure I can make it. I'm fine."

He gripped my right elbow and was holding me steady. Aric was still watching me.

"I'll feel better if I walk you over to your seat," Jamie said. He put his hand on the small of my back and led me over to my table where Gabriel was talking to some blonde haired golden eyed woman who had a body like that Latin singer Shakira. Gabriel looked at me when we got to the table.

He and Jamie exchanged greetings. "You okay Chyanne?" Gabriel asked me.

I nodded and sat in the chair Jamie had pulled out for me.

"Yeah, I'm fine."

Gabriel stopped a passing waitress and asked for a glass of water. The Shakira look-a-like was looking at me like I had interrupted them or something. Jamie brought my attention back to him as he kneeled in front of me to make sure I was okay. I listened as he handed me his business card again and told me to call him. My attention was thwarted as I saw Aric and April walking back to the table. She was walking in front of him but his eyes stayed on me and then turned to Jamie. Jamie stood as Aric neared the table. They exchanged greetings, but there was nothing pleasant about Aric's demeanor and it wasn't lost on Jamie. He looked from me to Aric and then back to me. Aric didn't sit until Jamie said his final goodbye to me and walked off.

Aric sat down beside me as I was trying to slide Jamie's card into my clutch, but he caught my hand under the table and took it from me. I kept my cool and looked over at him, but all he did was speak to the blonde chick across from Gabriel.

"Shelley, it's good to see you again. How are Robert and the kids," he asked like he hadn't just ripped up Jamie's card and discarded it on the floor.

"Great, Aric and how's Stephanie?" Shelley responded.

I didn't know what was going on but it was something about the way Gabriel chuckled and Shelley cut her eyes at Aric that let me know something was going on there. Aric's eyes darkened when he looked at her but he didn't answer. She quickly turned her attention back to Gabriel. Aric turned his attention to April, and for some reason, I felt like I was out of place. The waitress finally came back and handed the glass of water to Gabriel and he passed it to me.

"What's wrong Chyanne?" April asked. I could tell it wasn't genuine by the smirk on her face and the tone of her voice.

I shook my head. "Nothing. I'm fine."

Aric was talking to her but his hand was still on my leg. I knocked it off and his head snapped over at me. I arched a brow and stared back at him. I didn't know what kind of game he thought he was playing but I was about over it. I stood so I could go somewhere else. I wasn't about to sit there looking crazy. I grabbed my clutch and was about to walk off, until Aric grabbed my wrist and stood with me.

"Excuse us," he said to everyone at the table. I followed him, until we made it to a secluded area in the lobby. There was a black bench style sitting stool in the corner and I sat there. Aric stood in the little space across from me with one leg crossed over the other at the ankle. He slid his hands in his pockets while staring at me.

"Want to tell me what's bothering you?" He asked casually.

I looked up and caught the lick he placed across his lips.

"Nothing is bothering me."

"Could have fooled me."

I exhaled, crossed my legs, and looked around. Saw a man helping a staggering dark skinned chick to the door. It was obvious she had too much to drink. The guy didn't seem to mind as he was smiling and telling her something in her ear. She laughed loudly as they made their way out of the door.

I shrugged and looked back up at Aric. I shook my head and made a dramatic effect of pursing my lips up to say, "Nope. No problem."

He stood up straight with his hands still in his pockets and moved closer to me. "One thing you will have to learn about me Chyanne is I hate to be lied to and I hate to be bullshitted around and tried to be played like I'm stupid."

His eyes never left mine and his tone and demeanor showed the exact thing his mouth had just told me. I diverted my eyes down to his waist since his dick was now in my face. I slowly stood.

"Look, I said I'm fine. . . ."

He moved closer to me. I tried to step back but the stool only let me move back so far. His scent was like a drug and as much as I wanted to stay away from him, it kept pulling me in. I tried walking past him. Instead, he snatched me back into him and put my back against the wall before I knew what was happening.

His hands gripped my waist and he was looking down into my eyes. "What's wrong with you, Chyanne? My last time asking you. You either tell me what's wrong or I'm going to make you tell me."

"Excuse me?" My head tilted to the side and my eyes widened a bit as I moved a few inches away from the wall.

The only answer I got was his lips against mine. The kiss was so heated and primal that I lost all my senses. I didn't know what to do with my hands and when I felt his left hand raising my right leg to his waist and his hand coming around to grip my backside to pull me closer into him, I almost lost it. I could feel him getting harder against my body. The heels I had on gave me just enough height for me to feel it in the right area. My most private area was throbbing . . . aching . . . and jumping. When I felt his hand had found a way under my dress my breath hitched. I was so lost I had forgotten we were in a corner in a hotel lobby. When his hands came up and gripped my breast with a firm hold, I released his lips and almost screamed when he bit down on my neck.

"Oh God," was all I could get out as my eyes rolled to the back of my head. My body was hot. Blood rushing. . . .

"Oh, damn! My bad!"

My eyes shot open and Gabriel was there. I put my head down and covered half of my face in between Aric's neck and shoulders, attempting to fix the top of my dress.

"Ah . . . your presence is being requested back in the banquet room," Gabriel said as his eyes caught mine.

Aric didn't turn around and he kept my body shielded with his. My leg slowly slid back down to the floor.

"OK. I'll be there," Aric said over his shoulders.

Gabriel kept his eyes on me as he said, "OK. Cool."

He turned to walk away and something in his eyes bothered me. What he didn't say bothered me. I fixed myself and made myself look like I hadn't come close to having sex in a corner in the lobby of a hotel. I watched out of the corner of my eye as Aric fought to adjust his hard on.

"I'll be in. Give me a minute. Go ahead," he said to me nodding his head in the direction of the banquet room with his hand still trying to adjust himself in his pants.

I walked off, trying to look as normal as I could as I made my way back inside of the room and to the table. April and Shelley were talking like they were the best of friends until I got to the table and sat down. April looked at me and rolled her eyes before taking a sip of her wine.

"So, Chyanne," Shelley called out to me with a plastered smile on her face.

"Yes."

"April tells me that you have been at B&G for four years." Shelley took a sip of her drink, leaned forward, and smiled. "Surprised you hadn't filed a lawsuit yet. I mean it's no secret that the old execs had a thing for their employees."

"I don't, nor will I ever lay on my back to get a position," I said as I put my clutch on the table.

Shelley laughed over the soft jazz that was playing. "Girl, you never know what you can get on your back. You better try it! At least for some good dick. You feel me? It's a dog eat dog world out here in this big corporate world and as a woman you have to do what you have to do to stay one step ahead of the competition."

April chimed in. "You don't have to worry about Ms. Goody Goody doing any of that. Chyanne hasn't seen a dick since one spit her out."

April gave a little chuckle and Shelley's eyes widened as she tilted her head to the side.

April continued, "She's so busy trying to be perfect that she . . ."

"Just because I choose to keep to myself does not mean I am aiming to be perfect," I said. I sat back in my chair and folded my arms across my chest.

April had a smile on her face but the vibes coming from her were anything but friendly.

"Please! When's the last time you had a man?"

"About the last time you haven't had one."

I saw Shelley's eyes widen even more and she laughed out loud. April slowly sat her glass down on the table.

"What the hell is that supposed to mean? Since you have gotten this promotion you have been beside your fucking self. Don't think because you think Aric is sniffing behind your ass that you the shit now. You are still the same fat ass Chyanne that claims she doesn't want a man when in reality she just can't get one."

This coming from a woman who couldn't even keep a man! To say I was embarrassed would have been an understatement, but not because of what this semi-drunk hussy was saying to me. I was embarrassed because half of the whole side of this room was looking at us and Aric had introduced me to everyone as his assistant. So they knew I represented B&G Marketing and Advertising.

I slowly pushed away from the table and stood. "OK . . . you know what? I am going to leave. It's apparent that you have had too much to drink and before we both say something that we will regret . . ."

April laughed. "Trust me, Chyanne, there ain't nothing you can say to me that will hurt my feelings. Okay?"

I kept my composure and smiled. I could tell Shelley didn't know what to think, but judging by the slick smile on her face, it was clear she was enjoying the scene unfolding before her. I calmly picked up my clutch and started to walk away. I made my way over to the far side of the room where they had set up a bar and copped a squat on an empty stool. I was fine just sitting there and minding my business. Although some people were still looking from me to April then back to me, I kept my cool. From where I was sitting I could see Aric walk back into the room and I was hoping he was ready to go.

Right about then I was wishing I would have driven my own car. I sat there for at least another ten minutes and people watched. Aric and Gabriel had been caught up in a conversation with a group of white men across the room from me. I saw April and Shelley still chatting it up. Maybe April was just having a bad day or something. I didn't know what her problem was. I had noticed she had been acting like this from time to time but I blamed it on stress from her own problems. I had love for April but sometimes it was hard to believe she was a thirty-five year old woman with the way she acted. I was so focused on my thoughts that I didn't even notice her walking up to me. I jumped when I felt a hand on my shoulder turning me around on the stool. April stood there with one hand on her hip and a look on her face that let me know she was pissed.

"What is your problem, Chyanne? What was up with you trying to embarrass me back there," she snapped.

"Oh. I tried to embarrass you? You are the one who started."

"Started what? What did I say? What that you hadn't seen a dick since one gave you away? And that was reason for you to try and throw shade at me?"

She had begun to wave her finger and move her neck. Once again people in the vicinity were starting to pay attention to us. Why did she want to get in here in front of all of these white people and act an ass?

"Look April. If I said something to . . ."

"If? Bitch, you know what you said was fucked up!"

"I am not about to be too many more bitches, April."

"Oh, so you bad now, huh? This job has really gone to your head. Or you really think Aric wants your ass or something. One or two men show you some attention and that goes straight to your head."

"OK April, I think it's time for me to go. When you want to talk or ask me something, I will tell you . . ."

"Oh, like you told me Jonathan tried to fuck you?"

I stood. "What?"

"Don't get stupid now. Thought I didn't know huh? You weren't going to tell me either were you? You wanted attention so bad that you would take it any way it came huh? You think I don't know about him having you against the wall in my garage. Camera's bitch. My house has cameras."

"Look, April. Nothing happened. He was drunk . . ."

"Oh, I know nothing happened. And look at youuuuu," she said with very clear dramatics using her hands. Her face carried a smile mixed with a sneer. "You making excuses for him now? You are a thirsty heifer, you know that? You let him kiss you before you pushed him away but now you want to stand up here and act like you all innocent and shit. Ever notice I don't bring any man around you now?"

She had pissed me off. "That's fine, April. Trust me I don't want anybody you have been with. So we are good on that. Now, if you will excuse me . . ."

I tried to move past her, but what happened next came as a total shock to me. April picked up a glass from the bar and threw its contents in my face. Before I could react to the shock, her opened palm connected with my face. She slapped me so hard that it knocked my head back. All I heard were the gasps and *'oh my God's'* coming from the room. I was seconds away from messing her up! When I was able to release myself from the shock of what had happened, I went to grab for her but Aric had blocked me before I could. I didn't even get much of a glimpse of her after that. Aric had grabbed my clutch from the floor and was escorting me out of the room. That didn't stop me from still trying to get around him.

Only when the cold wind pierced my eyes from outside did I allow myself to calm down. My eyes were already watering from being slapped. Add my anger to that and I was in tears. I folded my arms across my chest as he gave the valet his ticket to pull his truck around. I guess because my anger had me shaking Aric thought I was cold. He took his suit jacket off and wrapped it around my shoulders. Once they pulled his truck around, he held the passenger side door open for me to get in.

For a few seconds, I was in the truck, behind his tinted windows watching him as he tipped the valet. I quickly covered my face and let out a muted scream and an exasperated breath. No matter how I tried, I couldn't stop my nerves from making me shake and I couldn't stop the tears. I had a full frontal headache and the left side of my face stung like a thousand killer bees had attacked me. Aric climbed into the driver seat and turned left onto Peachtree Street. He adjusted the heater at the light and some jazz played on the radio. It wasn't until we got on the expressway that he interrupted my thoughts of kicking April's behind.

"Want to tell me what happened?" He asked as he turned the music down a little.

"I don't know what happened. One minute I was talking to that chick Shelley. The next minute April is talking mess. I get up and leave the table. Next thing I know she is in my face at the bar."

I made a fuss of taking my shoes off.

"I could be wrong, but I thought you two were close." I turned to look at him at the same time his eyes caught mine. We both turned back to look at the road ahead of us.

"I thought we were too," was all I responded.

I was thinking back on that day in her garage. I had stopped by to chill and talk with April but after sitting in her front room for thirty minutes and she still hadn't showed up, I got up to leave.

I walked out through the garage and Jonathan was sitting on the hood of his Lexus. He was as drunk as an everyday wino. Once he saw me come out, he spoke and I spoke back. I told him I was leaving and to tell April to call me. I didn't know what he was thinking, but the next minute he was telling me how beautiful, sexy, and educated he thought I was. The closer he got to me the further I backed into the wall. The next thing I knew I was up and around his waist with his tongue in my mouth. I would be lying if I said that I didn't feel some type of way about it because I did. Some kind of way his hands had found their way under my skirt and into my underwear. His fingers had made their way inside of me all before I even knew what was going on. I broke away from the kiss and yelled for him to stop and he did. He apologized over and over, and to this day, every time he sees me he apologizes. I chalk it all up to the fact he was drunk and didn't know what he was doing. I wanted to tell April, but how do you tell your best friend that her husband had his fingers inside of you in their garage?

"You okay over there?" Aric asked.

I nodded. We pulled into my driveway a few minutes later. I didn't wait for him to open my door before I grabbed my shoes and hopped out of his truck. I pressed the button on my keys to let up my garage so I could go in through my kitchen.

"Let me see your face, Chyanne," he said to me once I turned the light on in my garage. I stopped and let him turn my face into the light. I cut my eyes at him when he laughed a bit.

"What's so funny?"

"Good thing you are chocolate. Otherwise there would be a nasty bruise on your face tomorrow."

He touched it and I winced away.

"You should put some ice on it or something because she slapped the shit out of you!"

He laughed when I pushed him away.

"Go to hell," I snapped as I turned to unlock my door. He pulled me back to him.

"Stop being so sensitive! I am only trying to make you laugh."

"Not in a laughing mood."

He pulled me closer and into him. "Well, get into one."

"Whatever."

He placed light kisses on the part of my face that had been assaulted. Those kisses then went to my ear and then down to my neck and back up to my lips. Heavy breathing and the wind blowing is all that could be heard.

"OK. I'm going to leave because you got my dick hard and I may have to put you on the hood of this car and fuck the shit out of you."

My eyes bugged out and I gasped. "Oh, wow . . ." That was all I could get out.

His smile relaxed me. "Don't be afraid of me, Chyanne. You don't ever have to be afraid of me. You just have to come to grips with the fact that I'm a man that says whatever is on his mind."

"I get that . . . now."

We both laughed. "Go ahead and unlock your door so I can make sure you get in safe. Do I need to come and check for monsters and shit," he joked.

I laughed as I pushed my door open and deactivated my alarm. "No. I'm good."

"Cool. See you tomorrow."

Once we had said goodnight and after I was in my bed I had time to think. I wondered if April had made it home safe so I picked up the phone to call her. After two rings, it went to voice mail. I tried twice more and the same thing. So I called Jo-Jo's phone a little later and he told me that she was outside talking to some guy. I assumed it was Gabriel since Aric had said he had volunteered to bring her home. As long as she was home, I could sleep.

Chapter 5

Aric and I were sitting in a part of his office that I didn't even know existed. We had gotten to the office a little early and he didn't want to be bothered before the meeting today at eleven. Needing some privacy, he had asked me to step into this room with him that looked like a very small apartment. A small stall with a shower was in the far right corner with a toilet next to it. A small desk was on the other side of it. An oversized loveseat that turned into a pull out bed sat by itself against the other wall. We had been sitting there going over the agenda for the meeting and his schedule for the day. He was dressed down in a pair of loose fitting dark denim jeans, a red polo style shirt and he was bare foot. The sexiest thing I had ever seen.

"So, tell me again how many numbers we are away from being in the black again," he asked as he typed away on his laptop.

I answered. "Over two hundred million."

"Damn!" He had been frustrated all morning. "As soon as I get one thing fixed some more shit happens! How many days have we been in the red?"

"Four hundred and seventy-two days," I answered him. I watched as he shook his head and kept typing.

"Did you send the figures down to accounting this morning?" He turned to look at me.

I stood and stretched. "I sent them last night before I went to bed and I also hand delivered the disk before I came up this morning."

"So did Katie send the report back up yet?"

I shook my head. "No, but she said she had to correct something that she had overlooked before. She said she would have them up before the meeting."

He nodded. "What about production? How are they on things?"

I moved over to the files on the desk that I had brought in earlier and pulled out the papers on production, telling him what he wanted to know. He was pleased that they had come in under budget without slacking on the quality of things, but his happy mood didn't last long when I told him that the marketing side of things was going way over budget. He moved his laptop from his lap and removed his glasses before groaning his frustrations out loud.

"These fuckers are going to kill me early!"

I didn't even know what I was doing, but I walked over to him and straddled his lap, trying to kiss away his frustrations. I caressed his bald head and then his face as I slowly and methodically intertwined his tongue with mine. I moaned into his mouth and took the kiss deeper. I didn't have on my work clothes yet. Only a white T-shirt and some sweats. My kiss became greedy and I pulled his face closer to mine and him closer to me. He had fully sat up on the couch and it didn't even seem like the kiss broke when he removed my shirt. I quickly went back in to taste his tongue and just as quick he was removing my bra and had both hands gripping and squeezing my breasts. He pushed me up to look in my eyes.

"You better tell me if you are sure this is what you want because I don't stop once I get started."

The area between my thighs felt heavy and it was throbbing . . . aching. My mind really screamed HELL NO! But my body was saying otherwise.

"It's what I want," I manage to get out.

He quickly shifted us so that I was underneath him and he made quick work of removing my sweats.

"Damn, Chyanne! You are thicker than a motherfucker," he said as he looked down at me. My
hands were covering my breasts and he removed
them, taking my right, then left one into his
mouth.

While teasing me, he used his lips and tongue
to pull on each nipple. He kissed my neck down
to that area between my breasts and let his
tongue trail down to my navel before slightly
brushing his lips across the area hidden by my
lace thong. I hissed, arched, and moaned before
he came back up to kiss me. He used his hand
to stroke me through the lace. I reached for him
to bring him closer but he stood and my eyes
opened when I heard the sound of his belt buckle
clink. I watched as his jeans dropped to the floor
and he stepped out of them. His body was sick.
His abs contracted as he pulled his shirt off and I
giggled when he made his chest jump.

Then my eyes nearly jumped out of my head
when he pulled his boxer briefs down and his
dick sprang forward like it had new life. It had a
slight curve and it was two toned, like a chocolate and caramel mixed. The head was big like
the fattest mushroom I had ever seen. He had
thick veins going down the side of it and I could
actually see it throb. He was blessed beyond
measures. His thighs were masculine and yelled

that he was all male. I closed my eyes and inhaled when he turned out the lights and brought
his body back down over mine. He slid down the
couch and placed his face where I had soaked
my panties. His hands gripped my thighs as he
spread my legs apart and pulled my thong to the
side and sucked my clit into his mouth.

"Oh my God," I cried out. Against my will my
back arched and made me grind into his face.

When his fingers found their way inside of me,
and his tongue and lips continued to suck and
dabble on my swollen clitoris I was near tears.
Moaning, screaming and pulling on my own hair.
He removed his fingers and stuck his tongue in
and out of my body. I was so wet I could feel it
running down in between my cheeks.

"Want to see what you taste like," he asked
me before coming up to kiss me. His lips and
tongue were wet with my juices. Reaching down,
he ripped my thong away from my body. My
heartbeat sped up and I got nervous. I looked up
and into his eyes as he seductively smiled down
at me. Those hazel brown eyes were pulling me
in to his allure and seduction. He pulled my left
leg up and cupped the back of my knee with the
inside of his elbow. I wondered if he noticed that
my body was tensed and had started to shake. I
closed my eyes as he placed butterfly kisses on

my lips. I could feel the head of his swollen dick right at my opening and it gave me the chills. I almost yelled out when his head first tried to break skin.

Between bated breaths I gasped out, "Ahh . . . Aric . . . Ow . . . wait . . ."

I had almost come up off that couch. I didn't know if he had caught on yet . . . but he was coming close to killing me. He inched his way inside, before he finally broke skin. I was clawing at his back and beating on his shoulders. I had started to sweat and with every inch of himself that he pushed inside of me, it was more pain than I cared to take.

"Wa. . . . Wait . . . Aric, wait! Ouch . . . shit. Damn, please wait!" I yelled out loudly as he found his way all the way inside of me.

I almost bit half of my damn tongue off, and that's when I assumed he realized what was going on.

"Damn it Chyanne! Why didn't you tell me you were a fucking virgin?!"

I tell you no lie when I tell you me, a grown woman, was crying right now.

"Aric, it hurts. . . ."

"Fuck," he yelled out. I could feel his dick flexing inside of me and that made it worse. I cringed when he punched the arm of the couch.

I didn't care. I was in so much pain that I wasn't able to think straight and found myself trying to push him off of me.

"Wait Chyanne! Shit, I can't just snatch my dick out. Relax baby please. Just calm down."

"Just hurry up and . . . come out. Please!"

I cringed, groaned, and bit down on my lips as he started to slowly pull out of me. It hurt so badly that it made my stomach hurt, made me dizzy, and gave me a headache. I could hear him groan and cursing under his breath. When I thought he was coming out he slid back in and slipped deep into me. I screamed out and jerked myself forward to bite down between his neck and his shoulder. He growled and roughly stroked inside of me, making it hurt me worse.

I backed away from his neck and loudly called his name. "Aric!"

He said nothing.

"Aric . . . this hurts," I cried.

Yes, I was in tears. He leaned into me and kissed my tears.

"I know, but you really should have told me this before now . . ."

He relaxed into me and wrapped his arms around me almost like cupping my shoulders in his hands. My body tensed even more and I tried to squirm away from him.

"Do me a favor, baby, and calm . . ."

"This hurts, Aric . . ."

"I know, but you have to calm down so I can fix it."

I was still squirming and praying that he would get up as we both just laid there. I could still feel him flexing inside of me. My walls and muscles were contracting. Felt like my vagina was inhaling and exhaling. Aric placed his mouth on mine and began to slowly move in and out of me. I moaned into his mouth and still tried to move away but he kept me locked in place. He moved slowly with a disciplined motioned that broke through the pain and introduced me to pleasure . . . and then pain . . . and then pleasure again. He would pull out a couple of inches and go deep again, but when he brought my knees up to my shoulders, I literally backed away as far as I could, which wasn't far on that loveseat. I backed away enough to make him come out of me. I was aching and throbbing like jumping beans down below. He caged me in between his arms and hovered over me, while we stared into each other's eyes. No lie, I was scared . . . .nervous.

"You started this, Chyanne," he said to me. His eyes held me hostage. "Now you running? It's your first time, baby. Let me take you where you need to be. You got me chasing you like a junkie right now. You gave me a taste and now I want it all."

He brought his face closer to mine and moved my head to the side so he could nibble on my ear. A soft moan escaped from within, as chills shivered up and down my spine.

"Can I taste that fat pussy again?" he whispered in my ear.

That same feeling in my spine was shivering down amid my thighs.

"Tell me, Chyanne. Tell me I can taste your pussy."

All I could do was squirm around under him when I felt his hand cup my pussy and stroke me.

"Tell me Chyanne . . . tell me what you want me to do."

That baritone in his voice was messing me up. Mix that with the fact that his fingers were making my insides quake and sucking on my breasts at the same time—if I had the secret of the Nile I would have given it to him. I told him to take what he asked for and he went down south, taking me to a whole other level. My back arched and I felt like I was free falling. There was this aching feeling like I had to pee and then the urge to scream out and clamp my legs around his head.

"Oh my God . . . oh my God . . . oh shit! Oh. . . ." I panted over and over again.

Before I could come down from such an over-whelming feeling, Aric quickly came back up and slid so deep into me that even he moaned and growled out. He had pulled me close to him so that I couldn't run away and although the mix-ture of pain and pleasure was new to me, I wasn't sure if I wanted to get away. The way he moaned out my name on top of that thick New York ac-cent, and the way he was hitting that one spot as he systematically stroked and grinded his hips into me, it was enough to bring water to my eyes. He had control of my ample hips, moving them to the speed and tune that he wanted them. As he pumped harder into me, I felt him swell and get harder inside of my sugar walls. I bit down on my bottom lip and dug my nails into his back until he let out a primal groan, giving one last hard push into me. Exhausted we lay sprawled out on the couch for a long while. I thought he had fallen asleep while he was still inside of me. I actually fell asleep with him resting between my legs.

The sound of an alarm woke me. It took a while for me to gather my thoughts. The sore-ness in between my thighs and legs surprised me. I looked around and realized that I was in my boss's hide-a-way office at work and we had just had sex. I looked around for Aric and did not see him. I noticed his gym bag was on top of the desk and his suit was gone. It was thirty minutes past twelve and I had missed more than half of the meeting. I sat up on the couch and then tried to stand but I was dizzy. My legs were wobbly but I somehow managed. As I was walking to the shower, the door opened and Aric walked in with bags in his hand. I smelled food. It was obvious he had been to the meeting and it was over with. I realized I was naked and moved back over to the floor near the sofa and reached for my T-shirt to pull it on. At the moment, I wasn't sure how I was feeling. I was nervous. I had just had sex with my boss. How was I supposed to feel? I heard him maneuvering around behind me.

"You OK?" he asked as he stepped closer to me and enclosed one arm around my waist.

I lied nervously as I nodded. "Yeah, I'm good." I smiled and peeked back at him.

He kissed my neck before answering his ringing phone and I listened to him threaten to fire half of the accounting department if they didn't get numbers that made sense by the end of the day. He handed me a Target bag and I looked inside to find a pair of red cotton boy shorts and a pack of Maxi panty liners.

"Thank you," I said in a whisper to him.

He nodded and pointed to the Red Lobster bag on the desk and mouthed for me to eat. I was starving and had already opened the bag and pulled out two containers. They both had the same thing, lobster tails with shrimp scampi and brown and wild rice with those biscuits that were going to go right to my thighs. I gave one of the containers to him and I sat down next to him to eat. We didn't say much to each other since he was still on the phone cursing people out.

After eating, I jumped in for a quick shower noticing that I was bleeding a little. I was thankful for the panty liners and the black wide leg pant suit I would be wearing today. I hid behind the curtain that separated the couch from the rest of room and put my suit on. It was the shortest work day I have ever had. I gathered the rest of my things back into my bag. As I was about to leave, Aric put the caller on hold long enough to stand and hug and kiss me. I didn't know how to feel and what to expect, but I was glad that he had put my mind at ease. My heels clicked against the hardwood floor as I left Aric. I hid my bag on the side of the leather sofa in Aric's main office before walking out to my desk. My head and the spot between my legs were still hurting a bit so I popped a few Tylenols. The rest of the day went by uneventfully. It was back to work as usual. Although for the rest of the day my mind played back this being my first time having sex and I was still in a state of shock. The lower half of my body kept reminding me that she had been pried open. The throbbing never left and every time Aric walked past me, my lower region jumped. A nervous feeling took over and I wondered how he would look at me now. Wondered if his image of me would change? By the end of the day, my stomach was in knots and I had a migraine that just wouldn't quit.

That same night, at about ten o'clock, Aric was at my door. He had knocked on the door in my kitchen and as soon as I opened it he pulled me into his arms. All I had on was a T-shirt. The wind was attacking me left and right, but when Aric put me on top of the hood of my car, pulled my T-shirt off, and spread my legs, heat rushed all over my insides. I clawed at the car when his lips enclosed around my lower set of lips and he sucked, licked, and ate all around my wetness. All you could hear was heavy breathing, me moaning, Aric smacking, and the wind howling. It was like the wind was a voyeur and I didn't mind one bit. Aric and the wind were taking turns fondling my body. My hand grabbed a hold to both sides of his face and tugged at his ears. I pulled his face closer to my pussy. I guess I was trying to either saturate his face in my juices or smother the man. He didn't seem to mind though. He kept right on fingering and licking. Licking and eating. Eating and drinking. I looked down and saw my juices had his face shining. It made me come harder, especially when he used his fingers to spread my lips and suck down on my clit. I moaned so loud. . . . I knew the old man across the street could hear me. I could feel and hear Aric going for his belt buckle and I was scared, but antsy. I wanted it . . . but I knew I couldn't handle it. His belt buckle clinking alerted me to when his pants were down. As he came up to kiss me, he pulled me to the edge of the car, and I braced myself for impact. I let out a startled moan when his head broke skin.

"My fucking . . . God . . ." he roared out with his eyes closed with his head thrown back.

I was panting and trying to catch my breath as he slid in and out of me with precise motion. I was clawing at his back so hard, I heard his shirt rip. I was literally on the verge of slobbering out of the mouth if I wasn't already. Once he got the position that he wanted, his rhythm changed to a steady beat. One minute his mouth was open and the next he was biting down on his bottom lip. I pulled his shirt over his head revealing nothing but muscles. My ankles were placed on his shoulders and he pulled me closer to him without breaking a stroke. The coldness of the hood gave me chills, but the feel of him inside of me, hugging my walls warmed me all over.

"Damn, Chyanne . . . umph . . . good pussy," he said to me with one hand on my breasts and the other massaging my clit. My back was arched, head back, and my body was convulsing at the way he entered me. I knew when he was about to come. The harder he pumped and the fatter he swelled on the inside of me let me know he was nearing the edge. I placed my hand against the panel of his stomach to try and push him back a bit, but to no avail. He simply moved my hand and rode me deeper . . . harder . . . and faster. I yelled . . . no scratch that . . . I screamed his name out and it seemed as if it stilled the night with my orgasm. The wind stopped blowing and with one last push Aric fell against my breasts. I was already sore from earlier. Now my inner vaginal walls were twisting and shouting in pain, but the feeling that I had just experienced was well worth it.

Chapter 6

What was left of October went by at a speed that I couldn't keep up with. Between me and Aric having sex, at the drop of a dime, anywhere at any time, my body was becoming addicted to him. I had gotten cocky and decided that I wanted to have my first oral sex session and I'd like to think I got an A plus being that I made him come the first time around. He could look at me and my boy shorts or thong would drop in an instant. At work we had little conversations here and there. He would leave me notes telling me how much he wanted to be inside of me and how much he missed me.

We had been at each other's houses quite a lot too. His house could sit ten of mine in it and still have room to comfortably live. His home was in a private Buckhead Estate. I remember listening as he told me about the whole house including the layered stucco and custom cut limestone finishes. He told me about the imported mahogany doors and windows, elevator, smart home, wine cellar, media room, custom master closets and outside had an incredible 2.95 plus acre lot over-looking a lake. The landscaping was immaculate. I had become accustomed to his California king sized bed.

He had become accustomed to my cooking. I would find myself shopping and filling my fridge and his with the stuff he liked most. Chicken, salmon, steaks, fresh veggies, and lots of apple juice, just to name a few. Was there a title on what we had? No. Why? Because Aric said it would be better this way. No title. No drama was what he said. I guess. And to be honest it was all good at first because he was being receptive to me and we both liked the same things. He was easy to talk to but as of late he had been distant. Not that it was a big deal because he was known to get very quiet when work was stressing him. So I was trying not to make a big deal of nothing, but you know that feeling you get when you just know something . . . something just doesn't feel right? Well . . . yeah, I was feeling that way.

I hadn't talked to Justin in a while and he called me up today, filling me in on the happenings down on the first floor. Lola was still busy slandering my name. Justin said she was pissed about being down there, especially seeing how

Aric was making progress with the company, but whatever. Right now I had other things to worry about, like why in the hell April kept calling for Aric. Each time she called she seemed more impatient than before. She never spoke to me at all.

The phone ringing was what snapped me out of my thoughts. "Good afternoon. Aric McHale's office," I answered with the energetic tone that Gabriel had started to tease me about every time he called.

"I need to speak to Aric again, please, and thank you." It was April.

"Hey, April," I spoke. I was trying to keep it together. We hadn't spoken to each other since she showed her tail at that business function.

"Chyanne, may I speak with Aric, please? Thank you."

I put her on hold and transferred her call to Aric. His office door was open and although I couldn't quite hear what he was saying to her, I knew it was brief. When he was off the phone I walked into his office and closed the door behind me. I knew April didn't know the first thing about marketing or advertising and I wanted to know what she wanted. He looked up at me from behind his desk before taking his glasses off. I gave a semi-curt smile and stood at the door with my arms folded.

"So why is April calling you?"

He put the paper down and his right eyebrow arched a bit.

"So April can't call me now?"

That struck a nerve since I didn't know they had become close enough for her to be calling him at all. I unfolded my arms and moved toward his desk. The sun was shining but I knew for a fact that it was cold outside. It was about as cold out there as it had turned in here.

"I know it's not about business being that she doesn't know a thing about what we do. . . ."

"Oh, so the only time I can talk to somebody is when it's business?"

His face frowned and he stood up. He moved past me and toward his file cabinet. I felt like I had just been brushed off.

"When it's April, yes," I answered. My anger meter was through the roof.

He stopped messing with the file cabinet and turned to me. The look on his face said he was either annoyed or pissed or both.

"Chyanne, I am a grown ass man. You don't get to tell me who I can talk to and who I can't. Get that?"

I don't know. I guess I was just expecting some type of common courtesy or something. I mean knowing that April is . . . was my friend and he saw the mess she had done. We stared at each other for a while before I turned and walked back out to my desk. I wanted to cry I was so mad, but what would I be crying for? I plopped back down at my desk and I could hear my phone vibrating in my purse. I didn't bother to answer it though. I had let my mind drift off, until I saw April strut around the corner. She had on tighter than tight denim skinny jeans, a red sweater so tight it showed the complete outline of her nipples, and red Chanel caged booties. Her makeup was flawless as was her spiked pixie hair cut. She walked right past me and into Aric's office. She didn't even acknowledge me. My leg started to shake and I could feel my blood pressure rise. It didn't help me any when I turned to see her give him a tight hug and he embraced her back. It really hurt when he walked out of his office with her.

"Hold my calls for me," he said to me as he slid his arms into his leather jacket. "I'll be right back."

He looked at me and I didn't nod or acknowledge that I had even heard him. I rolled my eyes and looked away. I didn't even bother to look at April. When they rounded the corner and I heard the elevator chime, I blew out a breath like it was steam. No more than ten minutes later the elevator chimed again and I was hoping it was Aric, but no such luck. It was Gabriel. I must admit even though my feelings were hurt, Gabriel's sexiness wasn't lost on me.

Hello, Ms. Chy," he said, greeting me with a gentle, yet magnetic smile. "Your boss around here anywhere?"

His teeth were the same size and perfectly white. Those dark coffee colored eyes beckoned to me.

"No, he stepped out for a second," I answered him back with a smile.

He nodded "Must have been a woman. Only a woman can take Aric away from work. Any idea when he will be back? We were supposed to do lunch. Had some things we were supposed to discuss."

Part of his statement bothered me, but I answered anyway. "Nope. No idea when he will return."

He sat down in the chair across from my desk as I answered the ringing phone and sent someone to Aric's voice mail. I looked up to find Gabriel watching me. He was casually dressed in tailored black dress slacks and a royal blue long sleeved crisp dress shirt. No tie. Black square toed dress shoes that set off his whole attire.

"What," I asked when he kept staring. "Is my fro lopsided or something?"

He chuckled. "No not at all. In fact, it really looks good on you. Matches your personality perfectly. Wild and untamed yet innocent and got it all together. You look good too. Black suits you. It's just that you have this new glow about you is all. I've noticed you had that extra something in your voice lately as well and whoever has put that smile on your face has to be one hell of a lucky man!"

I blushed. "Thank you."

I had on an all black skirt suit with white accessories and black and white spiked Gucci heels.

"Have you had lunch today?" He asked as he crossed one leg over the other.

"No. Aric and I usually . . ." I caught myself. "Mr. McHale and I usually . . . well I usually go and get lunch for the both of us."

I could tell he had already caught on to my mistake. He only smiled a knowing smile. He didn't say anything though.

"Well, can I take you to lunch? After all, seems like you will be doing it alone today anyway right?"

I thought about it and I know I made the decision out of spite, but I said yes. Aric must be out of his mind if he thought I was about to sit there and cry and brood over him. I grabbed my purse and my jacket after setting the phone to office "out mode" and we left for lunch. We ended up at Maggiano's. It was an authentic Italian restaurant. I had been to a lot of places, but never here before. We sat silently as I looked over the menu. It was apparent that he had been here plenty of times because it didn't take him long to look at the menu and decide what he wanted. I finally made up my mind and ordered the spinach and chicken manicotti, a small glass of Moscato D'asti and a glass of water.

"So Chy, tell me something about you," Gabriel asked of me.

I shrugged. "Nothing to tell. I am twenty four with three degrees. Graduated high school when I was seventeen. Don't have much family and no friends at all it seems."

"Where's your family?"

I looked up at him and stared before answering him. "Long story and if you don't mind, I would rather not talk about that."

He chuckled and nodded. "I can respect that. Why no friends?"

I shrugged again and watched him take a swallow of water before answering. "It is what it is, you know? Keep your friends close and your enemies closer and it seems I do a bang up job on that last part."

I could tell by his amused facial expression that he knew I was referring to the incident with April.

"By the way, thank you for making sure she made it home safely," I added after taking a sip of my wine.

He nodded and took a piece of the bread the waiter had sat on the table.

"No problem at all. All I had to do was drop her off and keep it moving."

The bottom of my stomach fell out at that. Did that mean that the man Jo-Jo saw April talking to was Aric? Did he leave my house and go to April's? As if Gabriel had read my mind. . . .

"Aric told me he stopped by her place to make sure she had gotten in as well," he told me.

I didn't respond. Just turned and look at the ongoing traffic on Peachtree Road and listened to the noise of the old Italian music and the muttering of the patrons at the restaurant.

"Did I say something wrong?" he spoke up and asked after a while.

I shook my head. "No. I just have a lot on my mind is all."

Gabriel exhaled. "I hope it doesn't have anything to do with Aric. If that's the case, then I wouldn't worry. I wouldn't let him get to me. Aric will be Aric and he has been since I have known him."

"Who said it had anything to do with him?"

He leaned forward and clasped his hands together, looking me in my eyes. "Chyanne, sometimes we have to listen to what's not being said."

His eyes studied mine and it was like he could see past the whole facade I was putting up. I was so thankful that the food came at that moment. I don't understand how I let these unseen feelings for Aric sneak up on me, but this man had embedded himself into my DNA in more ways than one. Over the last month or so, everything he had done had deepened my feelings for him. The trips to the movies, the shopping, the sneaking away for lunch at work together, the spending the night at each other's places, and the sex! Lord the sex! Thinking about it right now had me squeezing my legs together and silently moaning.

This was something that I wasn't used to. I wasn't used to getting lost in a man. I never wanted to be there. I never wanted to be the woman who couldn't see past a man's smile. Yet, here I was. I barely touched my food. My appetite had been lost. I was tempted to sneak to the restroom and call to see if Aric had made it back to the office, but there was no need. Aric was texting me in the middle of lunch asking me where I was.

Gabriel and I made small talk for what time I had left of lunch. I liked talking to Gabriel. He was fun and his deep baritone and Southern accent sent chills through me especially when he called my name. I asked him questions about his LX 11 truck just to keep the conversation flowing until we made it back to the office. Gabriel was a comedian too. He kept me laughing, almost making me forget that Aric had left with April . . . almost.

Gabriel was a gentleman through and through. I hadn't had to open a door for myself this entire time with him. It was funny to see chicks gawking at him as he passed with me. He opened the door for me when we made it back to the office and hugged me. There was something in his hug. Something I didn't care to dwell on because that would require me to admit that I was sexually attracted to him. I didn't want to go there so when he leaned in for a kiss, I politely moved my head to the side and declined.

"I . . . I can't. . . . Not right now," I said to him as we stood hidden from the cameras in the parking deck.

"I understand," was all he said. He kissed me on my cheek, handed me my doggy bag from lunch, and walked me to the elevator. I stepped onto the elevator a little embarrassed.

"Chyanne," he called out to me and I had to rush to stop the elevator doors from closing.

"Yeah," I answered.

"I'm always around."

I watched as he walked off toward his truck. I let the elevator doors close and finally let the breath I had been holding out. Lord what had I gotten myself into? I stepped off the elevator and made my way to my desk. Aric was in his office and I hated to admit it but I was glad he was there. I was still pissed. However, he was not with April, so I was good. I dropped my purse in the bottom drawer of my desk and switched the phone back on. I left my doggy bag on the desk. It was no more than five minutes later before Aric's office door swung open.

"Where have you been?" he asked me.

Something about the tone of his voice startled me.

"I went to lunch." I said sarcastically pointing at the bag on my desk.

"With who? Your car was still in the parking deck."

I wasn't so sure I wanted to answer that question. So I tried not to.

"Look I went to lunch. Is that a problem?"

I was sitting in my chair looking up at him in the doorway of his office with his arms folded across his broad chest.

"Don't play with me Chyanne!" he said through gritted teeth. "Who did you go to lunch with? Don't think I won't fu . . . mess you up because we are in this office."

My brows furrowed and I looked at him like he had lost his mind!

"I am a grown woman and I go to lunch with whomever I choose. Get that?"

The way he was looking at me had me feeling some type of way and I don't mean anything good about that either. He had bit down on his bottom lip and was nodding his head like he was keeping from saying what he really wanted to say. He turned and went back into his office, slamming the door so hard other assistants were sticking their heads around the corner to see what was going on. I put on a fake smile whenever someone asked if everything was okay and hyperventilated when no one could see me. I picked up the phone and pressed one.

Aric picked up. "What?"

"I went to lunch with Gabriel."

"Who?"

I could hear something akin to disbelief and anger in his voice.

"Your friend Gabriel who was at the. . . ."

Before I could get the last part out I heard a click in my ear. I heard when he moved into his hide-a-way office a few minutes later. A few minutes after that, he called me to meet him in there. I slowly stood and walked into his office, locking the door behind me. I was not in the mood to fight with this man, especially when he was the one who didn't want to put a "title" on our relationship. I pushed the button on the wall to his hide-a-way office and stepped in. He was sitting on the couch, arms wide, legs spread with a mean mug on his face.

"So you fucking Gabriel?" he asked.

I answered with my face bunched in disbelief. "What? No!" I chuckled a bit. "I only went to lunch with the man. Since you decided that you wanted to go do "whatever" with April. . . ."

He stood and walked over to me cutting me off and making me back up against the desk that was on the wall by the door.

"You think I'm stupid, Chyanne?"

He was right up on me and had cupped my chin to make me look up at him.

"No."

"Are you fucking Gabriel?"

He asked that with clenched teeth.

"No. How am I having sex with Gabriel when I have been with you every day all day until today? Are sleeping with April?"

His grip tightened on my face and his eyes watered, becoming red. "Don't play with me Chyanne! Tell me the truth."

"Who's playing? I'm telling you the truth." The attitude I had copped was laced in my voice.

I tensed because he snatched my face closer to his and his grip tightened causing pain in my jaw. He picked me up and sat me on top of the desk. Snatching me close to him, his right hand found its way under my skirt and his lips roughly enclosed around mine. I felt my thong rip on one side and he used his knee to push my legs further apart. He kept kissing me and pushing his tongue in and out of my mouth. I felt the split in the back of my skirt rip. It was all going in slow motion. I heard his zipper come down, and seconds later, I screamed inside of his mouth when he shoved his way inside of me. I was scratching and clawing at his back. I tried to push him off of me, but he grabbed both wrists and slammed them into the wall before removing his mouth from mine.

Looking me dead in my teary eyes he said, "Your pussy had better always feel like this. I'll know if somebody has touched my pussy," he said before pushing hard and so deep inside of me that my legs started to shake uncontrollably.

I bit down on my lips to keep from screaming. His mood, the tension in the room, the way he was treating me, all caused tears to fall from my eyes. I tried calling his name to get his attention to let him know he was hurting me.

"Aric," I called out to him again. "You are hurting me! Aric, stop!"

I squirmed and moved around, letting out silent screams and clamping my legs around his waist to try and get him to ease up and slow down. No such luck. I was forced to ask myself what was happening here, but I didn't really want to know what was happening. Aric was like an animal that couldn't be tamed. I didn't know where the moisture between my legs was coming from because this hurt. Aric's thrusts were so fast and hard that I didn't know where the pain ended or where it began. After a while I couldn't hold in my sobs any longer and I began to cry out loud. When he heard me he abruptly stopped and looked intently at me.

"I'm sorry," he repeated over and over to me in a near whisper, kissing my tears while they slid down my face. I didn't know how I felt. I was numb. I felt nothing. The pain inside hurt way worse than what he had done to me. I sat silent as he kissed his way down to my thighs. I hissed out and tensed when his lips touched my now swollen and hurting lips down below.

He planted butterfly kisses there and gently licked, trying to kiss away what he had done. I hated to admit it but he made me come. I didn't want to, but I couldn't help it. When he was done, he laid there with his head on my lap for a long while. I didn't touch him. I couldn't bring myself to touch him. After a while, I pushed him away from me. It hurt for me to walk so I stopped for a second to get myself together.

After a moment I cried my way to the shower and got in with all of my clothes on. While in there I peeled my clothes off and sat there. I could hear him moving around. Did I want a man so bad that I would let him do this kind of thing to me? Was I no better than April or all of the other women that I had called stupid? I rocked back and forth as I cried and thought. After trying to wash away what Aric had done to me, I stepped out of the shower slowly and steadied myself. I didn't even look up when his naked body came closer to me. I let him pull me up and let him pull me into his embrace.

"I'm sorry baby. I never. . . . Forgive me. Please forgive me. . . ."

His voice sounded as if he was weak, but I didn't care. I had no words for him at the moment. I let him reach down and pull me up around his waist.

"Look at me baby," he called out, shaking me a bit.

I looked away and didn't say a word.

"Chyanne look at me."

Finally, I looked at him. I listened to him apologize to me again. At that moment he wasn't even sexy to me anymore. He could do nothing for me. Within an hour, I went home. I crawled into my queen-sized bed, thinking about my relationship with Aric. What had I gotten myself into and how would I ever be able to get out of it?

I didn't talk to Aric for the next week or so. He would call but I wouldn't answer. I took a sick week from work. Justin told me Lola had been all too happy to fill my seat. I had been moping around my house all week. I did a little winter cleaning and I had been helping Jo-Jo with a PowerPoint Presentation for school. One particular day I was cleaning my room and my purse fell from the dresser. It was a clutch that I often carried with me when going to clubs. Jamie's business card fell out. It was the one he gave me when we were at Club Miami. I felt better that day, but a little lonely, so I went against the grain and called him. I was happy I did. He brought my spirits up. I let him take me to dinner and a movie and we hung out for a couple of days after that. He came to my house to watch a movie or two. I had taken all of Aric's belongings and put them away in a plastic tote until I could get them back to him.

As for Jamie and I, we decided to take it up a notch. I let him eat the coochie because he wanted to. Let me tell you I don't know who could do it better Jamie or Aric, but Jamie's tongue was long enough for him to reach the depths of my soul through the opening between my legs. And that man licked everywhere, missing not one nook or cranny. He did it so good it had me fanning myself down below trying to calm her down. Basically, he had me running from his tongue, but the feel of it was so good—a pussy monster for real. I enjoyed his company and was looking forward to spending more time with him.

My phone was vibrating like crazy. I stopped dressing long enough to see who was trying so hard to contact me. I picked up my BlackBerry after I pulled my fro back into a big puffball. Five texts from Aric and two from Jamie. I erased all of Aric's texts without looking at them and went to Jaime's texts. He and I were supposed to catch a live outdoor jazz show tonight. I was actually pretty excited. Friday night and I was on my way out. In Atlanta, live outdoor jazz festivals were the best. Vendors served the best food and drinks and it was mostly an older mature crowd

so there was not a lot of mess to put up with. I
texted Jaime back and told him I was getting
dressed. Jamie was cool . . . laid back even. Very
artistic I had learned. I dropped my phone back
on the bed and finished dressing. I tugged on
some wide legged high waist jeans and buttoned
up my black collared shirt that flared over my
hips and back side. Around my waist I put on a
wide chocolate brown corset type belt, threw on
some big brown feathered earrings, and threw
on my brown caged Chanel booties. I stood in
the mirror turning from side to side to make
sure I had no muffin tops. Then I took a picture
of myself and sent it to Jamie. We were supposed to meet up on Piedmont so I was leaving a
little early. I picked up my bag and dropped my
vibrating phone over into it. Again, it was Aric.

I had slipped up and told Jaime about me and
Aric. Didn't tell him about that last incident,
but gave him enough details to let him know we
weren't seeing each other anymore. I wasn't going to lie, I missed Aric like crazy. I did. Hell,
don't ask me why. I guess I had let myself fall in
love with the man. As much as I hated to admit
it, I couldn't fool myself any longer. From the
moment I stepped foot into his office he had
worked some kind of magic on me. Still, I would
be damned if I let a man do what he had done to

me and still be running after him. I may be young, but stupid I was not. I hummed and grabbed my keys as I strutted to the door with a smile on my face. I was actually looking forward to seeing Jamie. I opened my door and stepped outside into the brisk breeze. My coat was already in the car. I noticed a movement out the side of my eye and turned to find Aric casually leaning against the grill of his truck. I stopped in my tracks.

"I have called you, texted, left messages . . . whatever. Trying to get in contact with you," he said to me.

No threat was detected in his voice. The leather jacket, black jeans, black D&G turtle neck sweater, and even the D&G white perforated leather lace up sneakers made the appeal of this man much more lethal.

"I've been busy," I said, turning to lock my door. With my purse hanging in the crease of my elbow, I walked toward my car which he had parked his truck behind and was blocking me in.

"Too busy for me, Chyanne?"

I stopped walking and looked over at him. "Apparently so."

He chuckled and stood straight up folding his arms and standing in his signature wide legged stance.

"Got a date?" he asked me. My body turned hot at the way he looked me over. It's like his eyes had x-ray vision or something.

"Why? Is there something you wanted? I'll be back to work on Monday. I have a doctor's excuse which I'll turn in to HR on Monday. . . ."

"I miss you, Chyanne."

I stepped back when he moved closer to me. I exhaled loudly and shook my head.

"You don't get to do this Aric. You don't get to pull what you did and then say you miss me. You don't get away with that and think you can come over here and butter me up . . ."

I was annoyed. I had been easily annoyed a lot lately. My blood pressure was going up again. I could feel myself getting jittery.

"Listen to me." He moved closer to me and put his finger to my lips to quiet me. "I fucked up. I fucked up bad and I know that, but at least give me a chance to make it right."

I pushed off and away from him. He caught my wrist and pulled me back into him. I could see my old neighbor eyeing us and tried not to create a scene.

"You don't miss me, Chyanne?"

His scent was making me dizzy or maybe it was because he had driven my blood pressure up. I looked up at him with a frown on my face and snatched my arm away from him.

"No, I don't. Now if you will excuse me, I have some place I need to be."

"I miss you," he called out to me.

I stopped and turned back around to him. I hated to admit it to myself but I missed this man. Why did I have to miss him? I had thought about him every day. We stood there watching each other and his eyes burned a hole through me.

"What do you want, Aric?" I said impatiently.

"Let me show you I'm sorry. Look, why in hell you got me begging you to tell you I'm sorry?" He was using his hands to talk. "I don't like to repeat myself and I am not the one to beg."

It was my turn to fold my arms.

"First of all I didn't ask for your apology. Second of all you can't. . . . How do you apologize for using your dick as a weapon? What? You think that you can roll up here, flash that dimpled smile, and everything will be cool again? Some stuff you do you just can't take it back once it's done. What you did was one of them."

I quickly turned and made my way to the driver side of my car. I hit the automated button and unlocked the door. I threw my purse on the passenger side and was prepared to get in.

"I admit it, I was wrong. I keep saying that shit over and over Chyanne, but why do you always have to make a nigga beg?"

I had never heard him use the "N" word before and that was the second thing out of his mouth that shocked me. He stood with his arms wide. "Damn! What in hell do I have to do?"

I got nervous and looked around as some of my nosey neighbors had come outside. Some pretending to be doing something in their yard and others just plain out looking and listening.

"You see me face to face. You can see I am for real. Why make me do this shit out here? I messed up! I said it again. Now what? A nigga got to stand on his head and do tricks? Come on, baby! Don't make me do this out here like this."

I sighed and looked away from him as he approached me. When his hands touched my waist I nibbled on my bottom lip and folded my arms when he pulled me close to him.

With his voice low and baritone deep he said, "You don't know what it has been like with you not around me every day. I messed up, baby. I know that, but I won't do it again. I can guarantee you that. I lost it. I don't know. I guess the thought of you with another man fucked me up."

I finally looked up at him. "Oh and I'm supposed to be okay with you leaving the office with my best friend?"

"She asked to buy me lunch . . ."

"And you said yes?"

My voice was a little louder than I intended. He shook his head and answered.

"Look, baby. April has been trying to get my attention since she met me. I went with her that day to tell her that I was with you . . ."

I gave a faux chuckle and shook my head. "And you couldn't do that over the phone? What about that whole *"I'm a grown ass man"* thing?"

He smiled. "I was already annoyed and I lashed out at you. I was wrong for that."

"So what did you and April do that day when you left the office with her?"

"Nothing. I came back into the office about twenty, thirty minutes later and you were gone."

I turned my head again and looked elsewhere. I tried to be stubborn when he gently cupped my chin and tried to kiss me. I moved my face and he did it again, this time connecting his lips with mine. I had missed these thick chocolate lips. Heat settled in between my legs and my resolve slowly faded. He gripped my backside and pulled me closer to him as our tongues touched. I don't know. It was like a different feeling washed over me as he kissed me. My mind quickly went to Jamie. I didn't know if I was going to make our date. I stood there as Aric pulled my purse from my car and locked my doors back. I followed him to my front door, but before I unlocked it, he captured my attention. After a lengthy kiss, we both walked into my house hand in hand.

It was two hours later when I got to my phone to text Jamie. I rolled out of Aric's arms and took my phone to the bathroom with me. I texted Jamie that an emergency came up and told him I was sorry I couldn't make it. After I had finished using the restroom, he texted me back.

It's cool. Maybe some other time we can hook up. BTW I drove to your house to make sure nothing had happened since it wasn't like you not to call or show up.

I sighed. I felt so bad all I could type back was, I'm sorry.

It's cool. Don't worry about it.

I could detect the sarcasm and nonchalant tone. I heard Aric moving around in my room and quickly put my phone on the counter. I washed my hands, dried them, and walked out of the bathroom. My body was sore. Aric and I had made love forever it seemed. I still had to get used the stamina that he possessed. He took his time and took me to places that I didn't think I could go. I had missed him and my body showed it. I was dripping wet before he even had my clothes all the way off. I loved it when he got behind me. I liked the way he let his head lay at my opening and let my muscles pull him in. Aric's magic stick was way too big for me, but I loved the hell out of it. Loved the way he moved in and out of me like he was looking to hit that one spot and create another one. Loved the way he gripped my cheeks and spread them so he could fall deeper inside of me. And it turned me on more when he would tell me to *throw it back*. I had learned what he liked. I listened to his moans and paid attention to the way his grip tightened when I moved a certain way.

I walked over to the bed. He was sitting up looking at his phone. He had a frown on his face.

"Everything OK," I asked.

He nodded and yawned. "Family issues." He threw his phone back on the night stand beside my bed. "I'm hungry baby."

My eyes washed over his naked frame as he laid back and propped his left arm behind his head as the other rubbed his stomach. His baby maker never seemed to go all the way soft after we would finish making love, I thought to myself as I pulled on my pink terry cloth robe.

"What do you want to eat," I asked.

That was the normal for him. After sex, he always wanted food.

"I don't care. I'm just hungry." He yawned again. "Will you pass me the remote behind you?"

I grabbed the remote from my dresser and tossed it to him. I went to the kitchen and looked around my fridge. It was going on ten-thirty. I pulled out the ingredients for sandwiches and small salads. I made sure I had all of the toppings that he liked. He probably wouldn't want tomatoes in his salad, especially if I put them on his sandwich. I put the late night snack together and set the table. I could hear him laughing in the room. He had this habit of watching Sanford and Son. I called out to him when I was done. A few seconds later he emerged from the room and after he blessed the food, we ate. It was hard to focus on eating when Aric was sitting across from me in nothing but black boxer briefs. He had a healthy appetite which was probably why he worked out the way he did. After we finished eating we sat outside on my back patio and talked about what had happened in his office. After telling him that I was still not feeling that whole thing because it took me somewhere I didn't want to be, he assured me that it wouldn't happen again. The love I felt for him made me believe him.

Chapter 7

I guess you can say the relationship between Aric and I was growing and all that, but we still didn't have a title and it didn't seem if he had any intentions of giving us one. Every time I said something about it, we ended up arguing or not saying anything to each other for a while. We were back to our old routine of spending the night with each other, although he had been at my house most of the time, which was cool because anytime I wanted a change of scenery we would go to his place.

I had tried to call Jaime back a few times and got no response. I just wanted to apologize face to face, but he wasn't answering my calls. I guess I wanted more so to apologize because Aric and I were arguing again. Little things he kept doing raised my suspicions of him doing other things. Sometimes he was warm and affectionate. Other times it was like his mind was somewhere else with somebody else and it was starting to annoy me. Like at that moment his phone kept ringing. All other times his phone vibrated, but then it was ringing to the tune of a Trey Songz hit. He had ignored the call about five times. Whoever she was, she was not letting up. We were sitting on my couch watching a re-run of NCIS on USA. I had been putting the finishing touches on Jo-Jo's PowerPoint presentation and after Aric and I had eaten dinner, we decided to stay in and watch TV. His head had been lying on my lap until his phone rang again. He had on no shirt and a pair of black sweats. I watched the muscles in his chest and arms flex as he annoyingly answered his phone. You know my eyes and ears were on alert.

"What?" he answered.

He didn't look over at me as he moved past me to the dining room area.

"What?" he snapped again. "Why in hell do you keep calling me? What the fuck do you want?"

I watched his body language between looking back and forth at the TV. I stood and tightened my robe, making my way to the kitchen as if I wanted to get some water.

"You want something to drink," I asked. I said it loud enough so my voice could carry. He ignored me.

I guess the person on the other end of the phone asked who I was, because he answered 'nobody' and my blood spiked.

I pulled a bottle of water from the fridge and slowly walked near him.

"Who are you talking to," I asked him.

He looked at me but it was like there was nothing in his eyes. He ignored me again. With the phone to his ear he tried to leave the dining room, but I blocked him.

"Aric, who are you talking to?"

I just knew damn well he was not doing what I thought he was doing! Again, I was ignored but he answered the woman on the other end of the phone. I knew it was a woman because I could hear her asking the same thing I was. He brushed past me and out of the dining room. I slammed the bottle of water down on the table and followed him back into the front room. As he yelled and talked to the woman on the other end of the phone, I stepped in front of him again.

I waved my hands in his face. "Hello, earth to Aric!! Who in the hell are you talking to?"

He inhaled and cut his eyes at me. "Not now!"

His tone backed me up a bit. That was all he said to me and he had the nerve to move me to the side and walk toward the front door. All I saw was red and I slapped him and the phone from his hand. His phone went flying across the room under my couch. Hell, I shocked myself! So imagine the look on his face. After the initial shock wore off for him, and it was quick, I found myself slammed against the wall so hard that it knocked the air out of me. I didn't even have time to get over the surprise of what he had done before his hand came up and around my neck.

The look in his eyes scared whatever boldness I had in me out. "Don't you ever in your fucking life put your hands in my face again, Chyanne. I will beat your ass! You hear me?"

All I could do was try and grab at his hand around my neck. His lips were twisted in anger and he was talking through clenched teeth. Tears started to fall from my eyes more so because I couldn't breathe. He moved his hand and I slid down the wall and watched through tears as he went for his phone. He snatched the door opened and stormed out. I knew he wasn't leaving because his keys, watch, and wallet were still on my nightstand in my room. I sat there in disbelief for a while before getting up and turning my TV off. I could hear him outside still talking to whoever she was on the phone. He had just shown me my importance to him. How in hell could he tell me he cared so much about me when he knew damn well he didn't? He couldn't care like he said and do the things that he did to me. I went into my room and crawled into my bed. My head was pounding and before I knew it, I had fallen asleep. What seemed like a few minutes later, I jerked awake when I felt him climb into the bed with me. I moved away from him when he tried to wrap his arms around me.

"Chyanne." He called my name slightly above a whisper. I didn't answer. He turned me over on my back. He was leaning on his right arm with his body semi covering mine. I looked up at him. It was dark in my room but the moonlight gave enough light for us to see each other. All I did was look at him.

"You mad?" he asked me.

Was this man crazy? How in hell did he think I was feeling? I didn't answer him. Only looked at him.

"So you're not going to say anything to me now, huh?"

I still didn't answer. He leaned down to kiss me and I turned my head away from him. He moved fully on top of me and urged my legs open with his. I tensed. He tried to kiss me again and I turned my head again. He pushed my robe up and around my waist. Then I spoke up.

"What? Are you going to take it like you did when we were in your office?" I asked him.

That stopped him dead in his tracks. His facial expression looked as if he was about to say something but he caught himself and got up. I watched as he turned the light on and found his white T-shirt. He gathered his watch, wallet, and keys then pulled on his Nike Air Force Ones. Once he was dressed, he turned the light back out. He kissed my forehead and then left. I didn't have to get up because he had the key to my door so he could lock it on his way out. As I lay there, my mind kept wondering who was on the other end of his phone. I couldn't believe he would disrespect me, in my house, like that! I guess you could say I was confused right now. Part of me wanted to get up and run behind him, beg him to come back. Aric had some kind of hold on me and as much as I wanted to break it at times, I just couldn't. I stood, quickly walking to my front room window to see if he had gone. It was good he was gone because I probably would have gone after him.

I woke up the next morning with the same headache I had gone to sleep with. I looked at my alarm clock after doing my morning hygiene thing and it was almost seven thirty. Dang it! I needed to get Jo-Jo his PowerPoint project. I pulled on a terry cloth sweat suit I had and some sneakers and ran for my door. His bus would be there soon and I was trying to get it to him before I missed it. Instead of jumping in my car, since April lived only two streets over, I ran through a pathway the kids in the neighborhood had made. As soon as I hit their street his bus was pulling off. My heart fell out of my chest. Not because I had missed his bus either. I kept walking toward April's house. I looked at the cream colored Escalade parked in her driveway as I pulled my cell from my pocket.

"Yeah," Aric answered when I called him.

"Where are you?" I asked him.

"Home."

"Really? You went right home after you left my house last night?"

"Yeah. Why?"

I jogged over to the Escalade sitting in April's driveway and pounded on the hood. The alarm went off. I looked up toward her bedroom and saw someone peek out of her blinds.

"Shit," is all I heard him say before his phone hung up.

A few seconds later he was coming out of her front door. She was not too far behind him, only she closed her screen door and stood behind it in nothing but her green bra and panties. There was that smug look of hers on her face again. I tried to move past Aric toward her, but he grabbed me. I pushed and swung at him, screaming for him to let me go. My mind didn't want to wrap around the fact that I knew he had sex with April. I could just feel it in the pit of my stomach. I could look at her body language and tell.

I bit down on my lip while shaking my head and asked, "Really, Aric? This is what you do?" I was talking with my hands and was so mad that I couldn't think straight.

He walked closer to me. "Chyanne, come on. We can talk at your place. Don't do this out here," he said while trying to grab my hands and pull me away.

Once again Aric and I were putting on a show for the neighborhood. I could tell he was annoyed by the way he was cutting his eyes at me and sighing. That pissed me off even more because he didn't have a right to be angry or annoyed.

"Why, Aric? Why would you do this to me and with her?" I screamed at him using my right hand to point toward April.

"It's not what you think, Chyanne," he countered. I could tell he was lying because he kept avoiding eye contact with me and he kept running his hands up and down his face.

"Well please tell me what it is!" I snapped at him trying to keep the tears at bay that were threatening to fall.

"Let's just go back to your place and talk."

"No, we don't have to go back to my place and talk. You can tell me all I need to know right here."

Standing there like he hadn't done a thing wrong with his arms folded across his chest, he sighed loudly and responded. "Look either we go back to your place or I'm going home. I'm not going to do this shit out here!"

My body was trembling and my mind was racing a thousand thoughts per second. April's screen door opened and she stepped out onto the front steps of her house. We stared each other down for a minute before my attention turned back to Aric. I would deal with her later. I didn't have it in me to stand in front of the neighborhood, let alone April, and have this conversation with him. So I gave in to his demands. No more than five minutes later we were back at my house. I didn't say anything to him. I jumped out of the truck and slammed the door so hard it shook! I knew he was following me into my house so I tried to slam the door in his face, but he caught it and shoved it back open. Almost immediately, I started with the questions. I barely gave him time to close the door.

"Why? Is that who was on the phone last night?"

He casually sat down before answering, "No."

"How long?" I was trying hard to keep my anger in check.

"How long what?" He arched one eyebrow, giving me a look that implied he really didn't feel as if he had to answer what I had asked.

"How long have you been having sex with her?"

He sighed. "Do you really want me to answer that, Chyanne.?

I knew steam had to be coming from my ears, eyes had to be throwing daggers and I had to be foaming from the mouth! "Yes, Aric! Why would you do some mess like that? And then you act like you don't even care that this is hurting me."

I wanted to scream. I wanted to yell, but . . . I just didn't have it in me. I was weak. He had weakened me. My love for him made me weak. "I . . . I cannot believe you would leave my bed and go straight to hers."

"It wasn't like that, Chyanne. You're assuming shit!"

"You keep saying that, but yet, you have been lying and were going to lie to me about it. So what is it like?"

"It was a spur of the moment thing. She called me when I was on my way home and . . ."

"Oh, so you gave her your cell number too? I guess that's why the no title thing works for you, huh? Got me walking around here looking as stupid as I want to be. Did you at least use protection?"

He frowned. "Yes, Chyanne. You don't ever have to worry about catching anything. I wouldn't do that to you."

"But it's okay to screw my best friend and all of this other mess you have been doing as long as you don't give me anything right?"

I could tell I was annoying him because he only stared at me. I shook my head and walked off toward my bedroom. I didn't even know why I was wasting my time with questioning him. It was clear that he didn't feel he had done anything worth being questioned about. To be disrespected by this man, not once, but twice in less than twenty-four hours had me ready to kill somebody. I grabbed my car keys so I could get Jo-Jo his work at school. I noticed I had missed his call as I grabbed my purse.

"Where are you going?" he asked me.

He saw the disk in my hand so that gave him his answer.

"It was just sex. Nothing else. April was a quick fuck that's it! She doesn't mean to me what you do. She doesn't mean anything to me at all."

"I guess the woman on the other end of the phone last night means a lot to you too, huh?"

His expression was unreadable. "It's not what you are thinking."

"Then explain it."

He walked over to me, bringing me closer to him and caressing my arms. "Listen to me. I have some things going on right now that I need to fix. Some things that I can't explain right now, but you are the only woman that I care this much about. These other women don't mean shit to me. I need you to always remember that, no matter what. Just chill and let me do what I have to do. In due time, everything will come together."

"And I guess I am supposed to accept that there are other women," I asked looking into his hazel brown eyes.

"Just accept the fact that I care enough about you to tell you the truth."

I don't know why, but at that moment Gabriel's voice was in my head. *Sometimes you have to listen to what's not being said.*

Chapter 8

For Thanksgiving the office was closed for a week. Aric and I spent that holiday together. It was just me and him for the day. Jo-Jo, Aaden, and Aaron came over and kept us company for a little bit then they were off to their dad's. Jo-Jo wanted to thank me for helping to get an A on his project. Yes, Aric and I had worked through that whole April fiasco. Don't get me wrong, I was still pissed that he had sex with her, of all people, but what was done was done. One reason I was not about to give up on him and let him go was because I didn't want April to think she had gotten to me. I was pissed enough to let him go, but I didn't want her to have him. I mean what exactly are the odds that I would even meet another man like Aric? A man like him could have a model type chick or a video vixen type, but he chose me.

He had kept his promise with leaving April alone, but other things were still bothering me.

Like who that other woman was on the other end of his phone that night. He still hadn't told me the deal with her, leaving me puzzled. Later on that night Aric and I had been invited to one of his boss's house for a holiday gala. I didn't mind going, but I never expected to see Jamie there. I would find Jaime watching me from time to time or maybe I am the one who had been checking for him. I hadn't seen him since the last time he was at my house, but we had a few phone conversations. He and I had established a nice friendship from our conversations over the phone. Maybe he kept looking because I looked different. Aric had talked me into straightening my hair. No perm, but I had gotten it pressed. My hair flowed down to the middle of my back once the stylist was done styling it. I had on very little makeup and my red dress had caused a lot of people to compliment me. It was a long red dress that complimented my full figured shape and the platinum accessories and shoes set it off.

When Gabriel complimented me I noticed Aric pulled me closer to him. I had caught Gabriel staring at me quite a few times as well. The look in his eyes was readable. There was no doubt what he would do to me if I would allow him to. Once Aric had been pulled into a conversation on target markets and what not, I snuck away and followed Jamie into the secluded area of the backyard.

I lost sight of him when he rounded the corner. I called out to him twice and got no response. I cut my losses and turned back for the house. That's when he scared the hell out of me. He was standing right behind me. I stumbled back and twisted my right ankle a bit. He caught me before I fell.

"Jamie, why didn't you answer me?" I snapped. "You scared the crap out of me."

We could still hear the music and the chatter coming from inside of the massive structure the owners called a house.

"My bad. You okay?"

He helped me to the bench that sat by a flowing angel fountain. "Yeah. I hurt my ankle though."

He kneeled down and unhooked the strap around my ankle and took my foot into his hand. "Damn, Chyanne! Why do you wear these tall heels?"

"Because I like them and I have never hurt myself in them until now."

I looked at him when he smiled. It warmed me. His locks were pulled back into a nice neat ponytail and he looked GQ ready in the black tux he was sporting. Those dark chocolate eyes were pulling me in. I started to feel bad about standing him up. I tried to apologize and he stopped me.

"I said it's cool. I'm good. You should be too," he said as he kept massaging my foot.

I could feel my foot swelling.

"You may have to get a doctor to look at this."

I nodded. "Probably so."

"You look out of this world sexy tonight. What made you straighten your hair?"

I smiled and thanked him. I didn't want him to know Aric had talked me into it so I shrugged. Over the last couple of weeks he had darn near changed my whole wardrobe. "Just wanted to try something different. You like it?"

It was his turn to shrug now. "It's beautiful. I mean you have beautiful hair, but I loved the way your fro looked on you."

I laughed because I missed my fro too and this hair was too much to keep in check. I told him as much. He laughed with me.

"I miss hanging with you, Chyanne," he said out of the blue.

I smiled and looked out over the vast expansion of the green landscape.

"I actually miss that too," I admitted when I looked back down at him.

We continued to gaze at each other until the noise from the house got louder. I looked up the surplus of stone stairs and Aric and Gabriel were standing there. Aric's face was as hard as the stone steps he was standing on. Jamie placed my foot gently down on the ground and helped me to stand when it was clear I couldn't stand on my own. My heart rate picked up a beat or two when I noticed Aric coming down the stairs toward us. Jaime picked up my shoe and handed it to me just as Aric was nearing us. Gabriel was still standing at the top of the stairs looking on with a drink in his hand.

"Hey, baby," I said nervously to Aric. "I twisted my ankle and Jamie helped me out a bit."

I was trying to ease the obvious tension.

"What are you doing back here anyway?" he asked me looking at my arm still around Jamie's neck. I quickly removed it and hobbled over to Aric.

"I came out to get some air. It was kind of stuffy in there."

I knew Aric could smell bull a mile away and I knew he was calling mine. Jamie didn't move. I wished he would.

"Maybe you should be worried about her ankle instead of why she is outside, don't you think?" Jamie casually asked.

My eyes got as wide as saucers. Aric glared over at Jamie. "Maybe you should mind your own business don't you think?"

"Maybe she is my business," Jamie snapped back. The cold look in his eyes chilled the already cold night.

If I could have been taken up in the Rapture right now, I wouldn't even care. I couldn't believe Jamie just said that!

Aric stepped forward a bit and said, "Say what?"

I could tell by the look on his face that this was not going in the best direction.

"Baby, please," I begged Aric as I limped in front of him to try and stop him. "Not here. Not in front of your bosses," I said so only he could hear me.

By now Gabriel had come down to give me a helping hand.

"Come on, Aric, man. It's not worth it," he said to Aric. "Chyanne needs to get to the doctor."

I was so thankful for that. Aric gave Jamie another hard stare before picking me up and carrying me around the house to the front area where the cars were waiting. A valet quickly took his ticket and brought his truck around. We were in the black Navigator tonight. Once in the car and on the highway Aric didn't say much to me and he didn't say much as we sat in the ER getting my ankle wrapped. But when we got back to his place, that was when he let me know exactly what he was thinking. After we had gotten undressed and had showered, we were lying in his bed when he broke his silence.

"You fuck that nigga?" he asked.

"No. I have never done anything with him," I lied because Jamie and I did have oral sex.

"He seemed too sure of that shit he said to me for ya'll to have never done anything."

"I went on a few dates with him. That's it."

He was quiet after that. To be honest, I was scared that I had said the wrong thing. You never knew what would set him off. My head would not stop hurting. I could hear the rustle of the covers as he moved around. He pulled me close to him and wrapped his arms around me. I could feel him hardening on my back. He loved to sleep naked.

"Chyanne."

"Yeah."

"I will hurt you up if you even think about fucking that nigga. Don't make me go there."

I didn't respond. I was just happy that was all he said. It wasn't long after that we made love. It was like heaven of course. Not the usual aggressive Aric. He made love to me slow and long. He had me climbing the walls and snatching sheets off the bed. Our bodies were wrapped so tight I didn't know where mine ended and where his began.

I was looking forward to spending the Christmas holiday with Aric. I had been making arrangements and preparations for the last couple of weeks or so. I had bought food and a couple of new outfits and we both had helped to decorate each other's houses, inside and out. I was falling behind on my Christmas shopping because I had gotten sick for about three days. Somehow I caught a stomach virus. But Aric took care of me. He had made me come home with him and he took two days off just so it wouldn't look suspicious with us both being out, but I was better now.

I parked my car in Aric's garage and pulled out the bags of food I had with me. As I unlocked the door and walked into the kitchen I could hear him on the phone. Whoever he was talking to had pissed him off. As soon as he heard me come into the kitchen he stopped talking and walked into his office. I heard him lock the door. I shook my head. He had been doing that a lot lately. I popped three Tylenol to help my headache and scratched my nipples. He didn't come back out of his office for another thirty minutes and I was too tired to argue with him. Instead, I cooked. We ate and we went to bed shortly thereafter. I could barely keep my eyes open and I didn't understand why I was so sleepy because I had basically slept all day and the night before. While in the bed that night he told me that he had decided to go home, to New York, to see his parents for Christmas. At first, I put up a fuss and I actually shed some tears. I had been doing a lot of that lately. It wasn't because he wasn't going to be here for Christmas. It was because I knew he was lying. I knew a woman had been on the other end of those secret phone calls, but what could I do? I had heard him tell her he loved her tonight and that bothered me more than anything. I was weak for this man and I hated myself for being so weak. He knew that I knew he was lying.

I could tell by the way he was looking at me when I was cursing and yelling at him and we were standing across from each other like opponents in a fight. I could tell when he pulled me close to him and tried to get me to calm down. I could tell when he stripped me of my clothes and placed kisses that ignited my insides all over my body. I could tell he knew when he spread my lips and sucked on that most sensitive part of me and when he licked, kissed, and sucked on my wet oasis. I could tell when he long stroked in and out of me. I could tell. . . .

For a week, I didn't see Aric. I didn't hear from him. Seven whole days. Seven whole nights. It broke me. I'm not going to lie. For the first few days I was sick about it. I stayed in bed crying myself stupid, but after a while I found myself calling Jamie. I needed someone to talk to and he had been that person for a while now. I had found that whenever I had problems concerning me and Aric, I called Jamie. Most times, all he did was listen, and only when I asked did he give me his opinion.

That night, he invited me to his house for dinner. He lived in Atlanta and I had to admit I was excited to see him as I knocked on his door. From the outside his place looked like an old firehouse or police station. You saw that a lot in Atlanta. Old buildings would be turned into lofts. I had on a Polo red velour sweat suit that Aric had bought me with a pair of Polo Brenly Leather sneakers. My hair was flowing down my back and around my shoulders. I was shocked when he opened the door. His locs were in disarray and he was only in a pair of cream linen draw string pants. He had on no shirt and that was the first time I had seen the tribal tattoos surrounding his upper chest. Jamie's body was the business. His upper body had the cut of a cobra head. Broad chest that fanned out and then curved down into the perfect V that had a nice package hanging beneath it. I could hear light mood music playing in the background.

"Hey, how are you?" I asked him as he embraced me.

"Good, come in."

He moved to the side and ushered me in. The smell of vanilla and peppermint hit my nose as soon as I stepped inside. The inside of his place was like a wide open space. This place was so huge I believed if I would have yelled there would have been an echo. He had stained cement floors and his sofas and art work were all earth toned colors. He gave me a quick tour of the place and I must say I was impressed. Everything was in place minus a few pair of his jeans lying around. After dinner, after everything had been put away, Jamie and I lay on his oversized sofa talking about nothing and everything all at the same time.

"So I take it Aric is not around? That would be the only reason you are here right now. Am I right?" he asked.

I looked at him. "No, he's not around, but that's not the only reason I'm here."

He chuckled. "Yeah, OK Chyanne. I was born at night, but not last night."

The only luminosity we had was by candlelight but I could still make out the offhand smirk on his face. I was about to try and defend my actions, but he stopped me.

"Don't play games with me, Chyanne. I am not going to be the man you can run to when you and ole boy have problems. I am not a toy. You can't put me down and pick me up when you feel like it."

His voice was raspy and deep as he looked at me through hooded lenses. It was eleven-thirty at night Christmas Eve and here I was with Jamie. I wouldn't have thought I would be here, but here I was.

"I understand that," I said back to him. "I am not trying to hurt you Jamie, but to be honest, I don't know where he and I are going to go. I haven't heard from him in a week. I'm lonely and I just needed someone to talk to."

Neither one of us said anything for a while. I knew I had probably made him feel some type of way about what I had said, but I hated to be lied to. So I was not about to lie to him. We laid with each other well into the night, sometimes talking, at times touching. The later it got into the night, the more intense our touches became. My mind wandered to Aric. I wondered what he was doing . . . wondered who he was doing. A few times I got this feeling that I couldn't shake along with images of Aric in between another woman's thighs, sexing her like he sexed me. I wanted to call him, but couldn't bring myself to hear another call going to voice mail or another text going unanswered. That's probably what made me turn to Jamie and place his hand between my thighs once more.

Only this time, he didn't stop at just touching. Before I knew it all of my clothes were on the floor and I was about to give to Jamie what only one other man had gotten. As Jamie worked magic between my thighs, images of Aric flashed through my head. Not to say that Jamie was lacking because he definitely was not. Jamie had skills that had me salivating from the mouth. He gave me what I needed to take my mind off of Aric for a while. Not just tonight but the next night and the next one too. Jamie didn't celebrate Christmas so I helped him to set up for Kwanza. I learned that he was a freelance photographer on the side too and I let him take snap shots of me that I thought I would never do. During one of our slow sexing sessions, I let him set the camera in front of his bed and snap pictures of us.

Although I was having fun with Jamie, I found a way to send Aric a text. Simply because . . . I was missing him like crazy. I knew he was probably with whoever that woman was on the other end of the phone, but I just needed to hear something from him. He had asked me to trust him, so that's what I was doing.

I love you, I sent to him. I stayed in the bathroom for about ten minutes, hoping he would text me back. I got nothing. My feelings were hurt. I wanted to cry until I was walking out of the bathroom and my phone buzzed.

Ditto was all he replied, but that was enough for me. He may have been with whomever, and as crazy as it sounds, in my heart I knew he was thinking about me.

Chapter 9

The New Year found me back to my usual routine. There was work and there was Aric. I took it upon myself to question him on his whereabouts over the Christmas holiday. We had a knock down drag out fight about that.

"Why are you always questioning me like I am your damn child?" I remembered him yelling at me.

I just shook my head and answered, "Whatever Aric. This coming from the man who will mess me up if I even think about being with another man right? Last time I checked, I was a grown woman too!"

I knew I was pushing the limit with that, but to hell with it. Yeah I had to endure him yelling and telling me, of course, not to try him, but I was not holding my tongue anymore. Forget that. He could kiss my whole entire juicy behind. So yeah I got hemmed up in a corner and I got him in my face, but he got a piece of me too. That was about a week or two ago. It is now the thirteenth of January, my birthday. Yesterday was his birthday. Yes, our birthdays fell one day after the other one. We celebrated his birthday yesterday and all he wanted to do was be inside of me all day. Not that I was complaining, but it was already a bit much to handle. He said he was making up for what he missed during the Christmas week. We went out for a while but all we could do was think about getting back home to his bed. Sambuca was a great place to celebrate with the live jazz and all, but with the romantic atmosphere and dim lighting, it didn't help our horny mood any.

While sitting at my desk, I was working on a memo to send to all of the executives. I opened my top desk drawer and noticed there was a small maroon velvet box. My heart raced and then skipped a beat. It was from Aric. I slowly picked up the box and opened it. The sight of the tear drop diamond ring set in platinum gave my heart a conniption. I almost jumped out of my skin. I calmed myself quickly, picked up the box, and walked into Aric's office.

He looked up at me and gave a smile when he saw it in my hand. "What does this mean?" I asked him. I needed to know because he was the one insisting we have no official title. "What finger do I put this on?" I asked before he could answer the first question.

I waited impatiently for his answer.

"You can put it on whatever finger you want. I don't care as long as you put it on," he answered.

Whatever thoughts and hopes I had went right out of the window. I was so sick of crying, especially over him. He walked around to the front of his desk.

He sighed before asking, "What are you crying for, Chyanne?"

I closed the box and looked up at him. "For a minute I thought maybe you actually cared about my feelings like you say . . ."

He cut me off. "I do. . . ."

"But we don't need the title right? Just as long as you can mark and tag your territory."

He frowned and walked over to me. "Why do you keep doing this, Chyanne? I keep telling you how much I care about you. My feelings won't change just because we don't have a title or just because you feel you need more to be secure. I told you there is some shit that I have to take care of first. You have to let me do that. Don't try to pressure this or try to force this into what you want it to be. The ring is not about me marking my territory. This ring is just another way to show you how deep my feelings are and how much I really do care about you."

I wiped the tears from my face and looked down at the box in my hand then back up at him. "What do you want from me Aric? You don't want us to have a title, but we do all the things that people in committed relationships do from the arguing to the love making. Is there even any future in me doing this with you?"

He pulled me into him and hugged me. "You're thinking too much about this and getting yourself all worked up over nothing. We'll talk later okay? It's your birthday, don't do this today."

I wrapped my arms back around him and we stood there until we heard the elevator ding. He removed the ring and quickly slid it on my left ring finger and then gave me a quick peck on the lips. A few minutes later we were in the break room where Justin had set up a surprise party for me. It did surprise me and we all were in for a surprise when Jamie was escorted in by security with a big flower arrangement of carnations and roses. He had about six balloons that all read happy birthday. He also had about three different gift bags. He had on dark denim loose fitting jeans, a red scoop neck sweater, and black Tims. His locks were braided back into two braids.

"Damn, bitch," Justin whispered to me. "You ain't tell me you were pulling them like that!"

The mouth of every woman in the break room had dropped to the floor. I could hear the whispers and the 'damns' traveling around the room. My eyes diverted to Aric and the smile he was carrying only a few seconds before had disappeared. If looks could kill, Jamie would be road kill. Jamie smiled and walked over to me and pulled me into a tight hug and Lord help me, but

I was not prepared for the kiss he planted on my lips. And I could have died a thousand deaths when he kept the kiss going so long that Justin started hissing and making cat calls with the other women in the room.

"I want one of him for my birthday," I heard someone say and a few other ladies laughed loudly and agreed.

When Jamie was done kissing me he handed me the gift bags and looked over to Aric. He gave a head nod and asked, "What's up Aric?"

I now knew how a person having a heart attack felt. Of course Aric gave a head nod back, since no one knew about what we had going on and now all of the rumors may stop since Jamie had pulled this stunt.

"Can I speak to you outside?" Jamie asked.

I didn't know what else to say so I nodded and let him lead me out into the hall.

"Did you get the pictures?" he asked.

I nodded. He had sent me the pictures he had taken of us and he made a few into artistic nudes.

"Yeah. I checked the mail this morning and they were there."

"You like them?"

"Love them. Didn't know they would come out so perfect." We were quiet for a minute before I asked, "Why did you do that, Jamie?"

He shrugged. "Because I could. What is he going to do? Let everyone know he's having sex with his assistant?"

I cut my eyes at him.

He held his hands up like he was being robbed. "Well, hey. You said you guys weren't in a relationship. Not me, but look I have to go. I'll get at you a little later."

We said our good-bye and he was gone. When I walked back into the room Aric was gone and a few of the other executives were as well. We finished up the party and then it was back to business. Aric didn't come back to his office for the rest of the day, and I didn't get to finish all of my work until about six. I tried calling him a few times but got no answer. I already knew what would happen as soon as he laid eyes on me and I was preparing myself for the fight. I stopped and picked up a few items for my house before going home. As soon as I saw his platinum colored 7 series BMW in my driveway my head started to hurt. I quickly got all of my bags out of the car and made my way inside. I headed for the kitchen and started putting away the items I had purchased. I was shaking and my nerves were on end. So much so that I knocked over the three glasses sitting on my counter.

"Damn!" I felt as if I was about to pass out.

I rushed out of the kitchen to get the broom from the small closet in my dining room. I didn't see or hear Aric, but I knew he was here. I could feel his anger. I swept the glass up and was going to go to my bedroom until I walked out of the kitchen and saw Aric was sitting on my sofa. I already knew it was about to be some mess. I could tell by the way he was sitting and by the way his eyes cast a despondent glance at me. Once again his arms were thrown across the back of the couch and he was sitting with his legs spread wide. He had changed into some gray sweats with a white thermal shirt and all white Nike Air Force Ones.

"Aric I don't feel like fighting . . ."

"You fuck him?"

Something in his voice unnerved me.

I lied. "No."

He stood and his eyes told me to try again.

"Don't lie to me."

I was balling and un-balling my fists trying to get my nerves together.

"I said no."

I panicked when he slowly began to walk over to me. I wasn't prepared for him to pull the brown envelope with the pictures of me and Jamie out and throw them in my face. I turned my head and put my hands to my face to avoid impact. I had left them on my dresser this morning because I was in a hurry leaving. I didn't think to put them away. I looked down at the pictures of me and Jaime having sex . . . Jamie's face between my thighs . . . me with my head thrown back enjoying it . . . me on top of Jamie . . . Jamie on top of me . . . and so on . . . and so on. The pictures had flown all around my living room. Before I could fix my mouth to say anything Aric was in my face. He looked like a mad man. His eyes were red and his breathing was rampant. With his hand gripping the back of my neck and my hair, he pulled me to him. I don't know but a certain level of defiance arose in me.

"Let me go, Aric," I screamed and struggled with him.

He nearly lifted me off of the floor and threw me across the room. I got up to try and run for my room but slipped on one of the pictures and twisted my ankle again. I didn't have time to re-live that pain because Aric had snatched me up by my shirt and yanked me to him. With the way he had me I had no choice but to look up at him.

"So did you fuck him?" he asked me again. His voice was deep, low, and lethal.

I was still trying to snatch away from him to no avail. So I stood very still and gazed at him.

"I did with him whatever you did with whomever you were with in New York!"

He pushed me back into the sofa so hard my back hit the base of it and it caused nerve wracking pain in my lower back. I didn't even have time to recover from the flashing lights behind my eye lids because he grabbed me again and started dragging me toward my room. I kicked, screamed, swung wildly. I was scared. One of my kicks connected with his thigh and I got up and tried to run for my front door. Before I even made it he grabbed me from behind by my hair and then picked me up by my waist. Once we made it to my room, he slammed my door, locked it, and slammed me against the wall.

"Aric please stop! It meant nothing," I cried. "He meant nothing."

My body was hurting and my ankle was burning. My breaths were coming out in spurts and I had become nauseous.

"You thought I was playing when I told you I would fuck you up . . ."

"I'm sorry, Aric! Damn! I don't even know what you were doing in New York and you want to be mad at me for being with somebody else," I screamed at him cutting him off.

I tried to duck when he went to snatch me up by my hair again. Images of my childhood flashed before my eyes and before I knew it my fist had balled and I was fighting back. Images of my father dragging my mother through the halls of our house by her hair haunted me. I could see my mother kicking and screaming, fighting for her life. My hand connected with his face and I guess that pissed him off even more because that's when he backhanded me. My head snapped back as I went flying across my bed. My jaw felt like it would come unhinged and I was so dizzy that the room was spinning. I saw him coming toward me and I moved so fast getting off the bed and trying to get away from him that I fell onto the floor on the side of my bed. It felt like I fractured my hip I fell so hard, but I crawled to my bathroom and quickly locked the door.

"Open the door, Chyanne!"

I slid down to the floor and rocked back and forth. My whole body was hurting. My head was pounding and so was my heart. I could not believe this mess. My breathing was labored and I felt as if I was about to throw up any minute. I ignored Aric's banging on the door demanding that I open it. I ignored his pleading that he didn't mean to hit me. I turned my light on and looked at myself in the mirror. My eye was already swelling and they both were blood shot red. I touched my jaw and winched at the pain. I could barely stand on my ankle and my hair made me look like a mad woman. I turned the water on to take a sip and as soon as I did I had to throw up. I made it to the toilet just in time. I threw up so much that all I could do was dry heave for a minute. Aric was still knocking on the door and threatened to kick it down if I didn't open it up. I loved this man, yes I did, but not more than I loved myself. He would not be putting his hands on me another time because this was it! I was done! This was too much to be putting up with for me not to even be in a relationship with him. I was a lot of things, but stupid I would not continue to be. I wanted to be mad at my mother right now. All I saw her do was get her behind kicked, sometimes just because my daddy was having a bad day. I saw her fight with woman after woman because my father just didn't give a damn and I always wondered why she never left. I promised myself that I would not be my mother. I was startled out of my thoughts when Aric beat on the door again.

"Aric, please," I screamed at the door. "Just leave!! Leave me alone and get out of my house!"

"Chyanne, just open the damn door," he yelled.

"No, Aric. I'm done. I . . . cannot do this . . . . This is too much. You put your hands on me too much!"

"Don't act like you haven't done that shit too! But that's how you are going to do me? You fuck that nigga and have him mail the pictures to your house! That shit ain't cool. . . ."

"But it was cool when you where screwing April right? And who ever . . ."

He kicked the door and I jumped. "Get out of my house, Aric!"

"Come make me get the fuck out," he snapped.

I never left my bathroom because Aric didn't
leave my room. I pulled my suit off and looked at
dark, purple, and red bruises on my side and back.
My hip and thigh were hurting and caused me to
limp. I was happy that my linen closet was in my
bathroom. I pulled down a pillow and two com-
forters and made myself a pallet in my oversized
garden tub. That is where I slept. Throughout the
night I could hear Aric moving beside the bathroom door. Every so often he would twist the knob
or ask for me to let him in. Each time I ignored him.

I woke up at about seven the next morning. I
heard him yelling at someone on his phone. I heard
when he slammed my front door and left. I called
out to him to see if he was still there and when I got
no answer, I finally left my bathroom. He was gone.
I sat down and wrapped my ankle and popped
some Tylenol for the rest of my body aches. I would
go see a doctor later about my ankle. I was having
sharp pains in my stomach and hoping the Tylenol would hurry up and kick in. I sat down at my
computer and typed up my resignation letter after
picking up all of the photos. No way was I going to
keep working there with him either. He could have
it all. I showered and put on a purple velour jogging
suit with my white DK sneakers. Once I got to my
job, I stopped by HR to drop off a resignation letter. When people kept asking why I was leaving, I

just told them that I had family issues. I made sure to keep on my glasses so my eye and face could stay hidden. I knew half of the bruise on my jaw still showed, but oh well. I hopped on the elevator and made my way to the seventh floor so I could leave Aric the same letter and clean out my desk. I waited for the elevator to stop and was surprised to see Lola talking to Gabriel.

"Hey, Chyanne," Lola spoke to me. Although I found it strange that she spoke to me, I was prepared to speak back.

Before I could speak out of nowhere somebody punched me so hard, I heard bells ringing. I heard half of the office gasp as I stumbled back. I only had a few seconds to see it was an exotic looking dark skinned chick. She was a tall skinny woman and she had long wavy black hair. She came for me again and I caught her before she got to me again. I threw a punch that knocked her backwards. She looked stunned but I didn't give her time to think about it. I had no idea who she was or why she'd hit me, but I caught that broad by her hair and slung her to the floor.

I was quite sure it looked like something off of a YouTube fight video, but I didn't care. I kept her down by the hair and beat her like she had threatened my life. Every slap, punch, stomp, and kick I gave her was from the pent-up anger

I had held inside of me. I beat her for the slap I never paid April back for. I stomped her for the mess Aric had put me through. Through her screams and yells for me to let her go, I imagined she was April and Aric and beat her like she stole something from me! Gabriel had run and tried to get me off of her giving her a chance to get up and kick me in my stomach. I maneuvered around him and punched her in the face as many times as I could before he was finally able to get some help in pulling us apart. One of the security officers had pulled whoever she was to one end of the office and Gabriel was dragging me kicking and screaming to get back to her. He had picked up my purse and shades, and by now, everyone had seen the big bruise on my face. Gabriel escorted me to the elevator and he pushed the buttons for the door to close. Once the doors closed, I let out a frustrated scream.

"Calm down, Chyanne," he said to me.

"Who in hell was that?" I yelled at him. I hadn't meant to. It just came out that way.

"That was my sister," he said to me.

I was confused. "OK, and what did she come after me for? I don't even know her."

Gabriel looked as if he was about to say something that I didn't want to hear. "She's my sister and . . . Aric's wife."

Even though the elevator was moving, my world stopped.

"No . . . no . . . no . . ." I kept repeating that myself.

I was so tired of crying, but I couldn't help it. I leaned forward and rested my hands on my knees then came back up to look at Gabriel.

"What . . . what do you mean his wife?"

Gabriel exhaled and held his hand to steady me. I guess I looked how I felt. Faint.

"She's his wife, Chyanne," he answered.

I looked up and squeezed my eyes shut as I tried to catch my breath. I don't know why . . . wait . . . yes I do. I know why my hand connected with Gabriel's face. He could have told me the truth.

He must have known what I was thinking because he absorbed the slap and said, "It wasn't my place to tell you, Chyanne."

"Like hell it wasn't! If not for me, then at least for your sister!"

"Not everything is always black and white."

"You are so full of it and you know it," I snapped at him.

That was the last thing I said to him. I stepped off into the parking deck and limped to my car with Gabriel calling out to me, trying to get my attention. I drove like a bat out of hell trying to get away from that place and all things Aric.

Through tears I barreled through traffic. Lord, please let this be a lie! Please tell me the man that I had fallen in love with was not a married man! I was so hurt. The physical pain bombarding my body had nothing on what I was feeling on the inside right now. I wondered how long his wife had known about me. Where had she been all this time? Was it her that he had been talking to on the phone? Was she who he was with in New York? All of these questions attacked my mind at one time. I felt deceived in a sense. Now I knew what he meant when he said he had something that he needed to take care of. It all made sense now, but it still hurt like hell! I had been an unwilling mistress, but at least now I knew that he was not just treating me like crap because of my weight. His wife was the complete opposite of me and it looked like he was giving her hell too!

I didn't hear from Aric for two days. My body was aching and my stomach wouldn't stop hurting. The pain had crippled me. I grabbed my stomach and toppled over in pain as I tried to make my way to the bathroom. The pain was so bad that my knees hit the floor hard and I yelled out. I was tempted to call the police and have her arrested. Just thinking about being sucker punched had me wanting to whoop that trick again.

My mind kept going back to that night that Shelley had asked Aric about 'Stephanie'. I wanted to kick myself for being so stupid and naïve. But the pain in my stomach wouldn't allow me time to think about it. I crawled to the bathroom as I heard my front door open. Through the throbbing pain in my ankle and the gut clenching pain in my stomach, I stood and limped back into my bedroom. Aric stopped at my bedroom door when he saw me. I guess the scratches all over my face and neck and the bruise he had left on my face stopped him. I knew by now that it was no secret what had happened.

Justin had already called me and told me the talk had started. I was so mad at the man standing in front of me all I could do was struggle to take the ring off my finger, and when I did, I threw it at his head. He easily dodged it and it traveled into the hall, hitting the floor. I heard it bounce a few times.

"You are a lying . . . I don't even have words for you right now. So why not just leave and do both of us a favor?"

My eyes were filled with tears and my throat already hurt from crying all night before. It felt like somebody had fisted the lower half of my stomach and was twisting it for dear life, but I refused to flinch in pain. I wouldn't let him see me in any more pain than he had already caused. He tried to come near me and I quickly picked up the thick glass vase on my dresser. He stopped.

"I know you are mad, Chyanne, but you are going to put that damn vase down so I can talk to you," he snapped at me.

I looked him over. He was still in business attire and what usually turned me on about him, his eyes, dimples, lips, build, accent, it now revolted me.

"Forget you, Aric! I hate the day I walked into your office. Curse the day I let you kiss me, the day I let you touch me! I hate you so much right now!"

I was screaming and yelling. I knew by now I was the talk of the neighborhood.

"Watch how the hell you speak to me first of all and don't act like I am not hurt by this shit too," he started.

I looked at this man like he had lost his ever loving mind.

"Hurt! You hurt? You lying son of a bitch!"

I yelled that in disbelief and before I knew it I had stepped forward and launched the vase at him. He ducked.

"Chyanne, you had better calm the hell down! Let me explain . . ."

"You don't have to explain a damn thing," I said through bated breaths.

The pain had me sweating, I was hurting so badly. I squeezed my eyes shut and then quickly opened them.

"Keep . . . your damn explanation . . ."

My vision was becoming blurry . . .

"Chyanne," I heard him call out to me as he inched his way closer to me.

"Don't . . . don't come near me, Aric. . . ."

My legs felt unsteady as if they were crumbling underneath me and all I remember is hearing Aric call my name and rushing to catch me as I hit the floor.

When I woke up it was to the beeps of the machines surrounding me. I looked around and saw I was in a hospital room. I saw Aric sitting to the left of me.

Although I was still mad at him I asked, "What happened?"

He leaned forward looking at me. "You passed out."

There was an expression on his face that I couldn't read and I didn't really care to try and figure it out. I was more concerned with what was wrong with me. I wanted to page a nurse or something but was too weak to move my arms.

"Will you page a nurse for me and then leave?"

I was so serious with him.

"I will call you a nurse, but I am not going anywhere."

He stood and I rolled my eyes. I was not in the mood to fight.

"They will be back soon anyway. They said they were running some tests," he told me before standing and walking over to the table where a pitcher of water was sitting.

"Tests for what?"

"You need to drink some water," he said to me before answering. "They said you were dehydrated."

Come to think about I hadn't eaten or drunk anything in two days. I tried to snatch the Styrofoam cup from him but he must have known I would have because he had a tight grip on the cup. I rolled my eyes again and eased the cup from his grip. He cut his eyes at me and pressed the button to let the bed up to angle it so I could drink. He removed his watch as he always did when he was going to play in my hair. I moved my head and side eyed him hard. He only adjusted my pillow. I tried to bring the cup to my mouth and my hand was shaking like I had Parkinson's. He watched me as I tried twice to drink from the cup, but wasted more on me than I did the first time. He removed the cup from my hands, poured

more water into it, and then held it to my mouth. I
didn't want to take anything from him. I kept my
lips tight.

"Drink the damn water, Chyanne! Stop . . ."

Before he could finish, I mustered up enough
strength and knocked the cup from his hand to
the floor. Water splashed all over his expensive
suit. I would die of thirst before I took anything
from him again.

Before he could retaliate or before I could finish my thoughts a tall black woman in a white lab
coat entered the room. She introduced herself as
Dr. St. Simeon. I listened as she explained that
they had run a few tests and asked when my last
menstrual cycle was. I had to think back and
told her it was in October. I also told her that my
cycle had a mind of its own and came and went
as it pleased. She nodded and I waited for her to
say more.

"Well that explains it," she said as she scrib-
bled notes.

"Explains what?"

She looked at me and smiled. "Why you are
twelve to thirteen weeks pregnant and don't know
it."

"Excuse me!" I shouted that at her. She looked
taken aback and I apologized. I calmed myself
enough for her to repeat what she had said.

"Your body shut down on you because you have not been getting the proper prenatal care and it looks like you have been in a fight or two. Do you need me to call the police? Is anyone physically harming you at home, Ms. Johnson? There are laws in the state of Georgia that protects a woman with child against any kind of domestic violence. Once again, is anyone physically harming you, Ms. Johnson?"

She looked over at Aric like she cared even less for his presence than I did. She slowly rolled her eyes from him back over to me.

I shook my head. "No." Although I wanted to have him and his wife arrested, I was more concerned with the life that was or was still inside of me. "Did I lose the baby?"

"No, but you were very close to it. We are going to keep you here overnight to keep an eye on you to determine if you get to go home or if we keep you in here until you have this baby. It is possible that you may still miscarry and just to be sure that we are out of trouble and in the clear we will run more tests. Your cervix is thin and your progesterone levels are low, and for that reason, it may be a possibility that you may have to either stay in here until you deliver or we may seek other solutions like the P17 shot. If it comes down to any of those things, I will explain everything to you thoroughly at that time. Cool?"

It took me a minute to register what she was saying to me, but I nodded. She gave Aric the once over again and walked out of the room. If I was twelve to thirteen weeks pregnant that meant I got pregnant around the first time we had sex. I fiddled with my fingers and held my head down. Here I was twenty five years old; I had quit my job, and was pregnant by a married man. How in the hell did I find myself here? I wanted to ask Aric so many questions, but my mind could only think about this life that was inside of me. Tears started to slowly fall down my face. I looked over at Aric and he was standing there with his arms folded across his wide chest.

I was about to ask him about this wife of his and what we were going to do about this baby, but before I could open my mouth, he asked "Is it my baby?"

I frowned and looked at him. "Are you really asking me that?"

He shrugged with a nonchalant look on his face. "I'm just saying, I did see pictures of you fucking another. . . ."

"Oh Lord! Here we go! Really Aric? So what do you want? A DNA test?"

"I don't care what you get as long as it's something to let me know this baby is mine," he said before wiping his hand down his face and exhaling loudly. "But, if it is mine, then I guess you will be having this *lying son of a bitch's* baby, huh?

I rolled my eyes, shook my head, and folded my arms over my ample breasts and sarcastically remarked, "Tell me about it."